Dark Matters

An anthology of dark fiction

by S.R. Woodward

Contents

Cover design by CreativIndie.com

Foreword

Know your enemies as you know your friends - so the adage goes; but what does it mean?

Is there a manual? Well, not until now. Dark Matters, this anthology, intends to divulge everything you wish to avoid, and should. But to know what to avoid requires the knowledge and to finish this little tome will be an education, and a step on the way to self-preservation, if you wish it to be.

Where there is light there needs to be darkness to create balance; dark matters. And where there is darkness there are dark matters afoot. This is the yin and yang of life's nature.

This anthology is a collection of flash fiction – sub-400 word stories in this case – verse and short stories, each identifying some aspect of humanity's darker underbelly or possibly from just the other side of the shadows. Some are tempered with a soupcon of gallows' humour.

Nothing You Want

The policeman leapt from his seat as the station's front door crashed open; at 3am no one turned up even if it was Halloween.

He recognised the 27 year old – one of Leigh's less pleasant individuals; known for his violence – but this wasn't the guy he knew. Darren Johnston looked feeble, his confidence gone. It was all the desk sergeant could do to stop Johnston vaulting the counter.

"Stop there, Johnston. Tell me what's going on."

"I didn't do it – no. Listen to me." Johnston turned to the door; it inched open as the fierce wind blew. Johnston paled and leapt across the counter. "I'll tell you – when you've locked me in a cell."

"Have it your way, Johnston, but I've got to charge you."

Johnston landed a blow on the sergeant's chin, just hard enough. "Assaulting a police officer," he said.

"You tosser, Johnston."

In the cell Johnston started; "It wasn't like I was gonna use me knife…"

***

Johnston was on Leigh Cliffs desperately phoning around; he needed more smack. He needed money – fast.

Looking towards Leigh train station he saw a man wearing a long black coat and dark sunglasses walking up the steps from the station.

"Oi! You," Johnston called, pulling his knife.

The man stopped. "I have nothing you want," he said.

"Who the fuck are you to tell me that?" Johnston stepped closer, blade glinting in the sodium street lamp light.

The man moved his hands and they blurred. When they stopped the man held Johnston's knife. Before Johnston could run the man spoke.

"Is this what you want?" The man drew the knife around his neck – jets of black-red fluid arced from the wound.

"No… NO!"

"Is this what you want?" The man dragged the blade down his abdomen. As his intestines cascaded to the ground he continued towards Johnston.

***

"Johnston, it was a bad trip."

"I didn't score."

The sergeant slammed the cell door's hatch.

At the counter the sergeant continued the paperwork then looked up when the station's door rattled. His jaw sagged; at the foot of the door viscous red liquid had started to pool.

Eighty More Years

Hey! You! What's that in your hand?
Some kind of sickle for reaping the land?
And why you wearing that dark cowl?
It's not in vogue you know, not really for now.
What? You've come to take me. Where? Can I ask?
To the other side? On a boat, to a cask?
Now hold on just a minute. I have an idea.
What about a nice country pub for a cold pint of beer?
Perhaps you and me could have a little chat.
About what? The meaning of life of course, and where we're at.
What are you having? I'm having a Stella.
You what? An orange juice with a green and yellow umbrella!
Laugh! I could have cried, but better cry than to die.
We chatted a lot and finally saw socket to eye.
He had more juice and I had more beers,
But in the end I walked away with 80 more years.
Result!

The Mark Royce Chronicle

30th December

Over the last nine days I've been gradually becoming aware of, but not really taking that much note of, strange visions; visions of shadowy folk in the periphery of my sight, only to turn and look and then see nothing. Because of this I've generally assumed that they're floaters, bits of debris that we all get in our eyes, until now that is.

The events of today have disturbed me somewhat and this is due to the fact that, this time, when I turned around, I got a brief glance at a fully formed shape which then disintegrated in front of me.

This last experience has pushed me into thinking I need to start a journal, just in case something happens to me. Not that I think it would, I mean, why would it? But just to be on the safe side I will have an account of the whole saga if and when it unfolds. Perhaps I'll publish it, if it ever gets finished, who knows?

31st December

Well it's New Year's Eve and there's not a lot going on for me.

Today I sent an email to senior management telling them that what they're trying to do (which is nothing in my opinion), is totally crap. I think I may lose my job because of this. But then who cares, they really don't know what they're doing, so, why shouldn't I say?

Went out with work tonight to drink in the New Year. Pretty tedious evening, nothing special, same old, same old. Oh well let's see what the New Year brings.

1st January

It's 3:30am and I am back here writing, trying to capture what has happened between leaving the party at half past midnight and now.

I'd only been asleep for a while when I was dragged from the blissful respite of dreamlessness to fully conscious!

It wasn't anything to do with my other half, (I don't have one), but because of the Shadow-folk wandering about my place. This is new; I've never seen them here before, it's only in the streets near my flat. They are without noise. I think it must've been the drop in temperature that woke me.

They show no acknowledgement of my presence but, once I'm awake, they're something I can't ignore.

I was shivering in my bed even though the heating was on. And they were just wandering about. So I'm up and typing away. Apart from my disturbed sleep there is just them; wisp-like things, irrelevant.

I'm going to get the extra duvet and go back to bed. I'm glad the thought of ghosts doesn't bother me one bit, they're harmless, it's strange how most people don't realise this.

***

Here we are again and guess what? New Year's Day is crap. Nothing going on, nothing is happening. No one wants to know, none of the local pubs are open. All I have is the telly to watch.

***

8pm now, telly is rubbish, the usual regurgitated stuff and that's why I'm writing again. Somehow the telly turned itself off and the radio turned on. This doesn't worry me; occasionally it happens to everyone doesn't it? Anyway it's probably due to some kind of electrostatic disturbance created by sun flares or something.

Tired now. Going to bed.

2nd January

Been to work, same old shit, I suppose its saving grace is that it keeps me in beer money.

3rd January

Work was acceptable, went home via the local watering hole, and then left at the dictated time.

***

About half an hour ago I was woken. It is now 3:30am (again). I've decided to get up, or at least get out of bed and add to this journal.

They've been back, the Shadow-folk that is. I've only been able to see their ghost-like presence. They're hard to describe. I mean how would you go about describing something as intangible as individuals, I assume they're individuals, made of smoke. This is not just your ordinary smoke however but the kind of smoke that burning tyres produce, thick, black, and almost transparent in places. And in writing this description it has made me realise they're more here, physical I suppose. Not like before. They've changed.

***

I've been up for hours now, it's 6am. Apart from the noise they've started to make, which is new, they've disappeared. I'm going back to bed; at least I'll get one hour's sleep before the alarm goes off. Best do that, I can't afford not to.

4th January

What a crap day. I'm surprised I functioned at work at all. So tired. Glad I made it through. Avoided the local, was too tired. It's now 8pm, I'm going to bed. Please, please, please don't disturb me tonight.

5th January

Been to work; what an amazing day. No problem with the email I sent. Management are okay about it, sort of, but at least I haven't got the sack. Best not do that again though.

I slept right through last night without any problem. Don't know whether I was visited, but if I was, I was not woken. It'll be great if I can get another night's sleep, just the same as last night.

Good TV tonight. I am certainly going to relax, may well crack a few tinnies.

6th January

It's bloody 3am and I'm up again. They're back, wandering about sighing, moaning. I am truly getting pissed off with this. What have I done to deserve this? It's bloody 3am Friday morning. This is too much. I've got to do something about this. The novelty has worn off. I'm fed up with having to tell my mates that they can't visit. And I want to dispel the idea that I am a total saddo.

What the hell was that?

For the journal, something has just crashed heavily in the hall I'm going to go and have a look.

***

Can you believe it nothing has crashed anywhere? I walked along the hall, dodging the Shadow-folk, and there was no sign of anything. What was that noise? God I'm tired. I'm going to have to be more proactive about this. Problem is I just don't know where to start. I think this Saturday I'll try the local library to see if that throws up any pointers. I dearly hope it will.

5:50am now and they've gone. Off to bed, looking forward to waking in an hour and ten minutes so I can get up for work (not).

***

Been to work, fortunately it was not too taxing, but I am, and was, truly knackered. The guys wanted me to go out to the pub "as it's Friday". So I didn't disappoint.

Surprised I'm still able to type; one or three too many beers and I could hardly keep myself upright which was strange as I didn't have that much. Not tired anymore though: probably the expectation of being woken. Best have a few scotches to see if that solves the problem.

7th January

I didn't get up until 11am. What a good night's sleep.

During the usual chores one has to do as a single person I mulled over the other night's visions trying to glean any clues from the memories. With hindsight and without the fear, which is becoming more tangible, I did notice things that are sort of familiar with the Shadow-folk. I think they were dressed in woollen clothing and most wore cloaks but that's as far as I can recall at the moment.

I'm off to the library now.

***

Well there wasn't much help there; loads of general stuff about Essex and the Normans, a little bit about the Romans, no detail though. And nothing about Manor Mews, which is just off Manor Lane (where I live). Anyway that's what the local library had. So helpful. Actually I'm being a bit mean, I did find a book with some pictures of Celtic clothing that rang a few bells and the librarian did suggest trying the Internet. Don't know why I didn't think of that in the first place, working in I.T., as I do.

***

Typing again, it's 8:53pm according to the PC clock and it has been a pretty standard Saturday, apart from the library visit.

No calls from the guys. Looks like a night in. I think I'll just pop around the corner and pick up a DVD, perhaps Altered States with William Hurt, haven't seen that in a long time.

***

Nearly 12:30 in the morning and the film was as good as I remembered it, the cans of cider were a good complement. Good night all.

8th January

I've been up now for about twenty minutes, the coat stand in the hall was on the floor. I expect its crash woke me and yes the bloody smoky apparitions are back having their fun. I think I only slept for about two and a half hours.

I'm really fed up. I've got to find out why this is happening. I can't go on like this. It's doing my head in.

I'm going to watch to see if they give any clues as to why this is happening. The time now is 3:47am

Well that was interesting, the ghouls/ghosts, I don't know what to call them, Shadow-folk is probably pretty accurate, mainly appear in the hallway. Some of them seemed to come from the airing cupboard. The rest just mill about as if they are not sure what they're looking for. Can you believe it?

Anyway, I decided to open the airing cupboard door for myself. You won't believe this but the emersion tank was no longer there, neither were the shelves, neither were my pillowcases or duvets or anything, just a very dark landscape. I think I saw a tree off in the distance; it had no leaves just scrawny and twisted branches. The earth was dark brown perhaps even scorched, I think, and grassless as far as I could see.

Whilst I was standing there, I heard a sound. Straining my ears I could just about hear something. It was almost like hundreds of people screaming in sheer terror. No. Not people. Souls seems to be a more appropriate description. Not that I can say I've heard screaming souls before but their cry imbued such a resonance of feeling, my soul and spirit, in the deepest depths of me, was almost crushed by their out-pouring. To be quite honest I had to shut the airing cupboard door a lot faster than I opened it. This situation is becoming very hard to deal with.

The time's coming up to 6am and silence is now pervading. I need to go to bed. I need to pretend that this is not happening. I need to be away.

***

Just got up, I've washed etc., it's now 1:37pm. Nice sleep but what a waste of a day.

I really have to find out what this is all about. The local library is not that good, as you may have gathered. If I want to get to the bottom of this I'm going to have to trawl the Internet, but what do I search for? I hope my supposition that the answers do lie somewhere is correct because if they don't, I'm really worried about my sanity. I know I've just got to keep going and hold on tight to my belief that there is something that will explain this; something documented, something that I can get to grips with to help me finally figure out this problem of mine.

Why no one else in these flats seems to be bothered by this problem I don't know. Perhaps they are. I've not actually asked them, but if I do and they're not, what then?

***

Just come back from my sister's place. She's as nutty as ever, which is fun, but fancy her being a doctor and as daft as she is. Brother-in-law is just the same as he always is, fit, straight forward and without strange happenings. Didn't actually mention what is going on in my life at the moment. Perhaps I should, perhaps I shouldn't. Who knows?

Oh well, I'm going to sign off now and watch a bit of telly (as usual). The Time Team is on soon and I hope that'll take my mind off things for a while.

***

Dear Journal,
I'm off to bed now. I really hope we don't have to meet up again in the next ten hours, but if we do, then I'm glad you're here and that you will not judge me.
Goodnight dear Journal, thanks for your help.
All the best
Mark.

9th January

What a beginning to a new week. Management have decided to address the problems that I highlighted earlier and they've asked me to direct the ongoing upgrades. I don't think I've mentioned this but I'm the company's internal I.T. consultant of sorts, probably not.

Anyway this has nothing to do with the new found strangeness of my life that I'm attempting to capture in this journal.

Got a big presentation to do tomorrow. All the European management team will be there. I'll have to finish the final touches tomorrow morning, most of the work I finished today.

10th January

The presentation went exceptionally well. We all know what has to be done. Everyone is happy with the year's plan. Let's hope it actually happens.

Not wanting to tempt fate but I've had two trouble free nights on the trot! Is it all over? I hope so.

Going to sign off now and watch a bit of telly. One question bothers me though; will I get a good night's kip tonight? I want one, but I am cautious in my optimism.

11th January

Work was great, again!

You've probably noticed that I didn't add to my journal in the morning. I mean who has time? I don't, I don't even have time for breakfast, mainly because that means I'll have to get up earlier.

Crap telly tonight so I'm going to watch my Dune video, been a few months since I've watched that. A damn good film if I do say so myself.

***

Hello, I'm back. Went to bed thinking all my woes were over, but guess what, it's 3:05am and I've had to get up and add to this journal. The bastards are back. They haven't touched me but now I have smashed pictures on the floor of my lounge. Their manifestation seems to be becoming more real, more physical, a true presence in this world, my world. This is not good.

The noises are worse; in fact they are terrible; the screams just pass straight through my head, piercing, wrenching screams.

The airing cupboard door has been flung open and the soil I saw before is alight, burning. Black smoke is billowing above the unreal scenery.

When I look out of my study towards what was the airing cupboard I get glimpses of withered, skeletal things writhing in the agony of the flames. The individuals I see are covered in a burning light. Their clothing, I think it's their clothing, is dropping off them, forming flame ridden puddles, flickering orange and red.

Others mill about with no interest in helping their own. Now they look towards me, mouths agape, seemingly yelling, seemingly imploring me to do what, I don't know.

How I'm keeping myself together I have no idea. It's almost as if I have been through this before, I'm used to it somehow. But how can that be? How can I cope with this presentation of hell on earth? Why does it not affect me to the degree that I would expect others to be affected? This is truly unfair; most people would have surrendered their consciousness by now. Is this not correct? I am forced to be an unwilling witness to the trauma of these Shadow-folk. What has it got to do with me? Why has it got to do with me?

Before I could walk amongst them not too concerned. Now I'm stuck to my chair in sheer terror, watching, feeling reviled, as some burn in abnormal flames and others just, just… it's so hard to describe, just mill about ignoring the pleas of their own kind. I am desperate for release from my unnatural participation. I don't want to view it anymore, but it keeps going on and on and on. I try shutting my eyes but I still see. I see limbs dropping from bodies alight. I see blackened skulls, mouths open in screams of total pain as the smoke, or is it steam (?), pours forth out of the darkened orifices of their faces and all the while the flames lick greedily around the oval of their skulls. NO MORE PLEASE!

12th January

I don't know what happened for the rest of the time since my last entry.

It's morning now and I must have passed out, thank God.

I've phoned into work saying that there has been a family bereavement and that I won't be in. This will give me a few days grace.

It's only 8:30am and I'm going to bed now. I need some rest. I hope the memory of the previous night does not interfere.

13th January

No problems last night and no work today. I'm feeling a little better.

It's strange to note how a decent night's sleep can make you feel.

It's times like this that make me question the reality of the previous weeks' experiences. Everything now seems so normal. Have I just imagined the whole thing? Is it an overactive imagination that is causing me these problems? At this moment in time this is exactly how I feel, what a stupid imagination. But when I look about my lounge and see the smashed pictures of my family, I just shudder.

No, I haven't cleared the mess up yet and this is only because I fear that if I touch those broken pictures, those pictures of my family past and present, it will bring the Shadow-folk back to test and taunt me again.

***

Just back from shopping. I don't know whether you, the reader, have realised this but it's Friday the 13th. God help me.

I'm certain that, if anything terrible is going to occur, it just has to be tonight. Who invented Friday the 13th?

It's only 4pm and I'm trying to think of ways that I can knock myself out for one purpose only and that is to allow me to forgo the traumas of tonight's inevitable visitation.

It's not as if I can go out and avoid the whole thing. Nothing ever happens until the early hours anyway.

***

Back from the offy; I've a full bottle of Famous Grouse and twelve cans of Scrumpy Jack. Oblivion is not far away I hope. It's now 6:35pm and time to start my journey towards blissful annihilation before anything can happen. Cheers.

14th January

4:47am and I'm typing once more. This is the first time I've been able to get back to the journal and add this entry since I was awoken by some invisible presence dragging me from my bed, from my slumber.

I think it started around 2:30am.

I got into bed after completing half a bottle of scotch and four cans of cider, 10:15pm I believe.

At about 2:30am I was dragged, by my neck, out of bed into the hall. I remember trying to recoil from the strong fleshless, tinder dry fingers around my neck, but I couldn't, fear had paralysed me. I was pulled onto an unnatural earth and dumped, let go. From then on all I could do was watch, and even though the experience of being physically manhandled was worse than the previous were, I felt calmer. My fear probably muted by alcohol, I suppose.

The hallway, including the airing cupboard, was no more. What lay before me, and under me, was damp brown earth with gloomy green hillocks just visible in the distance.

Night was wrapped around the land holding the darkness fast, just as it had previously when I looked on from the other-side.

In front of the hillocks were wattle and daub roundhouses with a few cattle in a paddock off to one side.

A trumpet, of sorts, sounded. But it wasn't a trumpet, as you and I would truly know it, the noise was something more akin to the noise a bass wind chime may make, being blown continuously.

Some men emerged from the roundhouses in front of me, about 100 metres away. They seemed very worried. Their women appeared, leaving the roundhouses. Those with children were holding them close to their bodies covering the children's ears against the eerie sound.

Then there were two floating fireballs on the brow of the hill and a regular clump, clump, clump sound forced its way through the viscous night air, perhaps the sound of many feet on soft earth walking(?)… marching(?) in unison(?).

The little peace that was left was then shattered.

The men in their hide(?) coveralls ran to each of the roundhouses ushering out the remaining women and children, screaming at them in some language or another, to go, directing them away from the oncoming… I don't know what.

Then silence and there was nothing apart from the lowing of cattle and the occasional cry of a child. The air was still. No more clump, clump, clump, no more eerie guttural wind chime.

When I looked back at the men they all had their swords drawn and were facing the raised ground, facing the hillock behind their huts looking at the floating balls of fire. The women and children had gone.

While I looked on, wondering what was going to happen next, the men talked amongst themselves occasionally pointing toward the hillock. There was a tension in the atmosphere which was almost palpable.

The silence of the night was interrupted by a light whistling sound, a sound which imperceptibly increased in its intensity.

All of a sudden the roundhouse, just in front of me, cracked loudly as its roof disintegrated and its wooden uprights supporting the roof were smashed to pieces. The wall fronting the roundhouse opened up in an explosion of daub and straw, as a burning rock exited.

Cattle went mad and crashed through the willow fences that had contained them. Then there were more light whistling sounds, more loud cracks, more huts were smashed to oblivion before spontaneously erupting in flames.

I tried to get up but for some reason my legs were not responding. It was as if I was not completely of this terrible world; part in and part out. I tried rolling to my right and this worked, I rolled over and over until I was out of the line of fire. I stopped when I could roll no more. I had ended up next to a pile of rocks. All I was now able to do was to watch the ongoing destruction of the settlement.

In the flickering shadows cast by the floating fire on the hill top I could see one or two hide covered individuals beckoning to the soldiers(?), beckoning for them to make their way further into the settlement. This was very confusing and before I could think anything else of it, another projectile came out of the sky and smashed into the rock-pile in front of me. The rocks fell upon me.

That's what I remember from the last two and a bit hours.

And now I'm back here attempting to put, on paper, the memories of what had just happened.

Everything in my flat is quiet again and the airing cupboard is just that.

***

Not feeling well today, totally shattered, feeling so tired. The early hours of this morning were grim. This situation has got to me so much that it has made me vomit. I want it all to be over.

15th January

Resting, that's what I'm doing today, resting. I need to rest. My mind is still reeling from the other night's forced excursion into that bleak world of fear and resentment.

I try to make sure I keep adding to this journal though I have no energy to do so.

It's difficult to get back to the computer; my legs still feel as if they're not with me.

If I cease to exist at least there'll be something, some explanation why, something for my family and friends explaining my demise/disappearance. They will have to take this journal on face value. I hope they don't think this is just the ravings of a non-descript person, their brother, their friend, who lost his mind and disappeared for reasons unknown.

Yes. I am certain now that there will not be a good outcome to this. I am resigned to my demise.

***

I've just come off the phone from my boss. I've told him that my family bereavement has affected me more than I thought it would. He has said that within the company rules I can have another 3 days off. I thanked him and said I would be back on Thursday.

16th January

Bleak as the last few days have been I am beginning to feel Okay. Not brilliant, just Okay.

After re-reading my journal from the 13th, which was very difficult, especially so soon after the event, I think I have understood where I ought to start looking to understand why these awful visitations are happening.

I remember the people in their animal skin clothing, the wattle and daub homesteads and the foot soldiers. These things are all pointing to a Romano-Celtic era. Why I'm being torn from the present and dumped in this awful manifestation of pre-history, I have no clue.

But at least I can feel fairly confident about the "when" of it. I don't just watch Time Team, I do listen as well!

And however much I wanted an insight, I could have done without this baptism of fire.

At least now I have my seed, my kernel, the beginning of my understanding. I truly hope it's the beginning. And I pray my understanding will deliver, at the very least, an explanation.

***

I'm going to log on to the Time Team forum and ask a few questions; things like how do I find out about the history of my area, who can I contact for more information? I hope that the people in this forum will respond and give me some idea of what to do next. Not that I'll let them know why I'm asking.

***

Well I've done that, logged on, set myself up on the forum and asked the questions. All I need to do now is wait. I hope their answers aren't a long time coming.

Going to watch a bit of telly before I go to bed.

Hopefully, tomorrow, I'll be able to sign on to the forum and get some guidance.

17th January

Gooood morning Haaadleigh, that's Hadleigh, near the sea, actually. Decent night's sleep, had breakfast already and it's still only 9:45am!

Received a strange letter post marked Italy; its contents knocked me a bit. There was one sheet of paper containing a single sentence, "I will avenge my family." It wasn't signed. Is it my imagination or are there really more loonies these days? Anyway I threw it away.

Once I've finished this little entry in my journal I'm going to sign on to the Time Team forum. I really hope there'll be some answers to my questions.

***

Well, well, well, some answers. In order not to bore you with all the information the bottom line is; call the "Sites & Monuments Record Office, County Hall Chelmsford." Apparently they're the best place to start. Any enquiries regarding ancient goings on in my area they're the people to ask. This is good, I'm feeling the most positive I have in a long time. 'scuse me while I get on the phone.

***

Oh well, a little bit disheartened now. Spoke to a nice young lady called Sarah who told me that she wasn't the best person to talk to for the details I was after.

However she did say that her colleague, "Janus", was the right person but his shift did not start until 3pm, "would I like to call back?" I said "of course" and thanked her for her help.

This gives me about four and a half hours before I can do anymore so it looks like the Hoovering is beckoning.

***

It's 3pm, I'm going to make the call.

***

The call was very peculiar, so much so, I'm going to have to enter it in this journal just as it happened.

"Hi. Can I speak to Janus please?" I said.

"This is Janus speaking." Was the reply.

"Good. I have a few questions, did Sarah tell you?" I continued.

"No." Was the response I got, which was a bit surprising to say the least.

"Oh! Do you have some time?" I always ask this because I'm never happy intruding on anyone's time.

"Yes. What is it you want?" The man called Janus said.

"Well, my name is Mark Royce and I would like to know a little about the area I live in now, especially relating to its history." I informed him.

"Mark Roize? Is that spelt R.O.I.Z.E?" At this stage I was truly unsure of where the conversation was going but carried on anyway.

"No, it's spelt R.O.Y.C.E. Does that make a difference?"

"Yes."

"In what way?" By this stage I didn't know what was going on because I'd phoned to ask questions not the other way around.

"Where do you live?" Janus went on.

"I live in Hadleigh, almost opposite the Norman church. Now, as to my question…"

"Do you live in Manor Lane?"

"Yes. And now, can you please tell me why the spelling of my last name has any relevance? Actually how the hell do you know what road I live in?"

"Because I have some information you need, some important information that should put a stop to your current predicament." By now his stance was beginning to rile me.

"My predicament! What the hell do you know about my predicament? I don't know you from Adam, I've just made this call and there's no way you can know me. I'm sorry you're talking total bollocks."

"Sir, I implore you… just listen for a few minutes"

Well, against my better judgement I listened and when he got to the bit about his spirit guide I just turned off until he finished.

"And that's it?"

"Yes, please take my advice."

"Thank you Janus. I'm sure we won't be speaking again." That's when I put the phone down.

At that stage I went into the other room and put the telly on, I was fuming, vowing never to take any notice of Internet forums and assuring myself that tomorrow I would seek out other lines of enquiry.

Suffice it to say, after watching the box for a bit I'd calmed down and got to thinking it was possible that there may have been an essence of truth in what he was saying – no on second thoughts probably not.

I'm thankful for you, my journal; it certainly seems to be a good way to get things off my chest. It makes me calmer, apart from the typos I am continually struggling against.

But it can be said that it is better to have typos to thwart than the demons of a bygone age. Where am I getting to now? Am I becoming some kind of philosopher or something? Best not worry about this.

Okay, it's only 7pm now so I'm going to do something normal and put a DVD on. I think I'll go for Blade Runner.

18th January

It's just gone 12am and there is a fairly intense smell of smoke. It's triggered something in my head. It's not your usual kind of smoke smell, like paper burning or rubber, something else… something that I remember deep down… something I can't quite put my finger on at the moment.

Obviously I've got up and turned the computer on to write this, but there's nothing to see, nor hear, just the smell.

Sitting here waiting… it's an awful feeling. Not knowing what is coming. I hope nothing.

Just waiting and waiting.

I think now is a good time to get a drink, probably scotch, before the next mind wrenching episode. Something to help me deal with what is to come. (I pray to God it's not, not coming that is.)

Got the scotch from the kitchen now. Not a glass, I've got the whole bottle. 'scuse me while I have a slug.

The worry is getting to me again. I need to throw up, my stomach is churning.

The smell is back, that acrid, awful smell, it's so much stronger now. It vaguely reminds me of pork in some way, perhaps a bit sweeter, but burnt pork at that, not truly burnt sweet smelling pork, but almost.

Still no sounds, just the smell. I think it's getting stronger, if it isn't my imagination making it so.

Just so you know, I'm sitting here at my computer with a bottle of scotch and everything I do is illuminated by the computer screen.

I haven't turned the lights on because if they return I just hope they'll miss me, not see me.

Sitting in this darkness, being anonymous in the blackness, helps me focus on getting everything written down.

I don't want my peers or my family thinking I've lost the plot, someone they no longer want to be in contact with. So I write and wait... and wait.

***

Oh no, it's started, I'm awake again, I must've dozed off. The clock on the PC says 2:14am. The airing cupboard door smashed open violently (I assume it's the airing cupboard again, I haven't looked yet) and I'm awake. No noise though, complete silence, the clock on the wall no longer ticks. I cannot hear the fridge making its usual sounds. There's just me and silence in the glare of the monitor's LCD backlight.

My vaguely illuminated hands hover over the keyboard.

I'm finding it difficult to type, I'm afraid that any movement will bring them straight to me. I am pressing the keys as slowly and as quietly as I can, struggling to override the fear that wracks me, that attempts to paralyse me.

Oh God how I wish this was over.

It's no good, I've got to look. I can't take the silence and the smell any longer. I'm going to look.

And I will. I just need to lean forward a bit so I can see out through the door of my study, into the hall and towards the cupboard, and now I've seen it, it's a cupboard no longer, more of an entry into Hell on earth, I think.

From my study I can see the scorched soil is there again but still there is no sound, no Shadow-folk either.

But... I now hear an estranged noise growing, getting louder in its intensity. It's a unified noise, a unified chorus of voices growing louder, a chant.

"Animus" they say, "Animus" over and over again.

I am oddly thankful that the silence has been broken and, along with it, my total fear. I think I let my imagination go in the forced immersion of silence.

I must get more information, something that will lead me to understand the situation I am in.

I'm not going to wait until the chant sounds as if it is in my flat. I'm going to cross the threshold and move into that other world and see what I can find out.

I pray that this is not the last entry into my journal I ever make.

19th January

What has happened? My head feels like it wants to split open. I can hardly type but I need to. I need to write my diary. 19th, where did the last twenty hours go?

The pain in my head, what happened to me? The pain in my head is too much.

Pain, pain, pain.

2nd February

The geezer from the flat below, Dave, has brought my laptop in to the hospital. Didn't really know him that well but he must be a decent sort.

He said he hadn't noticed me out and about but my car was still there. Not on holiday he assumed.

Apparently he called to check on me, after work had sent someone round to find out what I was doing. All they did was knock, and having no reply, they knocked on his and asked if he'd seen me.

Still feeling dozy, but thank god for Dave, he found me.

After the person from my work left, he forced open my front door, and there I was, unconscious in front of my computer.

After the ambulance had got me to the hospital I apparently came round long enough to tell the doctors about the things that had happened to me over the last few weeks. They told me that everything I had felt and seen, the hallucinations, the weakness, the tiredness, the smells, my bouts of anger and rage, were all classic symptoms.

The doctors rushed me to have a brain scan and found a tumour, benign, thank God.

Now I'm sitting here in bed, bald as a coot, feeling a bit woozy.

If it wasn't for Dave, goodness knows what would've happened, I'm glad he's a perceptive chap. The fact he brought my laptop to the hospital, means to me, he must have read my journal and understood what I was attempting to do. The best thing is that he hasn't mentioned anything about the entries.

Keeping up these entries is tiring, I'm worn out now, so I won't add any more today.

3rd February

Feeling better. Can't wait to get home. The food here is awful. Not sure when I'll be allowed to leave.

Not a bad bed though, got an excellent view of the grounds. Right next to the window I am. Don't like lying around though. I'm in my own side room, which is good. Not much in it, just a TV, a cupboard that could do with replacing, and no en suite.

I think it must be midday now. The winter sun is shining through the window.

***

The nurses have just informed me that it's lights out in a few minutes. This doesn't mean I have to stop typing on my laptop but I will. They tell me I need the rest. Been through a major operation I have, but it's a good day tomorrow, I've been given the okay to go home, can't wait.

***

Just woken up, don't know what disturbed me, it's dark and silent. For some reason the door of the cupboard is open.

I'm starting to breathe faster; I can feel trickles of cold sweat running down the middle of my back and an insuppressible sense of terror welling up inside me making the skin of my scalp feel like it's being pulled taut. The hairs on the back of my neck are now prickling. I am suddenly chilled to the bone.

The hell of the last few weeks was all down to the tumour. They assured me it was. It was; wasn't it?

4th February

Passed out again and I'm not going home yet. Not sure why I passed out last night but when I did I dropped my laptop on the floor and the nurses heard the crash. They rushed me to have another brain scan and the results showed that there was nothing untoward going on. The worst news is that I may have to stay in another night. I can't stand it here, I've never liked hospitals. Let's hope when the doctor comes round, I can convince him that I really am okay to leave.

***

In the doctor's opinion I just fell asleep. He told me in no uncertain terms, that if I don't rest he will make sure that I have a few more days in here just to make sure I do.

Of course, I promised him that I would, so the news is that I'm going to be discharged in two hours or so, once they've got my medicine ready.

***

Just got in from the hospital. It was pretty eerie opening the front door after all that's happened, or apparently happened. I'm not certain any longer whether it did happen, but it certainly feels like it was real. Least it's still light. Going to take my pills and rest. Probably have a little read in bed then straight to sleep.

5th February

Slept well last night. Going to email the boss at work and let him know that the doctor's signed me off for a month, then take it easy for the rest of the day.

6th February

NO! NO. NO. It was all meant to be over but it's started again. The time now is 1:15am. About 20 minutes ago I was brought out of my sleep by uncontrollable shivering; the temperature in the flat must be zero now.

The door to the airing cupboard is wide open, and the smells of damp earth and smoke are saturating the air. I can hear the clash of metal on metal and the woomph of fireballs crashing into the ground. I have to see what is going on.

***

I've only been gone about three hours but it seems like an eternity.

Whether it was stupid or not, all those hours ago I walked straight through that doorway into that unholy land.

Although I want the images and sounds to be gone from my memory I feel I must commit the whole thing to writing before I forget, if I ever will.

Once I was through that gateway to hell I fell to my knees as my legs gave way for no fathomable reason. I ended up belly down next to a familiar pile of rocks.

The legion of Romans (which I had come to the conclusion they were) weren't a legion after all. More like a squad (I don't know the proper name) of about sixty men. From what I could see the battle seemed almost over as the remaining Celts were greatly outnumbered. But just as the final few Britons were about to be subdued a hellish guttural scream pierced the air.

The Roman soldiers paused in their culling of the Celt warriors, being distracted by the noise. The Celts that were left seemed oblivious to this new noise; in fact they seemed to gain strength. They thrust their spears into the bodies of their opponents and followed through with their short swords, slashing and chopping.

Just as the noise reached its peak, hundreds of painted naked warriors appeared over the brim of the hill to my left, carrying more spears, shields, and swords. Now the Romans were in the minority.

Their ranks were reduced easily and most viciously. Some of the Celt warriors not satisfied with the fact that their opponents had died because of their attack, continued to cleave bits from their bodies, in a kind of gleeful mania, eviscerating them as they did so.

Gobbets of human matter were strewn across the dank ground, the earth darkened further as the blood of the defeated soaked into it.

I lay there fixated, paralyzed with the unrelenting horror that was playing out in front of me.

Suddenly one of the Roman soldiers shouted what seemed to be a command and those still standing made a sort of salute to their enemy and put down their weapons. The Celts stopped their onslaught and rounded up the invaders.

Relief crept through me as the tension in my body, a tension I wasn't aware of before, dissipated. I was glad it was over; no person should ever have to witness what I had seen.

A few Celt warriors stood guard around the remnants of the Roman squad whilst the Celtic chieftains discussed something amongst themselves. The discussion finished and one of the Celtic chiefs barked a command to the guards

The Romans were pushed and manhandled into a single line and the chief walked along it as if inspecting them.

When he got to the end he pointed to the third soldier back. A Celt warrior walked up to this man drawing his sword. He stood and faced the soldier eye to eye and raised his sword above his head. The Roman centurion did not move.

The chief barked another command and the warrior brought the sword crashing down onto the centurion's skull slicing it in two.

A cheer went up as the Roman's body collapsed to the ground. The other soldiers in the line charged the Celt warrior, all barring one that is. The first soldier in the line made a break for the open ground. None of the Britons took any notice they were more interested in the final annihilation of the attackers.

I tried not to look, but I felt that if I did not watch then I would be discovered and undergo the same fate.

The centurions managed to kill two more warriors before they were overpowered and sliced from the abdomen to the throat.

One by one the Roman bodies had their mouths sliced open then levered wide for the chieftains to defecate in. Once that abhorrent rite had been completed the soldiers' genitals were carved from their bodies and stuffed into the gaping excrement filled holes.

I was sick to my stomach, needing to retch. I only just kept my silence.

The warriors left and I was alone with the mutilated corpses of Romans and Britons alike.

Then I was back in my flat ready to start this entry. I didn't blink; I don't think I passed out. I was there then here. It's almost as if some incorporeal power was trying to show me something in that land.

Oh god, what sickening memories are being force upon me? What is its purpose?

I think I am going to try and rest.

***

Didn't sleep at all well last night. I'm surprised I'm up and it's still before midday.

Now the phone's bloody ringing.

***

That was a phone call from the "Sites & Monuments Record Office, County Hall Chelmsford." Janus in fact.

He asked me if I had done what he told me to do during the last phone call. I told him "of course not," he said his spirit guide had revealed as much and this was his reason for calling. He insisted I should follow his instructions from the previous call if I really wanted to put an end to my ordeal.

Anyhow, as I don't think there is anything on this earth that will lead me to the resolution of my problem I am now going to go downstairs to take my shovel from my shed, and wander down the lane to the spot he has directed me to. I have some digging to do.

***

I couldn't carry out anywhere near as much as Janus has said I should. I'm still weak from the surgery.

One thing though, after two hours of digging, I did get down to some human remains, but I couldn't carry on. The earth was very hard. I will have to carry on tomorrow.

7th February

No disturbances during the night, I'm feeling quite refreshed today actually.

Although what Janus told me yesterday seems utterly ridiculous I'm going to carry on. There's not much else I can do really.

***

I loaded up my car with the remnants of old furniture I had stored in my shed, stuff I'd decided to take to the tip but never got around to.

Janus had told me that I need to create a pyre, something for the remains to be consumed by. This was all very well but I had no clue as to how I was going to avoid any official questioning of what I was going to do. However, this question did not last in my mind too long because the other choice was much worse. I decided that a spell in prison was worth me performing this rite; the alternative was not worth contemplating.

At the bottom of the lane I unloaded the car and dragged all the craggy furniture to the pit I had dug the other day.

I piled everything up as Janus had instructed and placed the bones I had found on top. Once done I lit the pyre. Thanks to the paraffin the whole lot started to burn.

Within the smoke I thought I caught glimpses of shadowy people flowing towards the sky. Whether this was fact or just another manifestation of my unstable self I have no answer. I was just following Janus' dictate.

It's been a long day, but I can say it's done. Let's hope that's it.

8th February

Another good night's sleep and no evidence that anything malign has gone on.

9th February

Same as yesterday. Can I allow myself to believe that I'll not need to enter anything in this journal ever again?

23rd February

It's been two weeks since I've entered anything in this journal and I hate to say it, Janus seems to have been right.

All those weeks ago he tried to convince me that my ancestors had defiled some Roman invaders after they had surrendered to a greater Celtic army. Were they really my ancestors? I don't know.

He told me that in order to prevent the spirits of my ancient family showing me the whole horror of that time I needed to undo the dead soldiers' defilement; to do this I should give the Roman army's General an appropriate burial with the appropriate rites. Two weeks ago I completed this task.

Found a letter today, in the kitchen, post marked Italy. I seem to remember opening it before and throwing it away, perhaps I didn't. Anyway as it couldn't be for me, not knowing anyone from Italy, I chucked it straight into the bin.

And now we're here, the very last entry in my journal.

Who's going to read it? I don't know. One thing is for sure, I don't want to come back to this journal as its contents chronicle a period of my life I most certainly wish to forget.

The Invincible Man

In his underground lab Professor James Leest fired up his machine once again. He was sure he'd figured out the glitches and this time his theory on molecular encryption would be proven.

He placed another orange in the M.E.M's path, checked the control panel, flicked the "encryption key" toggle switch to "static", ensuring the encryption key used would not be a random number, then pressed the "fire" button. For a brief moment a golden beam reached out from the machine and cloaked the fruit, making it shimmer.

James picked it up. The orange looked the same, but felt slippery; frictionless. Interaction between the molecules of his fingertips and the orange was zero. He pulled out his pocket knife and tried to cut the orange open, to no avail; the blade slipped across the orange's surface.

Repeating the encryption process with his knife, this time the blade sliced easily through the orange. James smiled, picked up one half of the orange and threw it. It bounced off the walls, finally coming to rest on the M.E.M's console.

Now it was time for the ultimate test. Setting the timer for twenty seconds he pressed the button then stood in the beam's path. For a moment intense cold engulfed him, reaching down into his very essence; then it was over. Picking up a screwdriver he thrust it into his wrist but it glanced off his skin – he was now invincible.

As he pressed "power off" he noticed that the toggle switch was in the "random" position, but thought nothing of it; the orange must have flicked it when it landed.

***

He woke the next morning with an intense thirst but no matter how much he drank his thirst was not sated.

Then it dawned on him; his body would only be able to process water or food that had been encrypted the same way he'd been.

Taking a jug of water he fired M.E.M, but the process didn't work.

"Random," he yelled as he realised what he'd done to himself, knowing he'd never discover the encryption key in the few days his body could survive.

The Snake, the Duck and the St. Bernard

"You must do this."
And then she turned restlessly in her sleep,
fearing the instruction planted so deep
in her subconsciousness.

She knew not where the instructions came from,
but knew to disobey was against the law,
and not to whore herself to the rules would make her life
an even worse mess.

Upon awakening in dawn's early twilight,
and as was usual her brows furrowed at the night's
restless and disturbing sleep;
that had left her body forever heavy and resilience weak.

"Good morning," said the withered, silver-haired snake.
And through dark ringed eyes, and a sneer-smile she
pulled a chair out,
for a seat to take
– at the breakfast table.

On the opposite side and behind the toast rack
was a crippled St. Bernard whose big brown eyes, almost driven to tears,
stared at her silently... with melancholy... wracked.

In the past, when the girl first appeared,
the St. Bernard was well and not crippled by fear
and avoidance.

But as night terrors began to reign,
the St. Bernard's will failed and with legs becoming lame,
she was an unwilling accomplice.

The snake cherished the girl and everyday
bought her beautiful things to wear, and toys to play with.

And wrapped in the snake's charms that she liked,
the girl felt wanted and locked up the night,
in a dungeon...
in her mind.

Some months, even weeks or days,
Mrs Duck and Mr Ostrich called around on Snake to stay,
for tea, or a supper to eat.

And over the meal they talked prissy things

and Mrs Duck occasionally glanced at the girl, her offspring.
And saw the dark rings and happily... didn't mention a thing
– it wasn't her anymore.

As the meal continued to its second course
Mr Ostrich looked at the girl, then began to talk.
Fluffing up his chest, getting ready to boast,
he dismissed the haunted look of his offspring and rose
to tell of the design of a magnificent new nest,
made from twigs and branches,
but it was the sand that was best;
and it occupied him completely
– to the exclusion of all else.

And as time passed the girl's natural eye shadow
became blacker than black and a moan in her mind became a wail.
Forsaken by Mrs Duck and ignored by Mr Ostrich,
her mind... finally... broke.

And, like a statue, her body became taut
as the dungeon in her mind wantonly spewed forth,
the horrors of her nights.

For the girl there was only one recourse,

something that would help her, something that would stop
her presence at the talks
– across the breakfast table.

After being dismissed and told to go to her room,
to wait for Snake and the way he groomed her,
she'd managed to snaffle a large sharp knife
and with one quick slice she took her life.
And only then she smiled,
knowing she was free, forever.

In Defence of the Realm

Chapter 1

With all the downsizing going on, I'd decided to take redundancy from the army. I'd been one of the lucky ones, no family to consider, just myself to take care of.

I'd now been at the head office of Markent Marketing Ltd, just outside Gloucester and backing onto the Forest of Dean, for the last three months, having started in April. Although I wasn't in any significant position, and just worked in their post room, I was quite enjoying the job – not having to look over my shoulder, or check where I was about to place my feet, or any other intense crap I'd had to put up with whilst on duty.

It was a total and utter relief, and, believe it or not, the pay wasn't that much different, either, though I missed the benefits associated with my army career.

However, days flew by because Markent Marketing had major accounts with insurance giants, banks and loan companies, sending out and receiving all their junk mail, and we were in the middle of large promotional campaigns.

The guy, my mentor, Jacob Brizelthwaite, had been at the company since it'd been started by David Markent in the late '90s. But to me it seemed like Mr Brizelthwaite had been operating this particular post room even before Markent had taken over the building, and David Markent had just absorbed Mr Brizelthwaite's post room into his operation.

If I was to guess, I would have said that Mr Brizelthwaite was at least twenty years past retirement. Don't get me wrong, he seemed astute enough, mobile enough, but his grizzled face, unruly, almost white hair and circular specs atop his short nose, spoke of someone a lot older.

Since joining the company I'd watched Jacob intently; one thing was for sure, I was going to do this job and do it well. And I'd mimicked him, questioned him and done everything he'd told me.

But on occasions, when he thought no one was watching, he would do something he'd never mentioned during my three month probationary period.

On occasions he'd open one of the letters as normal, stare at it intently for a moment then file it in an unmarked lever-arch folder – making sure no one was looking. I don't think he understood the training we got in the army.

Chapter 2

It was getting to me and I hadn't slept well. Questions kept coming into my head; was I not good enough to be trained how to deal with those "special" letters Jacob dealt with? Was I untrusted? What the hell was wrong with me?

It was only 5am and the office was only thirty minutes away. It was way too early to go in, and there was no point in trying to get back to sleep before the alarm went off; I knew the questions would start up in my head as soon as it hit the pillow.

I turned on the radio and listened to the day's breaking news. More extreme weather it seemed, more corruption in the banks – some that went back almost half a decade. The journalists still attempting to break up the government even after two years of trying – they didn't get the idea of compromise, because each and every one of them were their own editors now, and all hung their hat on the back of morbid curiosity – the skill of engaging readers, lost, due to sheer laziness – I was certain the days of great reporting had been killed off in the late '80s with the advent of the scoop.

The world was going to pot and no one was stopping it.

My alarm buzzed loudly and I looked at the clock; 8am, it told me. This gave me an hour to get ready and get to work. Somehow the three intervening hours had melted away, but during that time I had resolved to query Jacob about his weird and unmarked lever-arch folder.

***

It was busy. The results of the ongoing campaign were bearing fruit and it wasn't until the mid-morning tea break that I was able to approach Jacob.

As I did, I was still in two minds; questioning one's boss about something, that really wasn't the done thing, at least it wasn't the done thing in the army, by a long chalk.

"Mr Brizelthwaite?"

"Ah! Young Derek. What can I do you for today?"

I didn't like this one bit. "I'm a bit confused."

"Confused? By the workings of a post room? You surprise me, Derek. You're an intelligent lad. What could possibly confuse you?"

"I could be mistaken, but I'm sure you've missed out something in my training."

Jacob shook his head. "Lad, you've been here three months now. I've shown you everything. And you're doing a great job. In fact, I can tell you this; your probationary period is over and you will be joining us fulltime. I pray this is acceptable?" As he spoke Mr Brizelthwaite arched his hands together, fingertips and thumbs touching.

That statement ended any thoughts I had as to querying him about his lever-arch folder. I needed the job and the money. "Thank you, Mr Brizelthwaite. Of course it's acceptable. Thanks."

The day continued and I was over the moon. And for a short while, the questions about the strange lever-arch folder slipped to the back of my mind.

Chapter 3

Before I knew it I was back home sitting in front of the telly with a cold can of Kronenbourg 1664, raising a toast to my newly confirmed position. Again the day had sailed through.

After the first time I'd noticed Mr Brizelthwaite snaffle away one of those letters, I'd started making notes in my diary. I pulled it out of my pocket and flicked through the pages; 22nd May and 17th June. Neither of the dates rang any bells with me.

I knew, now, that I had to get a look in that folder if I was going to quash the low buzz of the question that had become an irritant in the same way annoying jingles could. "What are those letters…what are those letters…what…?" and on and on and on.

"Right," I convinced myself, "tomorrow is Operation Dead Letter Day." I would work late and find out once and for all –

then approach Mr Brizelthwaite and ask. I nodded to myself acknowledging this was the only way forward, the only way to kill off the annoyingly recurrent question that was beginning to plague my every waking moment.

Chapter 4

As I trudged along the streets making my way to work, my usual cheery feeling was somewhat tempered. I stared at the gaps between the paving stones as they disappeared beneath my striding feet.

"Oi!" someone shouted from back down the road. "That's my bike!" I turned around to see some idiot in baggy light grey tracksuit trousers and a similar hoody pedalling a very red bicycle with a front mounted basket, coming in my direction. I then saw the postman appear from around the corner as he chased the hoody. I shook my head wandering what the world was coming to. Then put my arm out as if stretching. Unfortunately for the hoody he was unable to avoid my arm and collided with it just before dismounting the bike in an ungainly manner.

"You focking wanker," the twat mumbled before running off.

It was strange, during the whole episode I never caught a glimpse of the being beneath the cloth, and my memory kept telling me that the opening to the hood had been too black, too dark, as if light had been sucked out of the very air.

The postman caught up with me.

"Hey. Thanks, mate."

I shook my head, clearing it of its weird perceptions. "No problem," I eventually replied; though the delay seemed only to be in my mind.

"Are you sure?"

"Of course. Think nothing of it."

"Thanks again." The postman picked up his mount and wheeled it back down the road, and I carried on towards Markent Marketing, a bit happier, a bit disconnected and a bit late.

Chapter 5

"First day at work after being promoted and you're late, Mr Johns. Who do you think you are?"

I'd never seen Mr Brizelthwaite so angry before. Just as I was about to offer humble apologies he broke into a broad smile.

"Mr Johns, I don't doubt that after your good news yesterday you took it upon yourself to dabble in a jar of mead or some such brew."

I decided not to tell Mr Brizelthwaite about this morning's altercation with an almost living jogging suit, and nodded, leaving him with his peculiar notion that I was late because I'd been drinking some stuff from the middle ages, the night before.

He winked at me. "Just make sure it doesn't happen again, lad."

"Ok, Mr Brizelthwaite."

As I made my way to the sorting room, he gave me a friendly pat on the shoulder. I looked at him as I passed and he just nodded back at me with another wink.

I got the feeling that he knew something, though I couldn't for the life of me fathom what it was – it certainly couldn't be about Operation Dead Letter Day. That, had been furthest from my mind. I frowned as soon as the thought struck me, was I starting to believe in such mad things as mind reading? I sighed and shook my head. What an idiot I was being.

***

The clock swung quickly through lunch time and pounced upon mid-afternoon tea break. I made my way to the canteen with the others and sat down at an empty table. I didn't feel like being disturbed. The thought of this evening's special ops wasn't sitting well with me. I liked working here. I liked the people I worked with. And I liked Jacob Brizelthwaite as well. It felt wrong.

Next to the canteen was Mr Brizelthwaite's half-glassed office, the other side of which was the sorting room, where I worked. And at the back of the office, attached to the partition wall, were three room length shelves, the middle one of which held the enigma that was the unmarked lever-arch folder.

"Whoa!" I exclaimed as someone tapped me on the shoulder and propelled me out of my mental soliloquy.

"Derek, are you all right, lad?"

"Yes, Mr Brizelthwaite, just day-dreaming I suppose." I didn't like to lie and my reply didn't feel like one.

"I was a bit concerned there for a minute, lad. I've an appointment I can't get out of this coming afternoon and need someone to lock the place up. I pray you have no plans for this eve – if you have, no matter; I can ask one of the others."

I fought very hard to quell the look of complete disbelief that wanted to explode across my face. I was certain I'd succeeded.

"Erm. Yes, yes, of course. No problem. I need to make up some time anyway...due to this morning's little incident."

Jacob laughed and patted me on the shoulder; then nodded. "Thank you, Derek. Before you leave make sure there's no one left in the building – double-check by making sure all the time cards have been clocked out."

"Ok, Mr Brizelthwaite. No problem."

Jacob handed me the biggest bunch of keys I'd ever seen, picked his fedora from the hat stand and nodded at me again. "Anon," he said.

As he left, I got the distinct feeling, once again, that he knew more about everything than he let on, and certainly more than anyone else.

Chapter 6

Bill waved at me as he picked up his coat from the rack and put it on. He was always the last to leave.

I grinned as I waved and said goodbye. Sometimes I don't understand why people put up with the things they do. His real name was Vance, but I suppose everyone has to have a nickname; Vance was the offspring of Mr and Mrs Posters – but he never seemed to mind.

Now he'd left, I walked over to the time cards and clock. I checked all the cards and everyone had punched out except for me.

I locked everything, including the building's front door then turned to Mr Brizelthwaite's office – and stared at it.

I could see the lever-arch folder on the shelf, sitting there, taunting me. I really didn't want to go through with this, but I knew I had to know what the contents were.

I reached for the handle of his office door. I looked behind me, listened, and almost removed my hand. I shook my head; then twisted the handle. It didn't make a loud click as I thought it would. The door swung open and I stepped into his office.

Although I'd been here for my interview, although I'd been here for meetings, the inside of this glass office felt very different from those times when people had been buzzing around outside, getting on with the day to day tasks of processing mail. There was a strange feeling of otherworldliness. Although the furniture was modern, I felt like I'd stepped back two hundred years or more.

I mentally booted myself up the arse. The quicker I got this over and done with, the quicker I would feel better.

I stepped behind Jacob's desk, lifted the folder from the shelf, pushed the framed picture of a woodland landscape to one-side and placed the folder on his desktop. Again I paused before taking the next step.

I quickly grabbed the lid of the folder and flicked the cover open. There were dividers in the folder, numbered by year. The first divider was labelled "2003". The section was further divided into two months; July & August each.

I looked up. I was sure I'd heard the building door slam shut. I shut the lid of the folder and wandered out into the sorting room.

"Hello?... Mr Brizelthwaite?... Bill?" There was no response. I listened intently and the building felt as empty as it was silent.

I took a notebook from my jeans' pocket as I walked back into Mr Brizelthwaite's office.

There were about ten letters for each month in 2003, the last ones being sent on 26th July and 21st August, respectively – I made a note and skimmed through the letter headings, marking down the dates, for each of the years in the folder. There were no dividers for 2005 or 2007, but each and every other year was covered from 2003 to the present.

Another rattling sounded, breaking my concentration. I knew I couldn't risk being here in Mr Brizelthwaite's office any longer, though I didn't think he would be back.

I closed the folder and placed it back on the shelf in exactly the same place I found it and left the office.

I was gutted I'd not had the time to see any of the contents of the letters. Perhaps there would be another time. But enough was enough and I'd done way too much, risking the friendship I'd found and the only job I had.

"Tomorrow is another day," I consoled myself as I shut up shop.

Chapter 7

I was pretty shook up. I hadn't enjoyed any moment of operation "Dead Letter Day". It hadn't been anything like the ops I'd been a part of during my army days, then, though not so clear now, everything had felt just right.

I sat on my sofa supping at my coffee as I flicked through my notebook. The dates of the letters didn't mean anything to me. "Damn." I shook my head; what had I achieved? The list was meaningless without knowing the contents of the letters.

I booted the coffee table in shear frustration. It tipped over dumping the magazines and my empty plate onto the lounge floor.

Looking at the mess I calmed down, berating myself for getting so riled about something that wasn't my problem. I was glad that I still held the coffee cup; if that'd gone over then there would've truly been a mess.

Placing my cup on the side table I picked everything from the floor. With order ensuing, I began to feel calmer. There really was no need to get this worked up.

Perhaps in the coming weeks I could take another look, get the contents of the letters written down, and finally find out why Jacob didn't feel I was up to this final task of managing the dead letters, for this was all I could assume they were. They didn't go anywhere apart from Mr Brizelthwaite's unmarked lever-arch folder.

I took my plate to the kitchen, shoved it in the dishwasher, poured myself a glass of water and made my way to bed. A good night's sleep and everything would be better, or, at least, more understandable.

***

I rolled over and looked at the clock. It was 1:37am Saturday morning. Sleep had come quick, but now my brain was buzzing, electrified by the one question I'd hoped to avoid; "*What's in those letters?*" – bzzzzzzzzzzzzzzzzzzz.

Twenty minutes later I'd given up trying to go back to sleep, and got dressed. I looked at the bunch of keys in my hand.

"To do, or not to do?" my sleep deprived thought process considered. "For that is the question – sod it. I'm going to do it."

I left my home for the office and thirty minutes later I'd arrived.

The street outside the office was quiet, cars passed rarely and the sodium soaked street was pretty much deserted. I let myself into the Markent Marketing offices.

As soon as I was in I closed the door behind me; then listened. Relief! Not a sound. I made my way back to Mr Brizelthwaite's office, slid the key in the lock, turned the handle and let myself in.

I stopped again to listen. To make sure I was alone. There was only complete silence and me in this building. I nodded to myself and took the unmarked folder from the shelf. Opening it I pulled one of the letters from between the first divider – 2003 – and placed it on Mr Brizelthwaite's desk.

I couldn't make out the text in the gloom, a situation I wasn't used to, as my night vision was brilliant. But I was prepared. I pulled a small torch from my coat pocket and pointed it at the letter.

I was confounded by what it said.

> *Lle wethrine amin. Tanya nae n'quel. I'Ksherea tulien ten' ista.*

It was short and made no sense.

"Derek! What are you doing?"

My heart sunk. I recognised the voice. I didn't need to turn around to see who had spoken.

For some reason Mr Brizelthwaite had decided to come back to work at this time of the morning.

Chapter 8

I didn't know how to start. I didn't know what to say. I'd screwed up royally, and probably destroyed the best thing I'd ever had since leaving the army.

I turned to face Mr Brizelthwaite, desperately trying to think of a legitimate reason why I would be in the building at this time of the morning, and, why, I would be in his office, looking at papers he'd filed for no one else to see, holding a torch. Nothing came to mind.

"I didn't know why you'd kept these letters from me," I blurted out.

Mr Brizelthwaite nodded. I couldn't read his expression as the office was only illuminated by the torch I held and I certainly wasn't going to shine it in his face.

"I'm sure I'm good enough at my job to deal with these dead letters…," I trailed off with nothing else to say.

"Dead Letters is a good way to categorise them, lad," he said.

I was now utterly perplexed. This was the last thing I thought he would say. With my mouth hanging open, Mr Brizelthwaite continued.

"They're a warning; a message from the other side that something terrible is on its way."

The tone of Jacob's voice sent shivers through me. Whatever was in the letters was serious.

"And you have proven my choice as the right one."

I blinked a few times and my chin made motions. Eventually I said; “Choice?”

“Yes, Derek. Choice. I’m too old to do what is required. Although, if you hadn’t come along, I would have, as there wasn’t a choice for me, in that case. But you’re here now. And you’ve amply demonstrated the qualities required.”

“You’re not going to fire me then?” Since Mr Brizelthwaite hadn’t started to bawl me out, the more mundane had become important to me.

“No. You’re here because I chose you. And you’re here because what is going to happen in the next few days – is your destiny.”

I stared at my boss, shaking my head. Nothing was making sense. I knew he’d chosen me because he’d given me the job. But telling me my work over the next few days was my destiny, although true, was a little bit over the top. I worked as a clerk in the sorting office of a marketing company.

“My destiny?” I re-iterated.

Mr Brizelthwaite nodded, solemnly. I didn’t get the good feeling I’d expected, now that I was aware the position in the sorting office was mine until the day I died. I wasn’t even sure I wanted to stay there forever. Apparently my boss had other ideas.

He walked around the table and I moved back. Then he picked up the letter. “Here,” he said. “Watch this.”

Mr Brizelthwaite opened his desk drawer and pulled out a plastic vial of what looked like silver glitter. The kind of stuff you would use for making Christmas cards or something. He thrust it under my nose.

“Glitter,” he told me. It was glitter. I couldn’t believe it. I had no idea what was going to happen next.

He picked up the letter I'd put on the desk. "Shine your torch on this, Derek," he told me. I complied.

He pulled the top off the vial and gently sprinkled its contents across the meagre amount of weird words written on its surface.

For an instant I thought the words changed, and I could read them. For an instant I read the translation;

> *You deceived me. That was not good. The evil ones coming for you.*

And then the mirage was gone.

Chapter 9

I looked toward the letter and back over my shoulder at Mr Brizelthwaite then back to the letter.

"The evil ones are coming?" I said in a whisper, as the only illumination was still my torch, the dimness lending the atmosphere a conspirational air.

Mr Brizelthwaite sighed heavily. "I'm afraid so, lad." He shook his head then placed a hand on each of my shoulders.

Leaning into my ear he said, "What I'm going to tell you, you're not going to believe. All I ask is you ask this question of yourself, when I'm done; 'Of what benefit is it to Mr Brizelthwaite to tell me this rubbish?'"

I shook my head. "Mr Brizelthwaite, I doubt you're going to tell me any rubbish," I said.

"Young lad, you haven't heard what I'm going to tell you."

Jacob lent across his desk and turned on the lamp then sat down in his chair. "Derek, quickly make us a cup of tea. We don't have a lot of time and I have a lot to tell you. So you're prepared for when you cross over."

My eyes blinked and my chin sagged. The tone he'd used was really serious, I mean really serious. There was no smile waiting to erupt on his face, lurking in the background ready to demarcate his statement as a little jest.

"Sugar?"

Jacob nodded. "Five please."

I left for the kitchen.

***

"Ah, young Derek, there you are. I was getting a little worried. You've taken your time."

I placed our cups on Jacob's desk then dragged a hand down my face as I attempted to collect my thoughts.

"You sounded serious."

"Very serious, Derek. There are bad times ahead unless we can stop them."

"How..."

Jacob held up his hand. "Let me tell you what I have to say and I'll answer any questions you may have then, young lad."

"Ok, Mr Brizelthwaite."

"It started, oh, so long ago, Derek, and my bones are weary. As the years have gone on the responsibility has weighed heavily..."

I'd never heard Jacob talk like this before. He always seemed to be such a happy soul. I picked up my tea and continued to listen.

"It was the likes of Sir Isaac Newton, François-Marie Arouet, whom most know by the name Voltaire and John

Locke, who sowed the seeds, all for very good reasons, but were blinded by their own reasoning and logic.

"What I'm talking about is the birth of science – which was no bad thing – but when working in tandem with blind belief in the scientific method, The Enlightenment, began to erode mankind's received wisdom; knowledge acquired through thousands of years of living in harmony with Nature.

"Two hundred years ago around the end of the 17th century it started and has continued, though corrupted to such a degree, there is, now, mortal peril for all."

As Jacob paused to sip at his tea I frowned. "I don't understand, Mr Brizelthwaite…"

"Jacob. Please, lad, Jacob."

"Ok," I nodded. "Jacob, it is. How can science put us all in mortal danger? Apart from wars and stuff like that?"

"It's not science per se; it has more to do with how scientific knowledge is becoming the only allowed knowledge; with its evangelists, like Richard Dawkins, dictating the boundaries of scientific investigation, by stating which areas do not warrant investigation, to their way of thinking: completely opposite to the scientific method, in fact."

"I don't get it, Jacob. How can that put us in mortal danger?"

Jacob held out his cup. "A refill first, I need to gather my thoughts. Then I'll tell you the rest."

Chapter 10

I think this next part was going to be difficult for Jacob. His distress was very apparent. He wasn't the confident old man I'd come to know since starting work in his post room.

"Sit down, Derek."

I did as I was told.

"Remember what I said before you come to any judgement, about the tale I'm about to tell you."

I nodded.

"I was barely in my twenties when The Enlightenment started and where we are today is the same place I've lived since.

"As the movement began to gather momentum I was approached by representatives of the 'Other Realm' – a world that sits in the same space as ours but where the plane of life is slightly separated, at an angle if you will; together and apart, at the same time.

"Many people you may know of have taken inspiration from…"

I stood up abruptly, so shocked was I about the little snippet of information that had joined with another in my head.

Jacob looked at me concerned. "Are you all right, my lad?"

"You just said that you were in your twenties when The Enlightenment started!"

Jacob nodded. "Yes. That I did."

"And you said it started about two hundred years ago?"

"Ah! I thought you took that part of my tale in good stead, but it seems it has only just sunk in."

"You're – what? – two hundred and fifty years old?"

Jacob shut his eyes and shook his head; then stared at me. He looked very tired. "I don't know, Derek, something around that. I've given up counting… Please, let me continue."

"Who else knows?"

"Derek, enough questions."

I sat back in my chair absolutely stunned by the revelation.

"Now, where was I? Ah! Yes. Many people have taken, what you could call, inspiration from the knowledge of the Other Realm; though others might call it fact.

"Have you ever wondered where C. S. Lewis, Charles Lutwidge Dodgson and J. R. R. Tolkien drew their ideas from?"

"Who's Charles Dodgson?"

"Sorry. Lewis Carroll."

"What! You mean there really are white rabbits checking watches and decks of card marching about somewhere or another?"

"No, Derek. What I'm talking about is the historical recording of the Other Realm in written works such as the ones created by these people. It is my belief they knew what was at stake. But still science soldiers on depreciating the history and extoling the destruction of such knowledge. We're lucky that these works have become 'classics'. At least there is some level of assurance the record will remain."

Suddenly the room began to shake as if an earthquake had just started, and we were at its epicentre. As our tea slopped out of our cups the shaking stopped as abruptly as it had begun.

"What the…"

"I think they've reached the beginning of The Conversion, Derek. There's probably less than a few days left."

Chapter 11

I didn't know what was going on. There was too much weird information and Jacob was talking to me like I was going to solve everything.

"Mr Brizelthwaite, I don't get it. What you're telling me is beyond normal. If you'd been anyone else I'm sure the men in white would be here in a flash, strapping you up and carting you away."

Jacob rolled his eyes. "I know how it must seem, lad." He shook his head slightly and pursed his lips. He seemed resigned to continue, come what may. "Derek, you've seen the letters. You've seen how the words were revealed. I don't have it in me to do what is necessary. I'm too old and I've waited a long time for someone like you to turn up. Things would have been different if I could have sought you out, but it was against the rules."

Things were getting weirder by the minute. "What rules?"

Jacob shut his eyes and shook his head again. "There isn't enough time to explain everything; perhaps afterwards."

"After what? What is this 'Conversion'?" I almost shrieked.

"Let me finish explaining."

Jacob downed the remnants of his tea and took a deep breath. "When it was apparent that the scientists would attempt to purge 'natural wisdom' from humanity's knowledge and replace it with the new science and its discoveries, a council of the cunning folk and the Sidheóga was called. The council agreed to build a barrier to separate mankind from the Sidheóga. They were certain that the Enlightenment would lead a determination to 'resolve' all potential conflicts that could exist between the new thinking and the old."

"I take it 'resolve' is a euphemism," I asked.

"I'm afraid it was, my lad. We always spoke of it like that. The thought of mankind and the Sidheóga parting ways was bad enough, but the Enlightenment had given those humans with a blacker heart a way to shrug off the shackles of the Sidheóga, as they saw it.

"The Enlightenment was a greater enemy than Christianity ever was."

Our shadows were suddenly cast upon the back wall of Jacob's office as a brilliant light sliced through the gloom inside the building. A massive peel of thunder followed and it vibrated the partition wall that separated Jacob's room from the post room proper.

We waited for another strike but none came.

"Jacob, what do you mean by 'the conversion'?" I shook my head then said, "It's nothing to do with rugby is it?"

Jacob smiled and coughed a slight laugh. "No. Nothing to do with rugby, Derek. I wish it were. Our lives would be so much simpler than they are now."

Chapter 12

Greyness had begun to penetrate the dark of the night and dawn was on its way. Jacob looked toward the windows and sighed.

"I've still so much to tell, my lad. And I've yet to prepare you for your journey."

I was just about to open my mouth when Jacob held up his hand and shook his head. "Before you say anymore let me tell you about the 'Conversion'; it's part of a barrier made of human and faery majick, built by the Sidheóga and the cunning folk almost two hundred and fifty years ago; an enforced apartheid of sorts, borne of science.

"The Conversion blocks the pathway between the two realms, that of humanity and the Other Realm. It's called the

Conversion because it translates space between the two realms, from one to another. Almost."

Jacob stared at me, his eyes probing mine. I'm certain he was checking for a glimmer of disbelief.

"Well?" he said.

I was silent, not sure what to say or ask. Though lots of questions were racing around my brain they were intermingled and nothing would crystallise.

"Come on, Derek," Jacob said in a weary manner.

The first one coalesced. "How d'you know all this stuff? It's a bit fantastical isn't it?"

"The easy ones are always first," Jacob smiled as he said this. "I was there, Derek. I was part of the council when it was decided to separate the two realms.

"The council members couldn't see any good coming of the Enlightenment for the Sidheóga, especially because the scientific method wouldn't be able to comprehend, let alone explain, how the Sidheóga could manipulate the forces of Nature in the same way a shepherd's wife could turn the coat of a sheep into a jacket or kilt.

"This inability, the council knew, would only lead to fear and out of fear would come death and destruction."

"So the Sidheóga were made safe?"

"If being locked into half of a whole is safe, then yes."

"Why did the letter say you lied and the evil ones are coming?"

"Because your science has progressed, Derek: in a manner of speaking. Nearly all the building blocks of Nature have been identified, and this is the first step on the pathway to understanding how to control those building blocks.

"But this isn't the reason I, as one of the council, have seemingly lied to the Sidheóga. Each step on the path of discovery that narrows the gap in knowledge, between that of the Sidheóga's and mankind's, is a physical encroachment on their realm – and the methods used in Geneva, at CERN in the Large Hadron Collider, are destroying vast tracts of the Sidheóga's land every time it is powered up to smash Nature's building blocks.

"It seems to me that mankind has only a capacity to investigate things by the very destruction of the said things; the reason why jigsaw puzzles seem such an antithesis – you discover their beauty by putting all the pieces together! Why not for the state of being?"

Jacob shook his head at the unbelievable craziness then soldiered on with his tale.

"The council had promised they'd be safe after the Conversion had been built and, because I'm one of the guardians assigned to the Conversion Bridge, the Sidheóga feel I've betrayed them."

Jacob shook his head again. "The cunning folk tried to see this far ahead, but nothing was clear. We felt making the promise to the Sidheóga would be something that would remain unbroken in perpetuity."

"And the evil ones?" I asked.

"Let's just say they're soldiers of Akh'Mori; and discussion is not their preferred path to resolution, my lad."

I gulped at Jacob's dark description. "What is Akh'Mori?" Though I asked, I wasn't wanting to hear an answer.

"It's the Elven Army of the Dark, Derek. Not something that should ever be present in the mortal's realm."

"Is there anything that can be done?"

"Yes. Go home. Get some rest, Derek – a lot. Then come back here at one o'clock..."

"Ok. Sunday?" I asked hopefully as one o'clock Saturday was only seven hours away.

"Yes. One o'clock Sunday morning," Jacob nodded. "That would be about right."

"Morning? Sunday?" I said.

"Yes."

For some reason I felt I had no choice. Whether it was Jacob's tired soul or something else entirely, I don't know, but I concurred anyway.

"Ok, Mr Brizelthwaite," I said.

Chapter 13

Thankfully I was so exhausted by the time I got home sleep came immediately; none of the previous evening's surprises keeping me awake.

But now I was up, stuff I hadn't asked Jacob about was buzzing around my head; what was the journey he'd spoken about? What preparation did I need? In fact, why did I need any preparation? I hadn't agreed to anything... I don't think.

"Oh my word," I sighed out loud to myself. How had I got here? Everything seemed so unreal... in fact everything was bloody unreal.

Then it dawned on me: The last three months had all been a stupid trick. I don't know why, or the purpose. But, for sure, I'd been duped.

The whole thing a laugh at my expense; but the people at Markent's had seemed so genuine; especially Mr Brizelthwaite.

But if it was a complex joke then that would explain why Jacob had his special letters that no one was allowed to see; the whole scenario designed to catch out an ex-army guy who, through his training, had to be observant.

The more I mulled over the details of my employment, the more it became apparent that, for one reason or another, a nasty insidious joke had been played on me.

"YOU BASTARDS," I yelled at the top of my voice.

I'd heard of this, army personnel after demob having the piss taken out of them; no respect for the fact they'd laid their lives on the line for the country.

No dots would connect up in my head to provide a reason for this – just the certain knowledge it happened, there, ready to grasp and embrace.

I felt destroyed. They'd done it to me, and I'd been caught out. What a complete fool I'd been: what a complete fool I was. A survivor of Afghanistan; a person who'd stopped atrocities being enacted in the UK and a person who'd committed, in civvy town, to help those around him – everything being thrown back in my face.

I decided enough was enough; the joke stopped here. I took the writing pad from the bookshelf in my lounge, placed it on the coffee table and considered how I would phrase my resignation.

It had to be poignant; it had to crush the reader just as their sick joke had crushed me. But I couldn't be vitriolic; that would show they'd won. Any words I wrote had to perform like the motions of a surgeon's scalpel; dignified, precise and thoughtful.

***

I looked at the pad then looked at the clock; the clock had moved on, but the pad remained blank, even after all these hours. It was twelve forty-five Sunday morning.

It really bugged me; in my head I knew all the things I wanted to say, but none of them complied with the principles I needed to follow if they were not to get the better of me.

I wrote the word 'You' then put the pen down. I checked the clock again – 1am 'This'll teach you,' I thought knowing my presence would never grace the Markent's post room ever again.

Chapter 14

I sat on my sofa and stared at the telly – it wasn't on – but I still hoped for inspiration. The minimal light in the lounge, supplied by a small desk lamp, made a dim reflection in the TV's screen of the sofa I sat on, as I tried to figure out the correct words to use, to show them who was really in command of my life.

A flash of light drew my attention to the road outside. It illuminated the lounge and was quickly followed by a deep boom of thunder.

I wouldn't have thought anything of it had it not been for an after image of an old guy with long hair looking in at me. Mr Brizelthwaite? my mind queried.

I got off the sofa and looked out the window. Lightning flashed again and in the moment of that flash Mr Brizelthwaite appeared, standing at the dead centre of the road.

What a git. How dare he continue this façade. Just looking at the soaking bloke made me clench my teeth. I raced out of the lounge and out my front door. But in the few seconds it'd taken me to get to the front gate he'd vanished.

I stood in the middle of the road soaking wet, looking up and down, trying to see where Brizelthwaite had gone. He was nowhere to be seen. In that moment I decided to go back to Markent and give the old man a piece of my mind.

Chapter 15

I shoved open the door of Markent Marketing and it slammed against the wall. I stormed along the corridor to the post room. Brizelthwaite looked towards me and waved me in. He wasn't wet!

"Now look here," I began.

"Derek, you're late."

Oh my stupid head, I thought. "It's real. Isn't it?"

"The Akh'Mori? The Sidheóga? Of course it is, Derek. Why wouldn't it be?"

I didn't have an answer. "I don't know, Jacob."

"You don't look very prepared, lad."

I squirmed.

"Lucky for you I have made some preparations. Once you're through the portal…"

"Portal? What? Like a gateway or something?"

"Yes, exactly. As I was saying: Once you're through the portal you'll need some way to make contact from the Other Realm."

"I've got my mobile."

"Derek, there are no mobile phones there, no electricity, no mobile phone masts. They don't need it. They interact with Nature for what they need. Come on. Come with me."

Jacob left his office and made his way to the cloakroom, which wasn't a room at all really, just a piece of wall with a coat rack attached.

"This is something you'll need to remember; 'Just after twenty to five in the afternoon'. Well, at least that's the way I remember it. 1642 – the year Sir Isaac Newton was born."

I shook my head. "Ok, if you say so."

"Watch, my lad."

Jacob went to the first hook on the coat rack and turned it to the one o'clock position, then quickly turned the next three hooks; six o'clock, four o'clock and two o'clock. There was a dull thud and part of the wall started to recess revealing a staircase that looked as though it had been hewn from the very bedrock.

"Bloody Hell! This is all a bit Indiana Jones, isn't it?"

Jacob smiled. "Haven't you listened to what I've been saying, lad?"

"Of course I have, Mr Brizelthwaite."

We started to descend.

"Perhaps a little, my lad. Don't you ever wonder where writers get their ideas from?"

"Like Wonderland?" I said, now understanding what Jacob had been getting at.

He nodded. "Just so, lad."

"Is this the portal?"

Jacob laughed. "No, my lad. Portal's aren't manmade; or made by cunning folk for that matter. They're part of Nature, just as sunspots are part of the Sun. Eddies in Nature's fabric, if you will."

"What's down here then?"

"My workshop, young Derek. Where I've got a few things you're going to need."

"Where's the portal then?"

"About 137 miles due east from here; in Essex, in a park named Belfairs Woods." Jacob looked at his watch. "We've only got about an hour and a half to prepare and get there."

"Why do we need to be there by three in the morning?"

"Because that's when the portal's open for mere mortals such as yourself, young Derek. But even then there's not a lot of time. As the portal cycles through its eddies, it only leaves a window of three minutes for you to slip through. So you can see timing is of the essence."

I nodded. Jacob pushed back a huge rug that hung on the wall opposite the bottom of the staircase, and revealed another, less secretly concealed doorway. We walked in.

I now stood in a smallish cave and I gawped as I turned on the spot taking in the view. Candles flickered all around. Its dimly lit walls appeared to be of blackish-brown rock made of lots of thin layers, almost looking like slate that had been piled high by geology. In places the walls were covered by patches of deep green, where rivulets of water dripped and trickled.

Chapter 16

Jacob was leaning over an old wooden bench, its dark top deeply grooved by the wearing of the wood's layers. He was emptying the contents of a glass phial into, what looked like, a small, manky leather pouch. And he was shaking his head.

"I'm sorry I don't have a lot of this, Derek." His face looked ominous as he told me.

"What is it?" I asked.

"It's Emmenanthe penduliflora."

"Thanks, Jacob, that's very helpful." I know I shouldn't have been sarcastic but Jacob wanted me to do this, so I felt it appropriate, especially as I needed to know the information.

"Sorry, Derek, there's been so little time. It's the Whispering Bell. I've had this plant transported all the way from Arizona, but never thought I'd need it so soon, nor in the quantities I know you need. After all the set-backs I never thought I'd find my apprentice. Then you came along."

All I could do was nod. After the way Jacob had treated me for breaking in to his office I'd gathered he'd had a plan for me, and now it had been said – I was his apprentice.

"Ok. Whispering Bell. Fine. What's it for?"

"It's the herb the cunning folk use when they're apart and need to talk."

"But that's from Arizona. How did they talk before that?"

"Some of the cunning folk have telepathy. In the older times there were shops like your post offices, but, instead of leaving letters or telegrams, the cunning folk would ask the teller to send the message mentally – all of us could 'hear' tellers if we were the intended recipient, but two way discussion was limited to 'tellers', the rest remained 'hearers', until the cunning folk learnt of Emmenanthe penduliflora from the native American Indians."

"How does it work?"

"Penduliflora needs to be prepared if it is to be used. But you must remember that, when prepared, its affects only last for an eighth of a local day; here that means about three hours. If you don't use the preparation in the time then its quality is so deteriorated it's unusable.

"Whispering Bell travels best when it hasn't been prepared. In its natural, picked state, it can last many weeks."

Jacob set the pouch he'd just filled to one side of the workbench.

"How am I going to know how to prepare it?" I asked.

"I'll show you in a minute. I just want to tell you about the tools I'll be giving you for your journey."

I looked at Jacob solemnly. "I'm going over aren't I?"

Jacob placed a hand on my shoulder and looked directly into my eyes. "Only if you want to, Derek. This task can only be performed by the willing, and although I'm as willing as I've ever been, my bones and my heart are not; it's been too long.

"This duty has an importance so severe only those willing, through and through, have the chance to complete it. At least that's how the prophecy states its case."

"Prophecy!?"

"Yes, Derek."

"I guess there's no time to ask about the prophecy?"

Jacob looked at his watch and shook his head. "No. We've only an hour to get to the portal and I haven't nearly told you enough of what you need to know. No time now, my lad. Perhaps later if… sorry, when you get back."

I heard Jacob's slip of the tongue and, although my heart was beginning to race, I knew I needed to focus on the task at hand, so I pushed his slip to the back of my mind. But this didn't stop a level of despair start to weigh on my shoulders. Who was I to achieve this? Why did Mr Brizelthwaite think I was the right person? So many questions; and no time to get any answers.

Jacob left the table and walked to a shelf on the opposite side of the room. He rummaged through a few books and pamphlets then pulled out an old dusty cylinder. To me it looked like the only thing it could contain was a decent bottle of malt whisky. But this wasn't to be the case. Jacob removed the lid and removed a scroll of paper, equally dusty and also dark tan in colour.

He unfurled it across the table. It was a map, of sorts. Nothing like the kind I was used to.

Jacob punched a point on the map with his forefinger. "There you go, my lad. Once you've gone through the portal and crossed The Conversion, this is where you're aiming for."

"Great! But what am I going to do when I'm there – take out the entire Akh'Mori by waving some flowers called Penduliflora at them?" I waved an arm about, holding an imaginary bunch, just to demonstrate the futility I was trying to convey.

Jacob's eyes crinkled at their sides. Although serious he was amused. "No, Derek. You need to persuade the Queen of the Sidheóga to call back the Akh'Mori, or at the very least send their own army to stop them."

"I thought they were all the same!"

"No. Not at all. The Sidheóga prefer peace over all else. But if they're wronged, and there are some that want to exact revenge, then the Sidheóga will turn a blind eye. The Sidheóga aren't Elves, Derek."

"How will talking to the Queen help?"

"The Queen rules over the majority in the Other Realm. She holds sway over the balance."

Jacob opened a drawer in his workbench and pulled what looked like to be a small round piece of paper from it. "A filter, Derek. You must never drink anything in the Other Realm without filtering it first. Is this clear?"

"Of course," I said. I knew about filters and such like. It'd all been standard training in the army. And I'd used them many times in Afghanistan.

I put the filters in the canvas satchel Jacob had given me.

"Now, my lad," Jacob said as he retrieved a large knife from the wall cupboard he was now standing at. "You will need this to help you with your task." He offered me the shaft and I took it.

"Only use the Knife of Zarcesaan to kill in the direst of circumstances. And only in the Other Realm, for it will not work here, my lad, 'tis only for folk of the majick tribes. But I pray you never have to use it."

I took the knife and stared at it, turning it in my hand. I couldn't see any reason why it wouldn't work in good ol' Blighty.

I ran my finger along the blade's edge and no sooner had it touched my skin it'd sliced through the ridges of my fingertip; blood began to seep from the cut. How this knife would fail to work here I couldn't figure. I sheathed the knife and put it in the canvas satchel along with the filters.

As I withdrew my hand I checked the deep gash on my finger – it was gone; nothing of the cut existed. My eyes widened, this was a complete surprise.

"Derek!"

I looked away from my satchel and back to my mentor. "Yes?"

"Have this."

Jacob handed me a Perspex tub of something that looked like lard. "This is the salve you will need to get through the Conversion without much ado."

I frowned. "What d'you mean much ado, Jacob?"

He paused for longer than I could have wished for. I shook my head. I knew Jacob was trying to think of the best way to phrase what he was going to say.

"Depending upon how you're made, Derek, you will slip through easily, or not, and you will feel every change the Conversion places upon your body."

He paused for a moment then continued. "The Conversion remakes you to fit the rules of the Other Realm, the salve frees your soul for the duration of the change; without it you will feel the rules and how they change your very body."

I gaped at Jacob. It sounded quite severe.

Three letters flashed through my mind; OMG!

Chapter 17

Jacob had shown me how to prepare the Penduliflora. To use it was very simple, paste the preparation behind the ear. Then call out, in my head, to the person I wanted to communicate with. That was it! So simple.

"Derek, there's only fifteen minutes left to get to Belfairs Woods. You really have to be ready."

"I've put everything in the satchel. I have the map. Can't think of anything I've missed."

"Good. Time to move then, lad."

Jacob pulled a gas firelighter from another drawer in his workbench. I recognised the grey-handled device, with its steel tube; my mother used to use the same said thing to light the gas fire in our lounge.

"What's that for?" I asked.

"It's to get us to where we're going, lad. I need to generate a leap to take us to the portal's entrance."

"A leap?"

Jacob nodded, his brows were knotted. "Yes. How else do you think we'll get to Belfairs Woods in the time we have?"

I looked at Jacob nonplussed.

"A leap of faith or a leap in time and space, it's all the same thing, lad."

"Sorry, Mr Brizelthwaite, I'm not used to this. It's just not normal."

"I know, lad. I know." Jacob nodded. "Let me establish the bridge."

My eyebrows rose. I felt I was about to see something beyond my comprehension. Something I'd certainly never seen before.

Jacob waved at me to follow. We left his workshop, wandered up the stairs, walked along the corridor and entered his office. He sat on his chair.

"Derek, we're about to go to the portal's entrance; I hope you understand what this means?"

I looked at the satchel I carried and I looked at my mentor. "Jacob, I know what's planned for me. I know what I have to do. And I know that, potentially, I may not make it. And I know someone has to do this." I shrugged. "And I think it's me."

Jacob put a hand on my shoulder. "You have all the skills, my lad. Don't fear."

He opened his desk drawer and pulled out a feather quill, a small strip of blotting paper and a pocket compass from the pen tray.

Placing the pocket compass in front of a framed picture of a woodland landscape, which had been on his desk since before the day I'd joined Markent, he waited for the needle to settle;

then aligned the left and right edges of the picture frame with north and south.

Next he reached into the drawer beneath the pen tray and removed – nothing! Jacob then twisted an imaginary lid from an apparently invisible vessel. I didn't know whether this process was mime, or, through some weird magic, I couldn't see the pot.

Jacob placed the "invisible" lid on his desk and pulled the thin strip of blotting paper towards him. Then he picked up the feather quill and after brushing the feather between his thumb and forefinger he dipped the nib into the non-existent pot.

I was amazed. As Jacob tapped the nib on the edge of the make-believe pot I could hear a light metallic clink on a glass rim each time. All I could do was shake my head in awe.

Jacob started to write on the blotting paper and words formed at the base of the quill, no different from any other writing with real ink from a real pot.

shackles from here take us to there,
and cease to be our bonds,
the portal will open in the park,
where twin trees demarcate the long,
journey to the Conversion,
where an apprentice makes a change,
to be in the Other Realm,
so as to extinguish the dark flame.

He put the quill down and folded the blotting paper in two. The words were now encapsulated within the slither of absorbent material, but slowly partial curves and lines showed through exposing illegible text as the ink made its mark.

Jacob took the gas firelighter, clicked the ignition and melted some wax. It dripped onto the blotting paper making a seal.

Jacob looked at his watch and then looked at me. "Lad, only seven minutes left. Are you ready?"

As I shook my head, my mouth said, "Yes."

Jacob took the sealed blotting paper and started to rub it against the surface of his framed woodland picture. With every circle he made the already dim periphery of his office, and my vision, became dimmer, dissolving the office and post room.

I could not see anything but a blackish background containing twinges of earthy brown, an image that changed position in the blackness whenever I blinked.

Then a path came to the fore followed by a moonlit golf course on my right and a hedgerow on my left. Forward there was a tarmac road; both of us were standing on it.

I turned to Jacob. "How on Earth?"

"Do I need to answer, Derek? I think you must be sure of the 'how', by now."

Chapter 18

We were now standing on a macadam path. Behind us was a road and across that another large hedgerow.

"Where do we go?" I asked my mentor.

He pointed. "Along there. See those twin trees on the south side of the path?"

I nodded.

Jacob looked at his watch. "In five and a half minutes you need to walk between them and make your way to the Conversion. After that you will have about three hours before the Akh'Mori start deconstructing the Conversion and cross the bridge between the portal and our realm."

I checked my watch as well, and nodded. The situation was dire, but to hear Jacob call this world "ours" made me all the more determined to do my very best to fix the problem.

"Derek, I need to tell you some other information before you cross over."

I felt my heart sink. If this wasn't difficult enough, Jacob was surely to load me up with other bad news. "Ok, Mr Brizelthwaite, what else do I need to know?"

On seeing my face, Jacob shook his head and waved a palm at me. "Nothing so serious, young Derek. Don't worry."

"That makes a change," I said. As soon as the words had left my mouth, I could see Jacob grinning under the moon shadow light.

"What?!"

Jacob shook his head again. "Sorry, Derek. A little jest to lighten your load. Be wary of the Irdiroga – the in-between folk – you may or may not come across them. But they will certainly hold a resentment of your presence, should you meet."

"Why? Where? What have I done to them? I don't even know who they are."

"I'll start with the 'where'. They hold sway between the portal and the Conversion."

I looked around quickly. The park was empty. Only myself and Jacob to be seen, barring a few of the other regular earthly inhabitants – foxes roamed and owls flew. "There's no one else here."

"I didn't mean here. I meant on the other side of the portal, on the way to the Conversion. Sometimes they're used as scouts for the Akh'Mori."

I was afraid to ask, but in my gut I needed to know. "Why are they likely to 'resent' me?"

"They have no free will, lad, other than in the in-between space. They cannot choose to leave or stay. When they are able, it is only because some other power has made that choice. They will see you, and your presence, as an affront to their circumstance."

"Oh great! Thanks for lightening my load!"

Jacob looked at his watch. "It's time, my lad. In three minutes you will need to walk between those two trees."

I looked to where Jacob was pointing and a little way along the path, in front of us, stood two solitary trees; twins they certainly were.

As I looked I could clearly see a house in the distance, framed by the two trees, shimmer as if some unknown source had heated the air enough to make the light passing through it sway and shake like a lake's surface, disturbed by small ripples of a thrown stone.

"Give me the map."

I couldn't believe Jacob's tone, but I handed him the map anyway.

"Look!" Jacob thrust a finger on the unfurled scroll. "Don't go near there."

His finger indicated a jagged zigzag line. It was a little way from the path we'd already agreed I'd follow. I shook my head. "Why would I? It's not our route."

"Just in case, my lad. Just in case." Jacob rolled the map up and handed it back to me. "One minute to go, lad."

We had walked the path and were now standing next to the twin trees. The shimmering between the trees belied the fact that the air was much, much colder – no heat-haze the effect. I could also hear a noise; almost a sea crashing somewhere on a distant shingled beach.

Jacob grabbed me by both shoulders and pulled me close, hugging me. “You need to sort this problem out.”

I smiled. “I think it’s a bit more of a ‘problem’ than you think.”

Jacob nodded and winked. “You can do it, lad. You can do it – time to go.”

I looked at Jacob for the last time; shook his hand. Then turned and made for the gap between the trees, waving as I left him standing on the path.

Chapter 19

As I walked towards the gap between the twin trees the noise of the foreshore got louder – increasing – large waves crashing on a million pebbles, and then sparkling snaps and crackles as the invisible water receded.

There was no smell of ozone though; nothing to indicate a far off beach. As soon as I’d passed between the trees silence crashed in.

I rubbed my eyes. It seemed there was nothing but night here. Stupidly I hadn’t brought a torch. But gradually my eyes adjusted.

A dim light came from the horizon on my left. Where the horizon was and how far away it was, I couldn’t tell, but at least some light existed. I would’ve been stuffed otherwise.

It felt like I was in a huge cavern – the distance, and all around, demarcated by a blackness that was a few shades lighter than the dense, impenetrable black further on.

Wet looking slate-grey rocks edged either side of a grey path, its paving made of flat pebbles, myriad shades of grey but countable, more than fifty, I suspected.

The path I followed sloped downwards. The only noises that fluttered in the air were those of my footfalls on the scree path and my breathing. It was uncanny.

After the shock of the change had subsided I settled into a regular stride, and the millstone of responsibility I'd been passed lightened a little. I was on my way to do an important job and ahead lay the Conversion.

I attempted to check my progress against the map even though I thought it would be a fruitless task in the lacklustre illumination. But as I moved my finger closer to the marked out route, the lines and features luminesced on the surface of the map-scroll, and I could see it wouldn't be long before I reached the Conversion.

I removed the salve from my satchel and was about to unscrew the lid when, from the corner of my eye, a skittish shadow caught my attention.

I looked up. Then left and right. Nothing. I dismissed the distraction as something my mind had created out of the surrounding blackness.

Jacob had instructed me to cover myself in the salve, though not to what degree. I unscrewed the lid just before something landed on my shoulder; a heavy hand? I was thrown across the ground. My heart pumped.

I scrambled to my feet, twisting from my prone position, and crouched; both hands fingertips to the ground; a kind of sprint position. I'd no idea where the tub of salve had gone, but that wasn't my immediate problem.

Around me, in the periphery of my vision, in the darkness, strange creatures moved. They had elongated heads, almost hoody-like, rendering their mouths tube-esque, but bucket size in circumference, and lips protruding just the same. In this light the head looked dark-blue, much the same colour as their body. Small jagged teeth projected inward from the oval of the circle-mouth. Towards the back of their 'head' protruded lime green eyes, in the same way an alligator's eyes would stick up from its own head. The eyes phosphoresced faintly.

I was reminded of the unintelligible 'youth' I'd stopped from stealing the postman's bicycle – the few creatures around me and the one in my road seemed similar. Could it be that one or another of these creatures had been instructed to track me down?

I took the Knife of Zarcesaan from my satchel and removed it from its sheath. Although the light was limited it glistened, heartening me. I held the ready blade next to my right thigh.

One of the things came at me in a loping motion. Its arms bordered on vestigial, both held close to its chest. Further behind the lead creature I could make out many more. I assumed these were the Irdiroga Jacob had spoken of.

If I was going to get through this, I would have to make an example, and pray that they'd behave much in the same way any pack animal would do, after the alpha male had been slaughtered.

Brazen as any ASBO kid from the streets of Gloucester, it continued towards me. I watched unflinching and waited for a tell-tale. Then I saw it; its left leg tensed and I knew then it was going to pounce, or something similar. And it did.

It still caught me by surprise. I thought it may get a few feet off the ground. But it went straight up and disappeared into the absolute blackness that enveloped the limited cocoon of dim light that surrounded the area about me.

The rest of the pack stopped, as if waiting for the kill. I listened intently and my army training paid off. My hyperawareness affected all senses and I could hear the miniscule perturbations of the air the creature made as it fell back to the ground. I ran backward ten paces. I was certain it would now land in front of me. And it did.

If anything so weird could look shocked, I was sure this creature did. But not as shocked as it looked when I launched my blade into its underbelly. In a huge arching motion I scythed the Irdiroga from gut to clavicle, my blade clipping, what must have been its ear, as it exited the Irdiroga's body via its right shoulder.

Suggestions of orange embers delineated the path the knife had taken through this creature's form. For a few seconds I could feel a strangling cold wetness cover my hand like a vile glove; the creature's internal fluids having been spilt.

Then the Irdiroga collapsed into pieces resembling the burnt out remains of an almost extinguished Chinese lantern. The sensation in my hand dissipated in the same instant.

In my grip I could feel the Knife of Zarcesaan vibrate as it soaked up the ephemeral plasma-red tendrils that left the dying Irdiroga's body, before the remains finally vanished like soot being dispersed by the minimal of breezes.

I looked up from the empty space that had been the body and none of the other Irdiroga could be seen; no shadows moving and no ripples in the air hushing sounds towards me.

I let my breath go. Wow! I'd not experienced anything that intense since Afghanistan.

After a few moments to collect my thoughts I checked the map once more. I was half way to the Conversion.

I looked around in the darkness for the salve, but couldn't see where it'd gone. If I was to stop the Akh'Mori I couldn't spare anymore time. I doubled my pace. The sooner I was through the Conversion the better. Or so I thought.

A blue light flashed and I had to blink. Somewhere, not so far in the distance, an oblong, reaching from the ground into the air, had flashed. The light was of a pale blue and the object was squarish, and elongated heavens-ward.

I knew I'd come across the Conversion. I reached into my satchel for the salve then remembered. I hoped I was 'made' in the same way Jacob had intimated and walked towards the light anomaly.

As I stood in front of the phosphorescent doorway, I took a deep breath, knowing this would be the next boundary to pass, before I could contact the Sidheóga and their Queen.

Thinking a little test prod of the gateway would allow me to judge the translation of my body, I dipped my little finger into the door.

Pain sliced through my fingertip traversing my arm. I tried to pull back to relieve my body from the agony. But it wasn't to be. Once the Conversion had been entered, you were going through, I found out.

The bones in my fingers felt like they were being crushed as if in a washer-woman's mangle, and the rest of my body followed what had begun.

I wished for the salve. I screamed for the salve.

Every bone in my body felt as if it was being deconstructed, made into small pieces, then remade: And I had no way to stop it. I was dragged through the gateway. The only thought I had the time to consider was; what would my head feel like if my tarsals and metatarsals felt this way?

I found out. Crushed and pulverised with no death to offer respite.

It would have been better if I'd lost the knife.

Crawling around the ground, hoping to lose the pain, I gradually came too and discovered I was still in one piece – no physical damage to be seen. The more conscious I became, the more the pain was shed like slithers of a snake's redundant skin.

In moments the physical pain had left and I stood. Although the memory I had was bad, I knew I was free but the memory would be with me for some while.

I pulled the map-scroll from my satchel and studied where I needed to go next.

Chapter 20

Although there seemed to be nothing equivalent of the sun in this Other Realm, the further from the Conversion I got, the brighter things became.

Colour was returned to the path; flecks of green grass – emerald green grass – trees with brown trunks instead of the almost charcoal ones close to the Conversion, as if the colour had only been borrowed. This place was so different.

High above me the sky was pale pink in colour, with richer gloss-wet looking, glistening ragged strips of torn tissue-paper-like highlights moving through it. Each flickered like temperamental fluorescent lighting tubes, almost aurora borealis but less graceful and not vertical, but perpendicular to the ground. Although the effect was absolutely stunning, time was moving on. I checked the map. Somewhere ahead there should be a hill, *Mullach na Sidhe* or Fairymount as the translation, in brackets, next to the words declared.

I couldn't believe this otherworld I'd been brought to, but something was nagging at me. Something was not right – barring Nature's peculiar colour scheme.

I stopped and looked around. Rolling plains of grasses, trees scattered, a far off forest, I think – in reality just a dense patch of green many miles away – and sheer, oxblood-red, snow-capped mountains beyond.

Then it struck me; there was no noise. No sound of birds twittering, no sound of streams trickling, no sound of people talking. Absolutely nothing. The hair on the back of my neck prickled.

It was time to get off the path – everything screamed ambush. I shook my head; how could I have been so stupid?

Next to the path was a v-shaped ditch, hemmed in between two rows of strange looking shrub, one either side. I slid down the short five-foot slope to the bottom and waited. I needed to know if the silence that'd become so obvious was due to my presence in this Other Realm.

Fifteen minutes ought to do it, I thought.

***

As I leant against the furrow's wall, hoping my stupidity hadn't undermined everything I was aiming to achieve through this ordeal, I started to hear sounds. The sounds made me shudder, as if someone had stepped on my grave and recognised who was lying there.

The noise was made up of myriad floppy and leaden footfalls. In my mind I was not far from the Conversion.

I knew this eerie sound could only mean the Akh'Mori were not far from destroying the barrier between the Earth – my world – and this Other Realm.

I straightened my legs and carefully poked my head between the stubby trunks of the shrubs that lined the ditch top. I couldn't see anything – I could hear a lot, but there was nothing to see.

This place was doing my head in.

***

Then the sounds were upon me, on the roadway, and it was only now, when the noise was parallel with my position, that I could see dark shapes flick between transparent, translucent and opaque; each synchronous footfall acting like a switch changing the flanks of the Dark Army between each state.

The Akh'Mori were completely different from the Irdiroga, more human-like, beautiful and sinister at the same time. Each soldier, when at their most solid, appeared to have been sculpted by the most talented hand of all time, in pure Jet.

They were of classic Faery-form with pointed chins and pinched noses, but probably no more than five foot in height. The real difference between my childhood memories of what Faeries ought to look like, from the children's books I used to be read and what was before me, were their wings – no butterfly or dragonfly facsimile these, but feathered – like an angel's; pure black as if born of a raven. Stunning.

Their faces were grim though. The impression I got was that they knew they had a task to undertake, no matter how unpalatable. I knew that very same feeling – the Akh'Mori were truly soldiers, just as I had been.

As soon as the column had passed me, the *thrump, thrump* of their footfall continued but they ceased to be visible once again.

Time was running out. I had to find the Queen.

Chapter 21

Animal noises started and this world started to seem alive, more alive than it had ever been since I'd arrived.

I followed the ditch as it followed the path I was meant to be on. And I followed it, and followed it, and followed it.

I checked the map; I should have arrived at the hill already, hours ago. The distance between where I'd hid from the Dark Army and Fairymount had only been six or seven miles, max.

Even on the most arduous yomps during Army training I'd always covered twice as much ground in less time. The scenery hadn't changed one iota. Everything was the bloody same.

I dropped down onto the side of the ditch. I needed to have a drink and collect my thoughts. Things weren't adding up. I took the flask from my satchel, unscrewed the lid and took a huge swig. There was nothing to have. I'd finished it. This was not a good situation to be in; a person could operate without food for a while, but without water they'd be dead very soon.

I needed to replenish the flask. Looking over my shoulder into the vegetation behind me, multiple shrubs and small trees, I got the feeling that deeper into the maze of plants there existed a small stream or something – the dense vegetation had to be fed somehow.

I got up and started to push my way through. After a few minutes the shrubbery thinned and I came across a stream with a shallow on my side.

The main body of water rippled by, and I knelt to fill my flask from the still waters of the shallow.

As I bent over the glass-like pool I caught a glimpse of my surroundings in the reflection. An image that should mirror everything that was behind and around me. But this was not the case – the reflection showed an entirely different surrounding.

On the surface of the still water, my head was as plain as day. But behind me, replacing the thick shrubbery, was a huge grass covered hill.

I turned around – shrubs. I turned back to the mirror water – hill. Needs were must and I filled my flask, filtering it as Jacob had instructed me, and waited for the waters to calm again after my intrusion.

They stilled and the hill remained whilst I looked at the water mirror. But when I turned the hill ceased and the shrubs regaled.

I needed to reach the Queen on the hill, but the hill only existed in reflection, not in the reality of this world, as far as I could tell.

I wished Jacob were here. He would know what to do. Then I remembered the Penduliflora, the Whispering Bells. I reached into my satchel and pulled out the container. The plant stems were plain to see but I knew I needed to do something with them, before I could contact Jacob.

I struggled to remember. I was tired. I'd been in this place sometime and had not yet rested. Nor could I, I reminded myself. Time was critical.

What was it? I relaxed. I knew getting stressed would only push the knowledge further from my grasp.

I tried to remember Jacob's little rhyme.

A flat stone, for the stem to hone,
A wet leaf for the mix to breathe.

There was more but it'd gone. The only thing I could do was find a flat stone and wet a leaf and hope my memory would return, very soon.

***

I sat on the bank next to the stream and looked at the objects. There they were – a flat stone and a wet leaf – what next? I ran what I could remember of the rhyme through my mind.

The rhyme wasn't just about collecting the leaf and the stone. I needed to do something with them. If only I'd listened to the whole thing instead of interpreting it.

I took a stem of Penduliflora and started rubbing its stem on the stone. Small pieces of the plant broke from the stem peppering the stone. I took the leaf I'd soaked in the stream and pushed it onto the stone with my fingertips, covering the small pieces and rubbed the leaf back and forward, then waited.

Nothing! Surely something had gone wrong. I wracked my brains to remember what else I should be doing.

Something itched my ear and unthinking I scratched it with my forefinger and in that instant I heard Jacob's voice, loud and clear.

I don't know what the rest of the rhyme was meant to be but I now recalled Jacob telling me to rub the mix behind my ear if I needed to contact him.

I loaded up my finger and placed the mix behind my ear. Then, looking like some kind of CIA agent, I started talking to my wrist.

"Jacob, can you hear me?"

"Lad! You're Okay! Have you got to the Conversion yet?"

"Conversion?"

"Yes, lad. The Conversion. It's on the way."

"Jacob, I got there days ago. I'm past the Conversion."

"Sorry, son, my memory fails me. Time in the Other Realm is faster than your world."

"What?"

"It's only been half an hour here, lad."

I couldn't believe it; half an hour equalling what seemed to be a day and a half! This could be discussed later. But I did need some vital information to get me closer to my goal.

"Jacob, I'm stuck. Something is stopping me from reaching *Mullach na Sidhe*. I can see it in reflection, but that is all."

"You seem to be in a similar situation that happened to me, some many years ago my lad. Don't move from where you are. The contact through the Penduliflora will remain as long as you don't move." Jacob told me.

"What if I have to move?" I said.

"How much Penduliflora do you have left?"

"None."

"Don't move, lad. Wait. I need to find the answer. I'll contact you soon."

Chapter 22

The light had begun to fade. I hoped that Jacob's answer would not require the continuing reflection of the hill. Very soon there'd be no light and, with that, no reflection.

In the twilight, in the mirrored surface I could see flickering orange lights near the top of the hill. Like torches, partially obscured, as if set back into the hill itself.

A rustling in the shrubs across the stream distracted my gaze. The shrubs seemed closer and deep within vaguely visible purple and pale red luminescent pinpoints of light, bordering on invisible, flickered on and off. My eyes ached, struggling to focus on these motile dots.

In an instant there was a loud crack and I flew sideways. I felt as if I'd been shot in the ear.

"Derek, Derek? Are you still there?"

"Bloody hell, Jacob! Do you have to have it so loud?"

"Sorry, lad. You didn't respond. I think there's something interfering with the link."

"What did you find out? The light's fading and the reflection's not going to be there much longer; if it's needed."

"I knew I chose well, Derek. You are astute. The reflection of the Fairymount has to be captured, my lad – I don't know why I forgot this."

"How do you capture a reflection?"

"It's simpler than you think. Do you have a small vessel for your use?"

"I have the lid to my flask."

"That is good news, young Derek. Whilst staring at the reflection in the waters, dip the lid of your flask into the reflected image of *Mullach na Sidhe*. When you do, repeat these words in your mind; '*Be fast, behold, image of old Fairymount. Captured in this vessel, no strength to wrestle yourself free, image of old Fairymount, captured in this vessel, you will be*.' Over and over, Derek.

"Then gaze at the reflection in the lid and walk backwards towards the hill. Until you're at the hill don't turn around. The counter-spell will be undone as will your chance to reach the hill's crest and the mission will be over. Without a doubt a war will begin. It is better for all races that there be no war."

I had to agree with Jacob's sentiment. I'd experienced the fruitlessness of war; the killing of fellow humans, and, if the reality of what I'd seen so far in this Other Realm had any bearing, a war between my world and this one would render Afghanistan nothing more than an inconsequential Xbox game – the *Sidheóga* able to manipulate matter just through thought alone. "Absolutely, Jacob," I said.

"I think that's all there is to say, son. As soon as you start towards *Mullach na Sidhe*, the link will be broken. We'll talk when you get back. Good luck, my lad."

"Cheers, Jacob. Back soon. Over and out." I heard Jacob chuckle.

"Over and out, my lad."

After three backward steps, the link evaporated. I tried stepping back on the spot where I'd spoken to my mentor, but no sound was forthcoming.

I was now on my own.

Chapter 23

As I strode backwards I expected to be thwacked around the head by various twigs and twiglets; branches of the shrub I was entering, but there was nothing. I kept chanting the words in my head and staring at the small circular reflection in my flask's lid.

Within ten or fifteen paces I felt the ground start to incline upward and although I shouldn't have done, I turned. I couldn't help myself.

I was dumbstruck. There were no shrubs around me: At all. Just the incline of a hill covered in meadow grasses and small closed-headed flowers. Near the top I could see the flickering flame-light I'd seen before.

Far behind me a toy-like roadway and train set toy shrubs, and the place where I'd contacted Jacob. Looking at the distance, I guessed I must now be at least half a mile from where I'd started.

I replaced the lid on my flask and started the trek to the top of the hill and the obvious settlement.

I had no idea how I'd be received. But the answer was soon coming. The moment I crossed a path that followed the contour of the hill, seemingly circulating the hill in a spiral track-way to its top, my wrists and shoulders were tugged – by what, I couldn't see – and I was forced, face down, onto the ground.

As I lay there, I could make out a strange whispering that sounded like I should be able to make sense of it, vowels and consonants its constituent parts, but it sounded like no language I'd ever heard before.

As suddenly as the whispering had started, it stopped. I turned my head from side to side but still couldn't see a soul.

Just as I was about to stand up from my prone position a force lifted me vertically by my armpits. I was accelerated towards the top of the hill, my feet a few inches above the ground skimming tops of blades of grass and flower heads, then the eerie whispering returned.

Within seconds I could see small dark-sided holes penetrating the crown of the hill. Deep inside each, flame-orange torches flickered. The holes were not that large, probably just two or three feet from floor to ceiling.

As if on a whim, my direction of travel changed and, to my shock, I was now heading for one of those titchy holes at break-neck speed.

I tried to struggle free but my upper arms were locked in place by an unseen force – no movement I made able to free myself from this transparent air-glue.

In thirty seconds I would be down the hole with my head snapped back and my pelvis folded up against the small of my back – legs trailing behind.

I closed my eyes and gritted my teeth, waiting for the inevitable.

***

After what seemed to be too much time, my arms were freed and I knew I'd been slung at the hole.

I landed roughly on a damp floor and opened my eyes. I was kneeling with hands splayed on the ground. Turning to look behind me, I saw the circular "O" of the entrance some hundred yards away.

This had me stumped, how.

"You are lucky that your brain does not possess the power to alter the fabric of Nature, Mr Johns. If you'd had it your way, your neck and lower spine would have been snapped as easily as dried kindling."

The voice was female, commanding and wispy. I shook my head as I tried to figure out whether it emanated from the centre of my brain or whether it was coming at me through my ears.

I turned to look forward. In front of me was a small cavern apparently carved out from the mud of the hill. The cavern was illuminated by flames; shadows on the circular wall flickered and jumped.

At its centre was an intricately sculpted chair of wood, with a high back and sturdy arm rests, the sculptor obviously having used a single large tree trunk as the foundation for the chair's creation; dark, gnarled, oak-like bark remained on the external facets of the chair, whilst its exposed core was of the light and cream-like colours of heartwood.

As my eyes focused on the source of the flickering light, I could not stop myself from gasping.

The flickering light was coming from the fire upon the chair. The fire upon the chair was a slender woman with the same pointed chin and pinched nose physiognomy that I'd seen earlier in the Dark Army.

Her flame-red hair crested upward to a point. Two translucent wings, touched by the rainbow colours that usually cruised surfaces of blown soap bubbles, curved down across her shoulders covering her body, as if a cloak or high-necked gown.

Her face and hands were of the palest tangerine, but most striking of all were her wise emerald-green eyes.

The cavern's flinching and twitching light emanated from the pale orange aura that surrounded her body.

"You're here to stop the Akh'Mori," she told me. "Have you seen what you're doing to my lands and the lands of my people?"

"No... yes. No. I mean, yes then no, I think," I blurted stupidly.

"You will see what you have done."

The Queen motioned an outstretched pale hand from left to right and gradually the far wall faded to be replaced by moving images. The images showed swathes of strange coloured countryside chewed up and vaporised by an invisible force; arable creatures cut down and turned into charcoal, little people playing games, only to have their limbs scythed from their bodies by the continuing onslaught of the invisible blade/beam of destruction.

"Okay. Stop it. I understand. Surely, with your powers, you could have stopped this?" I pleaded.

"And break the agreement, absolve ourselves from the rules? The rules that were agreed all that time ago? What do you think we are, human?

"How do you think our species could survive if we had as little respect for our kind and our laws as your kind do for yours?

"We agreed to move away into our realm but now you have dissolved the accord. We can no longer accept that we have to live away from the world that was ours long before you arrived.

"Time is finished. The accord is finished. The Akh'Mori march to reclaim Gaia for ourselves once more."

"No. I can help. Please hear me." I knew nothing else I could say.

Chapter 24

The light coming from the Queen's aura diminished. The wall of the cavern lost its definition: And, although the shadows flickered less, the expectation of sound from the crackling flames was not satisfied. The cavern was silent and the Queen stared into the distance, not moving a muscle. I was certain she wasn't breathing. But perhaps this was normal.

Time seemed to stop and, the more I squinted at the Queen, the more certain I became that what was before me was nothing more than a statue carved from the most exquisite palest peach marble.

I got it into my head that it was time to take some action. I started to stand, though not entirely sure what I was going to do. Then the cavern was bathed in light.

"What is wrong with your kind is the fact you have no patience. Since your kind decided your science was the only science, you've wanted all and everything, faster and faster and faster.

"No time for rational thought or debate; destroy first, no questions later, eh?"

I was getting a bit riled. "We're not all like that."

"I believe you, Derek. I know. It's just the people that have the power."

"Yes."

"I wonder who put them there."

"It's..."

"That was rhetorical, Derek. No need to reply."

I was certain she was being snide. This woman-thing was really getting to me. But it had just dawned upon me the only real weapon I had were the words I could muster.

I recalled all the things Jacob had done and achieved the evening I'd left, it'd all been accomplished by appropriate words, put together in the appropriate order.

The way he'd moved us from his office to the park. The way he'd got me through the Queen's magic camouflage of the hill, and the few words I'd remembered to make the link for him to tell me how to find the hill in the first place.

I looked at the Queen. For some reason she was smiling.

"Very well, Derek. Convince me to stop the Akh'Mori."

Bugger! Jacob had not prepared me for a battle of this type. I felt sick to my stomach. If I got this wrong, at the very minimum, there wouldn't be any more Markent Marketing.

Then there was the idea that after the Akh'Mori had transgressed the Conversion, when everything had settled down, – peace?

Governments had done this exact same thing. Previously I'd been one of their tools to achieve the goal, though it hadn't been successful – I didn't think the Akh'Mori would be unsuccessful. Peace in my life time: But the sacrifice? At least poverty would be wiped out once and for all: But the sacrifice?

Questions and more questions went around my head. This was awful. In effect, I had the power of Nature at my very fingertips; the ability to destroy everything Earth-side of the Conversion. All I had to do was screw up this conversation. Should I choose to screw it up or do my damnedest to win the debate?

I made my decision. Although in my gift I knew it was humanity's choice whether or not to terminate itself, not mine. And, if they did, I was sure the Sidheóga could recover Gaia for themselves.

I started my argument for the recall of the Akh'Mori.

"Why don't you send someone to break the LHC at CERN? And stop the scientists destroying your land."

"Derek, at the first hurdle you fall. I thought you had listened. We are Sidheóga not human. We agree to rules and abide by them."

"The Akh'Mori are on their way," I stated.

"There are no rules anymore. The accord was annulled by your actions. And we still prefer to remain mostly invisible."

"But our scientists don't know what their machine is doing."

"Ignorance absolves everyone. Is this the case?"

"In this case it certainly absolves the scientists at CERN."

"Who agreed the accord in the first place?"

"It wasn't scientists," I countered.

"No. You are correct. Was there a record made of the accord? Were there not guardians recruited? Were there not people who knew of this?"

"Yes, there were."

"Who hid the knowledge for it was not us?" the Queen asked.

I knew there was only one answer – it was the scientists. If the Sidheóga were acknowledged, if the accord was acknowledged, then science as it had been created during the Enlightenment, could not possibly exist in the form it had taken.

I had to take another tack in this debate. "Give me the power to stop the LHC."

"We have never given mankind the power. It is inconceivable; you are too puny of mind to use it wisely. Only half breeds like the cunning folk in your realm have some of the power."

"Transferring the power to a human is against the rules?" I asked.

"If that was so, mingling between the Sidheóga and humankind would be banned. It is by received wisdom that humanity is prohibited."

I couldn't believe it; a chance, a small window of opportunity had opened. "You can give me the power?"

"Yes, it is possible."

"And doing so wouldn't break any rules?" I pressed.

"No, Derek, it would not. Barring the rule of common sense. Don't forget we've watched what you do and what you're capable of. There's no facet of human nature that can be trusted."

"I said: We're not all the same."

The Queen looked at me. I couldn't turn away from her eyes, and as she stared I felt something reach inside me, a strange tickling deep in my chest, then a withdrawal.

The Queen shook her head. I didn't like it. Despair weighed on my shoulders. Had I executed humanity due to a demeanour I could not control?

Chapter 25

The Queen bowed her head and the remaining light left the cavern. All I could see now was the silhouette of her body, cast by a very dim sunflower glow coming from the wood of her thrown.

As she lifted her head I caught a glimpse of her eyes, they had changed; they were no longer green, but completely silver, mercury-like. As she raised her head, two narrow tubes of light, almost as if produced by powerful LED. torches, but somehow more perfect, traced lines across the floor towards me.

I knew this was the end. I hadn't been able to convince her of my sincerity. She hadn't believed a single word I'd said.

The beams struck me full force in the chest. I fell backward. It was like being at the wrong end of the strongest untamed bucking horse and beneath the crushing power of the tallest breaking wave, all at the same time.

I opened my eyes and could see the cavern's roof. I had a black blank gap in my memory. For a moment I wondered whether I was in the afterlife.

"Get up, Derek," the Queen's voice echoed around the chamber letting me know exactly where I was.

The back of my head ached and I tested it carefully as I sat up. It seemed Ok; still intact.

"Against my better judgement, we have decided to grant your request."

I stood up. "How can I get the power?" I asked.

"You have just received it you foolish, puny human."

I looked down at my chest and rubbed it. "That?"

"How else did you expect the power of Nature to feel?"

I shrugged. It wasn't just that I had no answer, my chest felt like every rib had been broken and I was struggling to breathe deep enough.

"You have but to touch the circle of the LHC in four places; from that time onwards, until the humans build again, no power large enough to cleave our lands will be generated.

"But keep in mind, this power of ours will not belong to you until your death-day. You have one mankind hour."

"What? How do…?"

"GO!"

As she said the word she pushed her hand out towards me and the cavern faded away.

Chapter 26

A sudden chill ran through me. The atmosphere felt as if all life had been sucked from it – the air was icy cold.

Around me were feeble, brittle brown twigs of what seemed to be a dead shrub. A few browning leaves remained attached but mostly they littered the ground.

I rubbed my arms; it was freezing; and dark for that matter. I looked around from behind the feeble trees and dense bushes that made up the spinney I was now crouched in. Some one hundred yards away an illuminated red strip was shining.

As my eyes adjusted to the new levels of light I made out the letters; E. S. S. O.

"Esso? Esso!" I mouthed the letters. It's a bloody Esso garage, I thought to myself. Then beyond I saw the brown, almost basket-weaved, sixty foot high, representation of the end of a shuttlecock, and knew then where I was. I'd seen this shape before, during my past army-life, when I'd been moved between training camps in France and Switzerland. It was the 'Palais de l'Équilibre' encompassing the entrance to CERN and my target, the LHC.

There was a lot of traffic on the dual carriageway and I had to pick my emergence from the shrubbery with precision timing. The last thing I wanted was to be picked up by the police as some kind of technophile pervert, or worse, terrorist.

I wished I had a watch. I had no idea how long it had taken for me to get here, though it had seemed instantaneous.

I thought the best place to start would be in the Esso garage. Perhaps I could take a peek at the clock in there – there was usually one behind the counter.

I checked to make sure the road was relatively clear and scrambled out of the spinney.

Good! That was done; no one catching sight of me.

Just to be on the safe side I decided to take fifteen minutes from whatever the time was when I found a clock. I couldn't imagine the journey from the Other Realm taking any more than that.

I walked into the garage shop and pretended to look around the shelves of stuff as I attempted to catch a glimpse of the clock behind the till.

"Can I help you, sir?" came an accented question through the air. Unfortunately I was the only customer in the premises so I couldn't pretend it wasn't me. I never could understand how these foreigners could tell an Englishman at thirty paces.

"Erm!" I didn't think I could get away with the usual excuse that I was just browsing. I decided to go to the counter for some chocolate or something then "accidently" discover I hadn't any Euros in my wallet and get a good look at the clock.

My stomach growled and I could see in my mind's eye pulling a fifty Euro note from my wallet; I could do with a bar of chocolate.

I walked towards the man and checked the clock – 8:50pm – I pulled out my wallet and fanned through its contents. Not a single pound note in sight; all Euros.

"Sorry. I haven't any Euros," I explained to the man.

The man reached over and took a ten Euro note then waved it in front of me. "Oh! You English. Always joking. What do you have?"

I shook my head. "I'll have a Snickers and a large latté, thank you."

I left the shop confused but the food soon took my mind off the strange appearance of the currency. It felt like it'd been days since I'd eaten anything.

***

I walked along the pavement towards the peculiar upturned weaved basket. Somehow I needed to get in there and a little further beyond. The external fence was not too big a deal, being only waist height. I looked up and down the road, nothing was near, and I jumped over and darted towards the 'Palais de l'Équilibre'

I guessed another five minutes had passed and that only left me with forty more minutes to find the LHC and do something to it. Time was running out.

So far no one had been around. I went over to the entrance and looked through the glass. I could see security sitting behind their desk, looking ominous. There was no way I'd be able to slip through the door, past the reception and into the lift that obviously went down into the bowels of the facility.

Then the worst possible thing that could happen, happened. One of the guards behind the desk looked up and spotted me peering in. He called his colleague and pointed me out.

They both started towards the entrance and I decided it was time to leave. Quickly I skirted the circular building and made my way as fast as I could towards the complex behind, putting as much distance as I could between the road and myself as I made my way deeper into the mass of CERN buildings.

I heard the footfalls of two people chasing after me and vague calls of, "Arrêtez-vous."

This was all taking up time; time I couldn't afford. I reckoned I now had only thirty five minutes before I was rendered a powerless puny human once more, with no prospect of stopping the Akh'Mori's destruction of Earth.

A gunshot rang out and I ducked.

Chapter 27

Ahead of me was a large white building with a smaller one next to it and a gap between. I picked up the pace. One thing I was sure about and that was not getting shot. If there'd been a bullet with my name on it, it was still in Afghanistan and those days were done with.

I looked back. The two guards were gaining on me, but their fitness was lacking. I entered the short alleyway between the two buildings. All of a sudden alternating red and blue lights illuminated the path I was taking. A security van had turned up. I was cornered.

As I backed away from the men who had leapt from the van, I wondered whether this would be it, the end of this strange quest, the tunnels below remaining just out of reach.

I could see in my head where I needed to get to but very soon I would be in custody. I took another step back and my heel caught the edge of a raised manhole cover, unbalancing me.

I turned as I fell and put my hands out to break the fall. Both palms hit the concrete path simultaneously, but they didn't stop there. The concrete bowed then rippled like I'd just put my hands in a large bowl of thick porridge.

Something clicked in my mind and I re-focused once again on the tunnels below that housed the LHC.

Soon I was up to my elbows in concrete porridge. I took a deep breath and pushed further. The ground absorbed my entire body.

I controlled my panic, knowing not to do so would mean certain death in a concrete overcoat. The pressure on my hands gave way and then I was falling.

I landed heavily on the smooth pavement below. Before I moved, I listened carefully – there was only the hum of the electrical circuits that covered the walls around me.

I stood up and made sure that nothing had broken. It seemed I was Ok. I looked at the ceiling of the tunnel I was now standing in; nothing – not a single mark or sign that anything had come through it.

Though I had thought that the currency thing had been a bit weird, this was freaky. However, I was beginning to understand what was going on.

Then my whole body jerked as I recognised what I was standing next to; it was part of the LHC, a huge tube that led off into the distance around a barely noticeable curve.

I'd been told I needed to touch it in four places. I put my hand on its surface. A splash of purple rippled out from my hand's outline across the tube, like ripples across the surface of a pond I'd just slapped.

As the colour dissipated so did the ripples and then nothing.

I heard the distant clang of a heavy metal door as it swung shut somewhere behind me. I didn't believe security had any inkling as to where I'd gone but I started running in the opposite direction anyway.

All I had to do now was to touch the LHC three further times and I was done. I thought it best that I spaced out these touches as far apart as I could. I don't know why but this tactic felt the appropriate approach.

***

With the penultimate purple rinse of the tube complete I headed onward only to be confronted by a heavy, orange-coloured metal door. I pulled it open and entered a huge chamber, then stared. Rising to the ceiling of this chamber was a massive red painted octagonal cylinder. This had to be my last target. Large letters on its side declared: ALICE.

I walked towards it and raised my hand ready for the final touch, after which I had no idea what I was going to do, but my mission would be complete.

I was so awestruck by the view of this enormous device, I missed the sound the security guard must have made as he crept up on me. The first I knew about it was the neck lock he put me in.

The second thing I thought about was the time on his watch; 9:30pm – at worst I had only five minutes left, at best ten. I guessed.

I snapped myself forward, grasping the arm that was locked around my neck – the guard flew over the top of my head and landed hard on the solid floor in front of me. The impact and angle forced him to let go.

I dived for the red cylinder and touched it. There were no purple ripples this time.

"Shit," I hissed under my breath. My time was done. I'd failed and war was imminent.

Chapter 28

It seemed like the entire wall of the chamber was made of doors. Doors everywhere began to open and the gunmetal grey clad security guards entered from all of them.

I couldn't believe it; after everything I'd been through I'd not only let down Jacob, I'd let down the Faerie Queen and all humanity. I was beginning to wonder if I represented anything meaningful.

Male and female guards approached me from all points of the compass. I raised my hands, but this didn't affect their cautious approach.

Then, from the corner of my eye, I noticed sparks start to form and flicker on the side of the red surfaced octagon where I'd placed my hand.

It started in a small way but within seconds it was as if a huge Catherine wheel had gone off.

Suddenly I was at the centre of a sphere made up from, what seemed to be, iron filing sparks: The rest of CERN's chamber blotted out.

***

I came to. All my eyes could reconcile was vague and grey; everywhere. Yet again I was prone on the floor. I got up and looked around. Nothing – I was encompassed in grey.

As I turned on point, attempting to get my bearings, I noticed two vertical patches of grey that were slightly darker than any other point. With no other options I made my way in their direction.

Wherever I was it was like a permanent fog existed; everything vague and surreal. Now there were two vertical posts of darker grey in front of me.

I had no idea what I ought to do. But I knew I couldn't stay wherever it was that I was.

Do or die, I thought and pushed an arm between the dark grey trunks of thick etherealness.

Pinpoints of dampness licked the hand I'd pushed between the dark grey pillars and coldness stroked my hand.

Before I could make a decision about my next steps, a vice like grip grabbed my hand and I was yanked into another world. I held my breath and readied myself for yet another onslaught of the senses. I hadn't realised it but I'd also closed my eyes.

"Derek, are you Ok? What happened, my son?"

The voice was familiar, though I doubted its reality. I opened my eyes slowly, stealing myself for a huge disappointment.

I was stunned. It was Jacob. He'd pulled me through and I was back in the park.

"I think you could do with a cup of tea."

"I think I could do with something less boring," I told him.

Jacob smiled. "Follow me, son."

Jacob walked towards the road and I followed. Within seconds we were standing in his office.

"Derek, you have done more than I could ever have hoped to achieve."

I didn't know what to say – the whole journey hadn't been anything I'd planned. I just shrugged.

"Do you know the Akh'Mori have turned back?" Jacob queried.

I shook my head. "No. But that's good isn't it?"

Jacob smiled his smile once again. "Of course it is, son. You have done immense good."

"The LHC is fixed?" I said.

"The Akh'Mori have turned back – there is a reason."

I nodded. I knew the truth of the matter, just wanted to hear it.

Jacob looked at me – somehow his face spoke of happiness and sadness at the same time.

"You have been the perfect student, Derek."

"I just wanted to do the best I could," I said.

Jacob nodded. "I know. And you are now in the position I was when I started."

"What d'you mean?"

"What I mean, young lad, is that I was the best person when I started."

"Ok, that makes sense," I said.

"Now you are." Jacob told me. He took my hand and shook it. I felt a buzz of sorts travel through my hand and arm; then he let go.

"I'm so sorry. But this is the way," Jacob said.

I frowned. "What d'you mean?"

"You're the guardian now."

Those were the last words Jacob ever said to me. Having completed his statement, and seemingly his purpose, Jacob crumbled to dust, his shape collapsing as if it had been made from the finest white flour.

I sat on his office chair and wondered whether I would find an appropriate apprentice in the coming years.

The Queue

I was standing outside the corner stop queuing to get my lottery ticket. Without a doubt there wasn't a chance in Hell I'd win the bloody lottery but if I didn't get them…?

I checked my watch my – only seven and a half minutes to go until the cut-off. "Come on," I thought.

The guy in front of me leant towards his mate. If there was a gold medal for crap whispering he would've won it, but what he said blew away any thoughts I'd had about jumping the queue.

"When she tried it she died", the guy had whispered.

"Died?" his mate questioned. The conversation continued.

"Keeled over just like that!" The guy snapped his fingers.

"But she got the numbers?"

The guy in front of me nodded.

"You haven't, have you?"

He nodded again.

"How d'you know the same's not going to happen to you?"

"Can't've been to do with the instructions", the guy pulled a flimsy piece of paper from his pocket and flapped it in front of his friend. "She must've had a dicky heart or something. You know… the shock."

As he continued he went to place the scruffy note back in his jacket, but he didn't – it fell to the ground.

"You can't be sure," his mate said.

The queue moved and as I stepped forward I picked up the note. The guy in front of me coughed hard.

"Sounds like you've caught something," his mate said.

"Feel a bit rough actually. But sun, sand and sea are coming my way".

I read the note; then slapped my forehead. Of course! It was so obvious, so simple. I changed my numbers, then glanced at my watch – four minutes.

The guy's friend filled in his ticket and went to the cashier.

The guy in front of me completed his ticket but before he had a chance to replace the pen he coughed, clutched his chest and dropped to the floor.

It was now my turn. Two minutes to go, but all I could do was stare at my new numbers as indecision ran amok.

What I am Now?

You drew me into this.
I had no choice but to comply.
Your influence twisting and corrupting
my mind.

First you offered your sex,
so enticing.
And I had no idea what was coming next,
then that poor girl's death.

I thought it was just for fun
but when she started to run,
her arms flailing against the trees,
whiplashed by the boughs as she fled.
I thought this wasn't me.

You took away my choice.
The nick on my neck has made me something else.
And now I follow you without options,
darkness my mentor.

And although my conscious speaks to me,
my lust for slaughter and to make the sheep bleed
supplants reason.
What have you done?
What am I now?

Murders Most Foul

Chapter 1

It was an unusual entry into the village for John Devereux. In years gone by there would have been a parade with the villagers welcoming the new constable, wishing the constable well, but this was not the case any longer; the office of High Constable was on the wane and the rulers of England had many other worries to deal with. John Devereux had his own. He knew he was born to be a painter, but his uncle, a close friend of the King, had had other ideas.

In the north the Parliamentarians, led by Oliver Cromwell, were battling the Royalists and closer to home, in Suffolk, a lawyer called Matthew Hopkins, who was not in fact a lawyer at all, was on the rampage; picking on any woman he felt didn't fit his criteria for "normal" womanhood. 1644 was turning into one of those topsy-turvy years.

***

After crossing the bridge over Butley River John came to a slippery halt at the head of the village's high street. The rain that had persisted since he'd started his journey to East Scythe to take up his role as the new High Constable had rendered the rutted track a quagmire of mud and puddles. John pulled at the rope he was holding.

"Come on you stupid ass," he said to the donkey that had decided it was tolerable to carry his luggage, his easel and nothing more. "It's bloody cold and this damned rain is wet. What are you waiting for?"

The donkey ee-awed.

Pretending to understand he continued to berate the animal. "I don't care. I think...," John paused gathering his thoughts for a moment, he was now a practitioner of the law and as such he ought to start using appropriate terminology. "I think the precedent has been set. And as I have led you these three score and twelve miles from my home, you do not have a legal leg to stand on when determining who the rightful leader of this caravan is. Now move!"

The donkey ee-awed again and after a few tugs the unlikely duo trudged up the street.

In the October twilight the half-timbered houses, lining either side of the street, seemed to lean over and look at him. John shuddered. He hoped he would find the coaching inn very soon.

In the dark it was difficult to distinguish between house and establishment. John pulled his letter of appointment from his tunic and struck the flint of his torch.

He read the letter again; "Until the office of High Constable has been refurbished you will be residing in the lodging rooms at The Merry Widow."

John looked up the street and frowned. There was no sign he could see that spoke of The Merry Widow. All he saw was the stone walled cemetery to his left, abutted by a Norman church a little way up the road. And to his right a row of houses unbroken but for a small lane that led away from the high street. He wished for the old days when new constables were welcomed and appreciated. It would have been so much easier.

As he stood in the rain sodden street a lantern, not ten yards from him, was lit and a sign proclaiming 'The Merry Widow' was illuminated. John put the letter back in his tunic and after a little cajoling he and his ass made their way to the coaching inn.

John, standing at the door and shivering, knocked.

"Come in, come in, fair fellow from three score and twelve miles yonder," the landlady said.

"Why, thank ye, dear landlady," John said. "How doth the knowledge come to you that I hath travelled this far?"

"Aye, that be the question. You'll be expecting bedding and a meal, I suppose?"

John sighed with happiness. "A meal would be most welcomed. The weather is terrible and I am frozen to my core; but what of my ass?"

"Your ass poses no problem for this establishment. It will fit easily into our stables. I will have Serf take care of it. Please enter." The landlady bowed and made a sweeping gesture with her arm.

John entered The Merry Widow, dragging his luggage and easel behind him. As the door shut he spoke in hushed tones. "Dear, landlady, I have studied the customs of these parts and hath failed to conclude how further intercourse should be conducted."

"Don't worry, John Devereux. I've not been insulted by your verbal corruptions. It is something I've learnt to expect from foreigners to these here parts. And as such, they're done and dusted."

"That is good to know, landlady. If I may be so bold, one final question…"

The landlady eyed the new constable suspiciously. "Aye, and what may that be?"

"How do I address such a fair person as yourself in future? Will the title landlady suffice?"

The landlady relaxed. "My name is Elizabeth Clarke, but mostly people call me Liz. However, if you'd prefer, you can call me Clarkey of The Merry Widow."

"I think I'll use Mistress Liz, dear landlady of my week's abode, for it is simpler."

Liz Clarke nodded and led John Devereux along a candle lit hallway and up some creaking wooden stairs to the first floor. She pushed open the second door on the landing letting out two black cats and a small Gloucester Old Spot.

"Here are your lodgings, Mr Devereux."

John walked in and was surprised. The room was large and overlooked the high street. "Thank you, Mistress Liz, this is most satisfactory."

"I will bring your meal presently," she said and left.

John unpacked, setting up his easel in the bay window. He was certain, given good weather, it would be an ideal spot for him to take some sketches and capture, in oil, the realities of rural village life.

As he hung his shirt in the cupboard he was distracted by a moaning from the street below, which was promptly followed by a knocking on The Merry Widow's door and a murmured conversation. He thought he recognised his landlady's voice.

After a passage of time, with no accuracy he could determine, due to the fact that his wrist sundial failed to work during the evening, Liz knocked at his door.

"Come," he said.

Liz entered. "I have your meal, Mr Devereux. Where would you like it placed?"

"Over there," John said indicating the small table next to his easel in the bay window.

Liz set the tray down.

"Mistress Liz, I heard someone knocking. Do you accept clientele at this time of night?"

"No, Mr Devereux. That would be pure folly."

"I agree. It would be certain folly for a landlady, such as yourself, to take in persons unknown at this late hour. But it seems this may have happened."

"It is not unknown, in these parts, Mr Devereux, for the wind to take on such a demeanour as to sound like conversations," Liz proffered as she backed towards the door. "I, being just a humble landlady, do not offer remedies to cure the ills that normally afflict folk in these parts; nor hexes to blight ones foes."

"Yes," John agreed. "That would be unusual for a proprietress of an establishment such as this. I'll make a note about the wind too. Thank you for the meal."

Liz Clarke left his room and as John tucked into the hot game pie he contemplated what he'd discovered. After a few minutes he nodded to himself. He was certain that the light the bay windows offered would be a boon to his paintings, if the weather got any better and it was daytime.

Chapter 2

By nineam the whole village Council had gathered in Bill Gouge's smithy.

William Dell, East Scythe's butcher and Council Chairman, smashed his mallet onto the bench. "Order, order."

"Two rabbit fillets and a sausage," Bill Gouge's apprentice yelled over the hubbub.

"You stupid boy," Dell barked and the gathered Council members hushed, not wanting to annoy the rotund butcher who happened to be pretty handy with a meat cleaver. "As you're all probably aware, since the last High Constable's death of natural causes..."

"It wasn't," a voice called out.

"Who said that? Show yourself," William Dell shouted. Everyone looked at everyone else, but no one raised an arm nor admitted to the outburst. Conversations started again and very quickly the smithy was filled with the sound of rhubarb.

William Dell rolled his eyes. "Bloody hell!" He smashed his meat mallet on the bench again. "Shut up, shut up, will you."

The quiet was resumed.

"As you're probably aware we have a new High Constable in the village."

Ayes and yeses came from the crowd.

"Now, I don't know who informed who, but we are now lumbered with an outsider in this office. And whoever it was, you ought to be ashamed of yourself." Dell squinted and craned his neck forward as he looked around the gathered Council members sitting in the smithy's dimness. Most were shaking their heads and others were asleep. "This village can more than look after itself," he continued, "even with all the troubles; nay, especially because of the troubles in the north. But, until we know which side this new constable bats for, we have to mind what we do. No one is to talk of our *special* trade in the presence of this constable. Is that clear?"

Apart from a few sniggers everyone was nodding.

"Good. Does anyone here know anything about him?"

"Aye. I know 'e 'as a donkey," Bill Gouge said.

"Right! Thank you, Bill. Is that important?"

"I don't trust it," Bill said knowingly as he stroked his beard and nodded at the truth of his statement.

William Dell quickly moved on. "Anyone else?"

The smithy was quiet.

"Very well. Now, before the lazy dandy decides to withdraw from his bed we ought to go about our business as usual. But pay heed to what he does and where he goes. And if he starts prying into anything he shouldn't, be sure to inform me. The *special* traffic along Butley River is for us and us alone, no one else."

Again the crowd agreed with his comments, but this time just nodding.

William Dell picked up the meeting's scrawled agenda. "Ah! Any other business?"

Marie Lincolne, the vicar's housekeeper raised her arm. "Yes, Mr Dell."

"Miss Lincolne, what pray be that?"

"How does the investigation go into the removal of the vicar's chicken's leg, Mr Dell?"

"Are you referring to the chicken that is now known as, Hoppy, Miss Lincolne?"

"Yes, I am, Mr Dell."

"I'm sorry to say that there has been no progress. But with good reason, that being the death of our High Constable. I would suggest to you that you approach Mr Devereux, his replacement, at your earliest convenience. Anyone else?"

There was no answer.

"I declare this meeting of the Council of East Scythe thus concluded." Dell smashed his mallet on the bench.

Chapter 3

John stretched as shafts of light filtered through the gaps between the heavy curtains of his room; then yelled in pain. Being of the height he was he'd pushed his feet through the bedstead and detached the toe nail of his big toe on his left foot. In an instant he was hopping around the room clasping his foot in both hands.

To add to his predicament his right foot caught the ruck in the rug covering the otherwise bare floorboards. Not having a third leg to rely on for balance, or a fourth like his trusty steed, his face quickly became acquainted with the floor.

"Ow!" he yelled and rolled onto his back. As he spotted the quality of light streaming through the gap in the curtains all thought of the pain disappeared. "Forsooth, what wondrous light," he exclaimed, as questions of what his next painting's subject should be, flitted through his mind.

He gazed at the ceiling noticing every nuance the diffused light picked out; the way it had some kind of stationary wobble reminiscent of the satin surfaces of the nearby waterways. How its convex and concave elements spoke of a troubled history. How the circular patch, directly above his head, seemed to dull in colour and grow. He was in his element.

Then the leak from the room above finally detached the plaster and it came crashing down on his nose.

"Ow!"

There was a knock at his door. "Did you call, Mr Devereux?" Liz asked.

"Doe," John said, pushing the ceiling plaster from his face.

"Is there anything I can get for you before breakfast?"

"Doe fangs," John said.

"Right you are, Mr Devereux. Breakfast is available until ten."

"Than coo, Mistress Lidz."

John Devereux heaved himself up from the floor and hobbled over to his bed, his toe felt hot with a sharp light-emitting twang of pure lemon juice thrown in, just to heighten his experience. Slowly he got dressed.

***

Finishing the last morsel of his full English breakfast he placed his knife and fork on the empty plate and stood up from the table in the Merry Widow's dining area. He nodded to himself as he flicked toast crumbs from the lapels of his frock coat; it was time he met the people of East Scythe, and introduce himself to the kind village folk he was sure they would be.

"Mistress Liz," he called out into the hallway, leaning around the door of the dining room. "Mistress Liz?"

Liz Clarke scuttled her way from the kitchen. "Yes, Mr Devereux. How can I help?"

"I require my ass, Mistress Liz."

Liz looked up and down the hallway. "As far as I can tell you are with it."

"No, Mistress Liz, my ass from the stable."

"Please excuse my impertinence for correcting you, sir, but surely you mean your donkey?"

"It's a donkey?" John exclaimed.

"Most definitely, Mr Devereux."

John raised his eyebrows. “Well I’d never have thought. A donkey you say? That could explain a lot.”

“Yes, a donkey, Mr Devereux. Shall I have Serf ready it for you?”

John nodded. Within moments John Devereux’s donkey was standing outside The Merry Widow.

“Mistress Liz, please have your serf load my as…, donkey with my easel and the other accoutrements, for I am off to meet the fair people of East Scythe.”

“Your easel?”

“Yes, my easel.”

“And your other accoutrements?”

“Yes, my other accoutrements. Why do you question me so, Mistress Liz?”

“Forgive my stupidity, Mr Devereux, but these tools seem strange for a High Constable.”

“They may seem strange, but they are not. It is for the simple reason of my enjoyment of the pastime of painting that I have come to understand a serious application for these tools. And by way of illustration, if you would kindly forgive the pun, I shall explain; should anything happen on my perambulations, as I undertake my duties as this village’s high constable, it becomes a very simple task to take a quick sketch or oil painting to capture any wrong doing in progress. And as such render the prosecution of the crime that much simpler.”

“Is that so, Mr Devereux?”

“Yes it is so, Mistress Liz; ultimately saving this village the costs of long prosecutions that undoubtedly would be the case if such evidence was not presented in the prosecution of crimes.”

"I see, Mr Devereux. This is certainly an innovation in the prosecution of crime I have hitherto been unaware of."

"It is no surprise to me you should say this, Mistress Liz. For this is an innovation of my own making."

"Forgive me for saying so, Mr Devereux, but I have little faith your method will catch on."

"Mistress Liz, you are forgiven. As I know myself, only history will tell." With that said John doffed his Capotain, something not unlike a top hat but more conical and then left The Merry Widow.

Chapter 4

The clear skies and October sun had dried out East Scythe's high street and as John Devereux made his way up the rutted road, with his donkey in tow, he wondered whom he should visit first.

"Donkey, my dear companion, where to visit first? 'Tis a quandary. The Fox and Hounds or the church, the pie shop or the milliners, the cobblers or the vicarage, the working men's club or the…"

A curdling girlish scream shattered John's contemplations as the bald and bearded Bill Gouge ran out of his smithy waving his arms from side to side above his head.

"…or the smithy?"

The donkey huffed and nodded towards the black tarred building at the furthest end of the street.

"The smithy!" John said.

As the donkey rolled its eyes and nodded once more Bill Gouge, still screaming and with arms flailing above his head, zig-zagged down the high street towards John, then stopped.

"It's Tom Stutton," Bill exclaimed.

John blinked, his head shaking slightly. "Your style of movement; a *Tom Stutton*?" he offered.

"No, no. 'E's dead."

"Not a *Tom Stutton*, but some other kind?"

Bill dropped his arms to his sides and closing his eyes he breathed deeply, tilting his head. "Are ye the new 'igh constable, sir?"

"That I am. Who may you be, sir?"

"I am Bill Gouge, the blacksmith."

John let go of the rope and put his hands together in a steeple fashion. "What seems to be the problem, Bill Gouge, the blacksmith?"

"'E's dead."

"Tom Stutton is dead, I know, you have already stated as much. Is this the cause of your consternation, Mr Gouge?" John placed his hand over his mouth and with his index finger he stroked his nose knowingly; then grasped his chin.

The donkey butted John Devereux, exasperated. John turned to the donkey. "Will you please stop that? This man is obviously concerned about something you will never, in your donkey universe, ever understand." John turned back to Bill Gouge.

"Tom Stutton is…, was me apprentice, sir."

John clamped his mouth shut and raised his eyebrows. *Oh the foul ejaculations of a bovine's rear*, he thought. "Of course, Mr Gouge. I understand. Can you lead the way?"

***

Bill Gouge stopped at the entrance to his smithy. John reached into one of the saddle bags on the donkey and retrieved a note pad. After a second's thought he replaced the note pad and took out his sketch pad.

"Mr Gouge, if you'd be so kind, could you stand in the smithy's entrance for a few moments?"

Bill Gouge frowned, unsure of the reason. "Very well, Mr Devereux, if it will help."

John nodded. "That will help immeasurably, Mr Gouge, I can assure you."

John pulled a charcoal from his pocket and scribbled a few marks in the top left hand corner of the sketch pad. He shook his head; the external light did not penetrate the smithy that well. He exchanged the charcoal for one that was more burnt and did the test again. It was perfect.

"Mr Gouge, if you wouldn't mind turning your head towards the sun slightly, I will be finished in a few moments."

Bill slowly twisted his neck until he was looking directly down East Scythe's high street.

"Perfect. Hold it there, Mr Gouge." Quickly John captured the blacksmith's profile as he stood in the doorway to his place of work.

"Thank you, Mr Gouge. I'm done. Let us go in."

Reluctantly Bill Gouge led John Devereux and his donkey into the dark interior of the smithy.

"It's dark in here, Mr Gouge," John said.

"Aye, that it is," Bill replied.

The donkey nudged John towards the furthest left hand corner of the smithy and just as John was about to berate the animal once more he spotted the dead teenage apprentice.

"Oh my Lord. That's horrible," John said, not being able to keep his thoughts to himself.

In front of him lay the body of Tom Stutton, perforated by the many rusted blades of upturned ploughs, blades that were designed to furrow the land and not a human body. Almost congealed rivulets of shiny red fluid demarcated the holes in young Tom's tunic like strange wet halos that were there just to highlight the red-brown slithers of metal protruding from his body. But it wasn't only his torso that had been punctured. One of Tom's eyeballs stood out from his head on the end of a blade as if it was some kind of bizarre safety measure to protect all from the dangers of its point. Gore dripped from it and from the teenager's body. Directly above the perforated cadaver, attached to a beam that crossed the smithy's width, hung four scythes that were paired in twos almost horizontal to the beam they were attached to by their shafts. All were held in place by thin pieces of twine. All were waiting for Bill Gouge to sharpen them ready for use in next year's season.

As John stared at the macabre scene the girlish curdling wail he'd heard not so long ago, started again and Bill left the smithy at a pace with his arms flailing the air once more.

John looked at his donkey and grimaced. "Unfortunately, donkey," he said through gritted teeth, "I think I may have my first crime to investigate, though I suspect, from what I can see, this is nothing more than an unlucky accident."

The donkey butted John, forcing him head long into the blacksmith's quenching trough beneath the smithy's central beam.

***

John Devereux stood up from the trough and coughed out the water that had entered his shocked mouth. "What was that for you stupid ass?"

The donkey kicked out with a hind leg and John collapsed to the floor clutching his knee. "Very well, I mean donkey. It was just a slip of the tongue."

The donkey's back leg lifted from the floor.

"Very well, it wasn't a slip of the tongue. I apologise."

The donkey placed its hoof back on the ground.

John hobble towards his steed and patted the donkey on its neck. "Now we're on better terms, are you going to give me an idea as to why I had to look at the bottom of the trough?"

The donkey took a few steps passed Tom Stutton's impaled body and started nosing a patch of blood drenched straw.

John bent over and looked at the straw, as far as the eye could tell it was pretty fresh, possibly only two days old at most. John nodded. "I see. Two day old straw." John nodded again and steepled his fingers, then started tapping his fingertips together, vibrating them as if shivering. He looked at the straw and then looked at his donkey, then paused. He twisted his pursed lips from one side of his face to the other.

Standing upright, with fingers still steepled, he raised his eyebrows. "Very well, I give up." John shook his head. "What?"

The donkey huffed at the straw then brayed; a single pastel toned ginger feather wafted into the air. John reached into the straw and plucked a small shred of white material from it. Holding the material between his thumb and forefinger he turned towards the smithy's entrance to examine it in the light.

"Ah!" John said, "a clue. Perhaps this is less of an accident than I originally suspected. Possibly, donkey, I have discovered a murder most foul!"

John put the evidence into the donkey's saddle bag and took out his sketch book, quickly rendering the scene to paper.

Chapter 5

After a few more runs up and down the High Street Bill came to a stop outside William Dell's butcher's shop, the horrors he'd seen in his smithy dissipated, a tad, by his exertions. Bill closed his eyes and breathed deeply, shaking his head, but the respite from the shocks he'd endured did not last for long. A loud, *crack, crack, crack*, came from the window he was leaning on, making him jump. He turned around to see William Dell waving him into the shop. Bill entered.

"Bill, you all right?" William Dell asked. "You seem to have the devil upon your tail. What bothers you so?"

"'Tis, Tom, Mr Dell."

"What's that ragamuffin 'prentice of yours done now? Not been taking of the milliner's young strumpet?"

"Nah, nowt like that. 'E's dead, gone is 'e to the 'iverafter. Died on the blades of ploughs I was sharpnen. A mess, Mr Dell, truly a mess."

"An accident?"

"Soes the 'igh constable reckons. Or at least did when I left."

William Dell nodded. "I'm sure it was an accident. Can't have this John Devereux poking around business he has no business poking around."

"S'pose you're right, Mr Dell. Reckon young Tom must've been in the loft for some reason and just fell. Nothin' else can count for it. I s'pose."

William Dell grabbed Bill's shoulder and squeezed it. "I'm sure you're right. Go see Liz Clarke, she's certain to have something to take care of your grief."

"Wouldst it be like that, but it ain't. Times 'ave been hard."

William Dell took a few coins from his purse. "Here, Bill, take these, go see Liz."

Bill Gouge smiled. "Why thanks ye, Mr Dell. This is most generous."

"No problem, Bill. We're all part of the same team, apart from that John Devereux, that is. Has our constable been prying into anything he shouldn't?"

"Nah, Mr Dell. 'E's jus' int'rested in my Tom. That's all."

"Good, Bill. That's good."

Bill Gouge tapped his forehead with his index finger and left, making his way down the High Street towards The Merry Widow. He was in need of a drink.

Chapter 6

As John Devereux and his donkey made their way down the High Street, old grey-haired men, clad in suits of armour that had seen better days, appeared, each of them carrying a shield.

Though the heraldic designs varied greatly John could not help noticing a common theme. Each and every shield, without exception, had the stylised image of a feather emblazoned upon it.

He stopped outside the milliners shop to watch the strange procession. Most of the knights walked, stepping carefully over the ruts in the High Street, squeaking as the joints in their armour grated through lack of care. Some used their swords as walking sticks to help their progress. A few rode horses as decrepit as their armour, but all made their way towards the narrow side street that led from the village's main thoroughfare.

John Devereux pushed out his bottom lip and raised his eyebrows as he watched the ancient knights. Never in all his life had he seen such a strange sight.

His thoughts were disturbed by a light *tinging* of a bell, and as he turned he saw a young girl in the doorway to the milliners urgently waving him in.

"Donkey, I have been summoned. Stay here."

The donkey raised its head and looked at its master, then nodded. John entered the shop's dim wooden interior and just before the door closed the donkey kicked a lump of dung into the door jamb stopping the door from closing completely.

"Yes, Miss?" John said, "How can I help you?"

"You are Mr Devereux, the new constable?" she queried, glancing over her shoulder at a door set into the wall at the back of the shop.

"I am he."

"Mr Devereux, the village is all a fluster with the news of young Tom's death."

John steepled his fingers. "I see news travels fast in East Scythe."

"That it does," the young woman nodded and lowering her voice to a whisper, leaning closer to the constable, she continued. "Not that it's any of my business, but it is well known that…," she paused and looked towards the back of the shop again, "…that Mr Dell is involved with Miss Lincolne."

"That is interesting, young miss, *involved* you say? But I see not how that has any bearing on the incident with Tom Stutton."

"Miss Lincolne had eyes for Tom, possibly..."

A noise from the back of the shop stopped the young woman from finishing. A much older and rounder woman heaved herself into view, lifting her tatty dress as she walked up the creaking steps that led from the stock room.

The young girl paled. "How can I help you with your Capotain, sir?" she said, changing subject.

John, noting the young girl's distress, continued in the same vein. "For today, my hat is fine but perhaps you could answer this question; who are those knights I've seen entering the alleyway just yonder?"

Before the young girl could pipe up the older woman cackled, holding her sides, mirth halting her from answering the question but after a phlegmy coughing fit she spoke. "Mr Devereux, those knights belong to the Secret League of the Renowned Feather. And 'tis every other weekday they meets in The Fox and Hounds."

"Thank you, Mrs..."

"It's Mrs Baston, but my husband is long dead."

"I'm sorry to hear that, Mrs Baston."

"I'm not. He was a complete bastard and I pray to God that he's still burning in hell, the fu..."

"Thank you once more for the information, Mrs Baston," John interjected, quickly avoiding the Anglo-Saxon he didn't want to hear. As he left a thought struck him and he turned back. "Mrs Baston, one further question, if you'd be so kind?"

"Yes, me dear?"

"Why did you laugh so?"

"It's a *secret*...," she said, but before she could finish she started cackling again and waved John out of the shop, the irony being too much for her.

Outside John looked at his donkey and shook his head. "This is a very strange village, donkey. A strange village with a murder… and a murderer that needs to be caught."

The donkey swayed its head from side to side.

"I think it is time to go back to our lodgings and examine the evidence I've collected." John clutched the rope attached to the donkey and started his way back to The Merry Widow.

Half way down the High Street John's arm was nearly wrenched from its socket – his donkey had stopped again.

"What is it now, donkey?" John said as he turned to face the damned animal.

The donkey swayed its head to its left. They were now at the head of the narrow alleyway.

"Ah! You think some refreshment is required?"

The donkey stepped on John's foot.

"Ow! What was that for?"

The donkey huffed and in its usual four-footed manner entered the alleyway, stopping outside the entrance to The Fox and Hounds.

John looked at his donkey then looked at the door and raising his Capotain he scratched his forehead. The donkey snorted at the bottom left hand corner of the door. John squinted, there was something engraved there. He bent over to get a better look. "A feather!"

The donkey nodded.

"You think this may have some bearing on the case?"

The donkey nodded again.

"Why, donkey, why?"

The donkey re-enacted its huffing in the smithy.

John shook his head. "Very well, I'm not sure of your reasoning but I will go in." John tried the door, but it was locked. "It's locked," he said and started back towards the High Street.

The donkey didn't move. Instead it kicked the door and a slat in the door slid back.

"Password?" a voice demanded through the small opening.

Being well read John said, "Open Sesame."

The slat closed.

"Well, that's that then," John said and turned away from the door. But his donkey butted him, pushing him back to face the door once more and snorted at its lower left part then kicked the feather that was engraved into it.

As the penny dropped the slat in the door opened again. "Password?" the voice demanded once again.

"Feather," John said.

"What type of feather?" the voice queried.

John was lost for a moment, then recalled what Mrs Baston had said to him. "A renowned feather," he answered.

"Welcome, brother," the voice said and as the slat closed the door to The Fox and Hounds opened.

Chapter 7

It was dusk and Elizabeth Clarke had finished serving the early evening meal to Bill Gouge.

"Anything else I can get you, Bill?"

"No thanks, Liz, that mighty supper was well filling and I'll be taking my leave. Thank ye, Liz." Bill stood up and Liz showed him to the door.

"I'm sorry for your loss, Bill."

"'Tis a bad thing, Liz, a very bad thing when one loses an apprentice. I shall have to start over."

"An accident?"

"Aye, I reckon. Can't imagine why 'e was in the loft though."

"Fresh straw for the moulds?"

"Aye, possibly, but one can never know. Me thinks I'll take a long walk in Rendlesham Forest, a place for me contemplations and a place for me to collect the firewood for me furnace. And as happenstance may take, a place where justice may prevail."

"Aye, Bill, you do that. Rendlesham Forest can draw out the calm in troubled times." Quickly Liz closed the door, glad that Bill had left. She had things to do.

***

In the kitchen Liz looked out the window at the horizon, there was little time left to collect the herbs in the forest for her potions. Certain plants required picking during evendown to secure their majikal properties. Wrapping a large dark cloak around her and pulling up its hood she left The Merry Widow by the back. With wicker basket in hand she entered the forest beyond.

***

Richard Clayton, East Scythe's vicar, made his way from the vicarage down the High Street to his church. It was almost time for evensong. He had to ready the church, light the candles and choose the psalms his congregation would recite for the evening.

As he walked through the graveyard to the church's entrance the sound of a door closing stopped him in his tracks.

He was certain it hadn't been the door to the church. Turning around he saw, what could have only been, Liz Clarke leaving the back exit of The Merry Widow; a place of ill repute, he was certain, and a place that abutted the northerly wall of the church's perimeter. Although he was sure of her ilk nothing of her doings had ever spoken of the witch he knew her to be. He nodded thoughtfully to himself. One day, he would get the evidence he needed and on that day a messenger would ride out and find Matthew Hopkins and deliver the letter he intended to write.

***

In Rendlesham Forest John Ayers took the kill from the traps he'd laid a few days earlier. Whilst he worked his poacher's way thoughts of Tom Stutton crossed his mind. Tom had been good to him, fixing his old traps and crafting new ones, for far fewer schillings than that stingy git Bill Gouge.

John Ayers had seen Tom right for his help. He stroked the chicken's claw charm around his neck, knowing its influence was responsible for the harvest he was now reaping.

He would make sure Liz Clarke was all right for this blessing as he owed her for the charm. John Ayers was sure she wouldn't mind a late payment. Though to be on the safe side he'd stayed away from East Scythe but now he was ready to return after his final bit of business in the forest. The money he would raise from his poaching would more than pay for Liz Clarke's services.

John gathered up his mantraps; it was time to move them to a fresh area. After a time the animals he trapped always learned which places in the forest to avoid. He knew not how, but knew for a fact that they learnt the ways of men, the spirits of the wood educating them, he guessed.

After collecting the last trap he tracked silently through the dense forest until he was far enough away from the traps' previous killing fields and began to set the traps once again.

With the sun sinking below the horizon the shadowed darkness of the forest deepened but this did not cause any trouble for him. He'd been born and bred a poacher and Rendlesham Forest was a larder he could navigate almost blind.

As he set the last trap he heard the snapping sound of a twig or branch. He crouched down and held his breath. He hoped the King's game keeper had not decided to pick on Rendlesham to excise any potential poachers who may be taking advantage of his land. John listened intently. After what seemed to be an appropriate amount of time, with no other noises coming from the forest around him, he eased the jaws of the last trap open. It clicked into place. It was now time to make his way to The Merry Widow and pay Liz Clarke her dues.

Standing up he started his journey out of the forest, mindful of the traps he'd laid. But as he made his way to the path a clump of ferns rustled, followed by the sounds of snapping fronds. John turned to face the noise and although the sun was still just about visible there were no silhouetted shapes he could attribute to the unnatural sound.

Suddenly, to his left, another clump of ferns shuddered and a *whoosh, whoosh, whoosh* sound filled the immediate area. Then behind him the same happened and he turned to face the noise once again. Still he could see nothing but the agitated movement of the plants in the growing darkness.

Slowly the hairs on the back of his neck and arms began to prickle. After a few moments of indecision he ran helter-skelter from the noises surrounding him, offering murmured placations to the pagan spirits of the woodland, begging for protection, as he stroked the chicken's foot charm that hung around his neck.

After what seemed like many minutes he slowed, trying to listen to the forest above the sound of his own breath. And as his breath calmed he realised the forest had become silent. He took one more step forward and another sharp crack rang out through the woodland. It was only as he stumbled he realised the crack was the noise of his shin bone breaking under the crushing force of one of his traps. His body crashed down onto the forest's loamy soil and before he had any time to recover his head had sprung another mantrap, cracking it in two; the jaws of the trap acting like a nut-cracker on a walnut.

As his soul eased its way from his body his pursuer, with twitching head, lent over his broken skull and looked directly into his eyes. John's eyebrows, each on their own half of his smashed head, rose for a moment and as his consciousness passed into blackness he thought, *it's you!*

Chapter 8

John Devereux awoke suddenly as a beam of light bored through his eyelids. "Noooo," he yelled, "no more." He grabbed the counterpane and pulled it over his eyes. His actions had the desired effect. The sun's rays that were streaming through his curtains were pinched out and he swore never to take of the local ale again.

Under the counterpane he rubbed his forehead and massaged his temples hoping this would alleviate the continual thumping that echoed around his head but it wasn't to be so.

Mixed within the thumping he heard a voice calling to him. "Mr Devereux, Mr Devereux, are you there? John Ayers has been found dead in the forest."

John realised someone was knocking at his door and carefully sat up on the edge of his bed. "Please stop the banging. I'll be there in a moment." The banging stopped and John breathed a sigh of relief. Slowly he made his way to the bowl in the room and filled it with water from a large jug. Then he splashed his face.

"Enter," he said.

Liz Clarke walked in. "Mr Devereux?"

John raised a palm in Liz's direction. "Mistress Liz, what is so important that you rouse me at this early hour?"

"Forgive me for saying so, Mr Devereux, but it is eleven of the clock and a runner from Mr Dell has brought news of John Ayer's death."

"Eleven of the clock you say?" John made his way to the bay window and thrust his watch into the sun. The dial read eleven. John rolled his eyes.

***

Careful to stick to the forest path and avoid any of the poacher's traps, John Devereux, his donkey, Mr Dell's runner and Liz Clarke made their way to John Ayers' final resting place.

"Oh God, I think I'm going to be sick," John said as he surveyed the mangled head and leg of John Ayers. After taking a breath he continued, "Very well, I'll take it from here," he said to the runner and Liz Clarke.

"Are you all right, Mr Devereux? You look a bit peaky."

"I'll be fine, Mistress Liz."

"I have many potions that could ease your dis-ease, Mr Devereux. Not that I make them myself, of course."

"Don't worry, Mistress Liz, the fresh air will forestall my ailments. Thank you for your time." John Devereux bowed.

Liz and the runner turned to leave.

"One question, Mistress Liz, and I'm certain you'll understand why I have to ask this."

"What pray be that, Mr Devereux?"

John scrunched up his face. "I noted that you took us into these woods via the back entrance of The Merry Widow, can you tell me where you were last night?"

"Of course, Mr Devereux. After serving Bill Gouge a meal I remained in The Merry Widow performing the duties that would be expected of a proprietress of such an establishment."

"Of course, Mistress Liz. Sorry I had to ask."

As Liz and the runner left the blood strewn scene John turned to his donkey. "A most horrible accident don't you think?"

The donkey shook its head.

"Not an accident?"

The donkey nodded.

"How the hell do you come to that conclusion, donkey?"

The donkey huffed at the ground and John looked closer. The forest's loamy soil had captured a foot print, but it was a foot print that had only captured the balls of John Ayers feet. The donkey followed them, each were placed a large distance apart. After a few minutes the donkey stopped. On the ground were complete foot prints pointing in every direction, as if John Ayers had turned on point before he'd sped off along the path that had led to his untimely demise.

"So you reckon Mr Ayers stopped here for a moment?"

The donkey nodded.

"But what of those toe prints?"

The donkey trotted on spot.

"He ran!"

The donkey nodded again.

"He was chased?"

The donkey ee-awed.

Slowly John Devereux followed the poacher's tracks back to his body. John kicked the poacher's body turning it over onto its back with much of John Ayer's head remaining in its original position. The poacher's charm glinted as it caught the few rays of sunlight that had managed to bleed through the forest's canopy.

"Ah! John Ayers must have had pagan beliefs for him to have that charm around his neck." John snatched it up. "One minute, donkey, I must get a sketch." Quickly John removed his sketch pad from the donkey's saddle bag and using his least burnt charcoal he captured the scene.

"Not an accident then, donkey," John stated, once he'd finished.

The donkey nodded in agreement.

"But a contrivance to make out John Ayers accidently died by his own hand?"

This time the donkey didn't make any movement, its eye had seen something else lying next to John Ayers' body adjacent to his belt. Bending its neck down the donkey huffed at the ground and a single pastel toned ginger feather wafted into the air.

John plucked John Ayers' purse from his belt and opened it. Inside was a small piece of vellum with writing scrawled upon it. The writing said; "Charm: fifteen shillings, or at least something equivalent, I'm not fussy. E.C."

John nodded to himself. *Interesting*, he thought.

Chapter 9

As John reached down for his donkey's rope he noticed two letters, picked out by the morning sunshine, on the blood slimed mantrap encircling John Ayers' leg. But they were barely readable for the blood that had filled the engravings.

"Donkey, can you lick that clean? I need to get a better look at the engraving."

The donkey raised its eyebrows in an *you've-got-to-be-kidding-what-d'you-think-I-am-I'm-not-a-dog manner.*

"You're not going to do it, are you?"

The donkey shook its head.

John snatched a couple of fern fronds from the nearby plants and gingerly wiped the blood from the mantrap hoping not to get any of the wet viscous fluid on his hands. After a couple of swipes the letters T.S. were revealed.

"What do you make of that, donkey?"

The donkey considered shrugging but not having the musculature to achieve its goal it decided not to do anything.

John ran his thumb and forefinger down his chin. "Well, well, well. This is interesting. I think some oils are required to capture the nuances of this clue."

John set up his easel and placed a blank canvas upon it, then looked at the mantrap once more and shook his head. "It's no good, the light isn't quite right."

He had two choices, either cut down some of the vegetation blocking the sun's rays or, move the body. The latter made him feel sick to his stomach.

John started through the undergrowth and picked up a large stick, then attempted to bash down the foliage in the way. It was only when he heard a, *click, chang*, and realised he'd almost lost a leg, or at the very least a foot to one of John Ayers' traps, the idea of moving the body became his primary notion.

Using the large stick he poked and prodded John Ayers' body until the legs were illuminated by a beam of sunlight. *That's better*, he thought. Quickly he removed his palette from the donkey's saddle bag and began painting in earnest.

Two hours later, pleased with the facsimile he'd managed to capture, he loaded up the donkey's saddle bags with his equipment careful to make sure the drying oils on the canvas would not be smudged. With the evidence collected John Devereux made his way back to the village.

As he walked the leafy path he spoke to his donkey. "Donkey, I think I'm going to have to speak with Mr Gouge and Mistress Liz again. Something's not quite right."

***

Entering the village John started up the High Street to Bill Gouge's smithy, but before he'd even got past the church his arm was almost yanked out of its socket, his donkey having stopped again.

"What now?"

The donkey looked at him then made its way to the stone water trough next to the wall of the church's cemetery; John followed.

"You know you make me feel like a lemon," John said to his donkey.

The donkey lifted its mouth from the trough and nodded.

"Are you smiling?" John said. "Can donkeys smile?"

The donkey nodded and put its head back in the trough.

As John was contemplating what to do with his wayward donkey, Richard Clayton, the vicar, appeared from the direction of the church's entrance and waved.

John waved back. "Hello, sir. I take it from your collar you are the vicar of this parish… and perhaps the village?"

"Good to meet you, Mr Devereux, and yes I am." Richard Clayton offered his hand over the wall and John shook it. "I take it you're the new High Constable, sir?"

John nodded and doffed his Capotain. "I am," he said.

"'Tis troubled times we live in, constable."

"Very troubled," John concurred. "What with the war in the north and that madman Hopkins taking the law unto himself, very troubled times indeed."

"Those evil wenches deserve the wrath wrought upon them, Mr Devereux. But, in fact, sir, I was alluding to the deaths in the village. I've not known anything like it, especially the beautiful Tom. He was a sight to behold. A wondrous boy, with such beautiful locks, locks to be the envy of any woman in this village."

John's jaw dropped. *Very well*, he thought. "Perhaps, vicar, you could help me."

"Of course, of course, Mr Devereux. Anything I can do to assist, I shall do."

"Were you about the village between dusk and sundown yesterday?"

"In fact I was, Mr Devereux. I was on my way to prepare the church for evensong."

"Did anything catch your eye? Anything unusual?"

"I wouldn't say anything unusual, per se, Mr Devereux. But I did see that hag, the proprietress of The Merry Widow, leave for the forest. God only knows what she was up to; probably boiling babies in a cauldron of pig fat if I know anything of her ilk. Probably added the ash of desiccated newts too."

"Mr Clayton, vicar, just to get this clear in my mind; you saw her leave The Merry Widow, at dusk, for the forest?"

The vicar nodded. "That is correct, sir."

"Thank you, you have been most helpful."

John doffed his hat and the vicar nodded, making his way out of the cemetery towards the vicarage.

"You finished?" John said to the donkey.

The donkey licked its lips.

"Very well, back to The Merry Widow. Time to understand the intelligence I've gathered."

The donkey kicked out.

"We've gathered," John added, rubbing his shin.

Chapter 10

John Devereux walked up the three steps that led from the High Street into the hallway of The Merry Widow and called out, "Mistress Liz, I have returned." There was no answer.

"Mistress Liz, I require someone to stable my donkey and take my tools to my room."

After a few more moments Liz Clarke appeared looking somewhat flustered.

"Ah. Mistress Liz, could you facilitate the stabling of my donkey and have my accoutrements placed in my room? Are you all right?"

Liz Clarke had heard of the discoveries John Devereux had made. The village grapevine was second to none and should it happen that news could travel as fast through some strange mechanism in the air, it would still not be beat.

"Mr Devereux, I am fine and if you have heard any pernicious gossip I am here now to tell you it is a falsehood."

John nodded, then steepled his fingers. "Mistress Liz, fear not the tattle tales, my role is based in fact, something I bathe in daily. If, perchance, you have dallied in wrong doing, it will be my investigations that uncover this and not the hearsay of malcontents."

"Thank you for saying so, Mr Devereux, and may the blessings of the goddess Veritas be upon you. Not that I believe in that, of course."

"Of course, Mistress Liz. Can you have the serf take my accoutrements to my room?"

"Without delay, Mr Devereux." Liz turned and called out down the hallway. "Oi, Serf. Get this geezer's stuff to his room." She turned back to John. "Please excuse me for using the local dialect. 'Tis the only way to get things done."

"You are excused, Mistress Liz. When things have to be done the appropriate manner is always appropriate."

John walked up the creaky wooden staircase to his room and within moments the sketches, his painting materials and canvasses were delivered.

Once Serf had left, John Devereux crossed his room and faced the wall opposite his bed. As fast as he could he removed the pictures that hung there, and the looking glass, leaving the wall bare. Then he took his sketches and paintings from his day's excursion and tacked them into place on the newly denuded wall. Within the hour he'd finished his task. In front of him hung all the evidence he'd collated. All he had to do now was to tie all the evidence together to make a complete picture of the crimes that had taken place under his watch.

He stared at the wall, but he had nothing to link the scenes. Within minutes he'd made his decision and opened the door to his room.

"Mistress Liz," he called into the hallway. "Mistress Liz, I require your assistance." There was no answer. He sighed. If only there was some device in his room that could put him instantly in touch with the staff of his lodgings, what benefits that would reap.

John walked to the top of the staircase and tried again, a bit louder this time. "Mistress Liz, I require your assistance."

"What pray that be, Mr Devereux?" Liz called up the stairs.

Finally, he thought. "I need some string and some sealing wax, if you'd be so kind," he yelled back.

"You will have that in a moment, Mr Devereux," she answered from the kitchen on the floor below. John went back into his room and sat on his bed, contemplating everything he'd pinned to the wall.

After a time there was a knock at his door. "Stay there," John called out.

He got up and opened his door. Liz stood in the doorway with arms full of wax sticks and balls of string. John took the string and wax from her. "Mistress Liz, from this moment on I'll have to ask you not to enter my rooms without permission. And the same goes for your staff. As you must be aware I'm in the middle of an important investigation and no one should spy the information I've gathered, until such a time it is ready to be presented to the judge. Is this clear?"

"It is very clear, Mr Devereux. But as proprietress of The Merry Widow it is my duty to ask for such a view of the, what you call, evidence."

"I am sorry to say, Mistress Liz, that that request has to be denied."

"If you say so, Mr Devereux, then it shall be."

John nodded. "It shall be, Mistress Liz. Oh! And one other request, Mistress Liz."

"Yes, Mr Devereux?"

"On the morrow perhaps we could sit for a while, as there are some things that aren't clear to me and possibly you may have an insight."

"I'm not sure I have an insight, Mr Devereux, but if it helps I will comply with your request."

"Thank you, Mistress Liz. That would help greatly." John shut the door to his room and listened. After a few moments he heard Liz Clarke make her way back down the stairs.

John walked over to the candle next to his bed and lit it. Heating the sealing wax he drew the string through the hot fluid covering every inch. Once he was done he used his pen knife to slice up the string, ready to pin it between the pictures on his wall.

He linked Tom to the vicar, he linked the smithy to Tom, he linked Bill Gouge to John Ayers and John Ayers to Tom. And Tom to Bill Gouge. By the time he'd finished every sketch and painting he'd made linked to every other one.

John looked at the mishmash. *I don't think this will ever take on*, he thought to himself. He shook his head. *How could anyone unravel these connections to make something meaningful? Unless...*

John let go of the thought and got into his bed disheartened by the method he'd created to solve the puzzle of the murders. Staring at the sketches and paintings on the wall opposite, hoping for inspiration, he fell asleep.

***

Richard Clayton knew he had to approach the hag and confront her about her wrong doings, though he had no facts to base his accusations on. However, it was his duty, a duty bestowed upon him by God and told to him in his prayers.

He had no doubt that the recent deaths in the village were the responsibility of only one person, and that person was Elizabeth Clarke. He had to approach the witch and have her confess to her dabblings with the devil.

Though it was late he could not let the village's curse continue. It was incumbent upon him to stop the deaths and, to do that, he would have to exorcise Elizabeth Clarke and teach her the ways of God, allowing her salvation.

Taking his bible in hand and a vessel of Holy water he left the vicarage. Half way down the High Street on his trek to The Merry Widow, it began to rain.

***

In the early evening darkness a knight under the influence of the beverages he had taken, beverages particular to East Scythe, stood outside the Fox and Hounds lighting a cheroot. In the flicker of his flint lighter he noticed the silhouette of someone traipsing down the high street holding a large book to their chest.

***

Downstairs in The Merry Widow Liz Clarke was finishing clearing up the kitchen. As she'd worked on the cutlery she had taken time to put the kettle on the fire to boil water for a camomile tea. As was her regime she'd placed the cup on the work surface beneath her cupboard of tinctures. This was the way she always finished her duties for the evening. Once the cutlery was done she left the kitchen for the public lounge of The Merry Widow to close down the fire in its hearth.

As soon as she had left the kitchen a tapping started at the window and after a few moments it popped open. Then, after a quiet clicking sound, followed by a couple of whooshes, a packet of dried Birdsfoot Trefoil on a shelf above her tea tipped over, spilling some of its contents, adding a not so subtle twang to her calming beverage.

Having shut down the fire Liz Clarke made her way back to the kitchen and poured the boiled water into her cup. After a quick stir she sat down at the table in the centre of the kitchen and began to drink. Very quickly she felt sleepy, the natural cyanide from the Birdsfoot Trefoil making its presence felt.

She looked at her cup wondering why the camomile was working so well. The quantities she used never differed but this time there was something wrong with her tea. As her vision began to blur she realised it wasn't the camomile but something else that was affecting her.

Grasping the table to hold herself steady she glanced around the kitchen shaking her head, not only in disbelief, but as a way to clear her clouding mind. Finally she noticed the packet of Birdsfoot Trefoil that had been knocked over, but it was too late. She slipped to the floor, unable to breathe, her lips turning a nice shade of cherry red. In her last living moments she recognised the head and eyes that were staring at her over the edge of the table she now lay beneath. The head was twitching.

"It's you," she exhaled with her dying breath.

***

Richard Clayton decided not to knock at the door of The Merry Widow on the High Street. This thing, this confrontation with the witch was between him, her and God alone. He made his way to his church's cemetery. From there he could use the gate that linked the church to the back garden of the pub.

Opening the gate in the church's wall he saw that The Merry Widow's kitchen was still lit and guessing that Elizabeth Clarke would be working in the kitchen, he walked up the muddy flagstone path to the back door.

Noticing the kitchen's window was slightly ajar he opened it further and peered in; then jumped back. The sight he saw was nothing he'd been expecting. Elizabeth Clarke was lying on the floor motionless. Slowly he retreated from the view and decided there would be a more appropriate time to confront the witch. She'd obviously possessed one of her familiars and was out seeking another victim from his flock.

If he was going to do his job it would be better if he locked himself in the vicarage, so as not to become her next victim, as the witch made her rounds in the guise of one of her familiars; the decision to take this tack coming very quickly to him.

Chapter 11

John Devereux awoke ready for the day. He was happy with his new role, but then he saw the oils and sketches he'd pinned to the wall the previous evening. His demeanour sunk as a melancholy struck him; nothing made any sense. If his new method was to be believed everyone had a reason to murder everyone else, at least out of those he'd spoken to. And apparently, according to his new method, even the people that were already dead were in the frame.

He swung his legs out of the bed and trudged over to the washing table, picking up the folded flannel to dab his face. But before he'd had a chance to wipe his forehead, let alone anything else, there was a knocking at his door.

"Mistress Liz, what is it now?" he said in a monotone. "You've told me in the most recent past of the breakfast arrangements. So what can be so important as to interrupt my ablutions, madam?"

A timid voice answered. "It's not Mistress Liz, sir. It's Serf, sir."

"Serf, why do you knock on my door so?" John called through the door.

"I think Mistress Liz is dead, sir."

John dropped his flannel, shaking his head in consternation, then made his way to the door pulling it open abruptly. "Mistress Liz is dead? How so do you determine this, serf?"

The young serving girl, with greasy lank hair in her best tattered clothing, answered the query. "Sir, my mistress is lying on the floor and will not be roused. I have tried many things, even dripping the hot wax of a lit candle in her ear, but still she does not move, sir."

"Let me get out of my bed attire and I will join you. Where is she?"

"My mistress is on the floor of the kitchen, sir."

"I will join you there, serf."

"Right you are, sir."

"Does anyone else know of this circumstance?"

"No, sir. Just you."

"Thank you, serf. One more thing."

"What pray be that?"

"Get my donkey from the stables. I'm sure to need him."

"Your donkey?"

"Don't question me, serf. Just do it."

"Aye, sir. Sorry for my impertinence, sir."

***

John entered the kitchen from the hallway and the donkey entered via the back door. They both looked at the body lying beneath the table. Serf hovered in the doorway.

John turned to the serving girl. "You can go now. I'll call you when I need you. No word to anyone. You understand?"

"Aye, sir," and with that said Serf left the crime scene.

John rubbed his chin and as he looked at what lay in front of him he turned to his donkey, nodding. "Obviously an accident," he stated. "She must have fallen from the kitchen chair and in doing so, she was afflicted by death."

The donkey looked at its master with its jaw sagging.

"You don't think this is an accident do you donkey?"

The donkey shook its head from side to side and began to trot around the kitchen. After a few moments it had stopped and started braying. The donkey was now beside a worktop beneath some cupboards at the back of the kitchen.

John joined the donkey. On the surface of the worktop was a fine powder and within it there were strange three pronged markings; four of such.

"You think this is important?"

The donkey nodded.

"Very well, donkey. I think I need to record this. Go to my room and retrieve my sketch pad. Be sure to bring the correct charcoals."

The donkey nodded again and trotted out of the kitchen.

John went over to the table and picked up the cup that was there. He sniffed it gingerly. *Ah! Camomile*, he thought before placing the cup back. Supporting himself with his hand he leant over the table and looked at Elizabeth Clarke's still body. She could have been alive if it wasn't for the fact she took no breaths. Leaning further he touched her face with the back of his hand. And the fact she was stone cold. This was a puzzle to say the least. As he stood up, letting go of the table, a single pastel toned ginger feather wafted down landing in Elizabeth Clarke's open mouth.

John frowned. There was something familiar about the feather. He was certain he'd seen it somewhere else, but before his thought could congeal a loud clomping on the stairs brought him out of his reverie. His donkey entered the kitchen with the tools he'd asked for. Taking the pad and charcoals from the donkey's mouth he quickly rendered the scene to his sketch pad.

"Are we ready?" he said to his donkey. "We need to inform the Council."

The donkey looked around almost ready to nod, but then it spotted the feather resting in Elizabeth Clarke's mouth. The donkey shook its head and bashed its hooves on the flagstone floor.

"What?" John questioned.

The donkey huffed at Elizabeth Clarke's face and the feather wafted into the air.

"The feather. I know. I have rendered it in charcoal."

The donkey went mad, bucking and kicking, shaking its head, nodding, braying.

John eyed his trusty steed carefully. He was not used to this kind of behaviour. Slowly tilting his head to one side, he said, "You think the feather has some significance?"

The donkey relaxed, breathed in and nodded.

Chapter 12

At the moment John Devereux was attempting to get to grips with the revelation that the feather was a crucial part of his investigations, there was a loud knocking on the door of The Merry Widow.

"SERF?" John called out.

Serf appeared. "Yes, sir?"

"Get the door."

Serf nodded. "You want the door in the kitchen?"

"No, serf. I want the door answered."

Nodding again Serf left the kitchen to answer the insistent thumping of The Merry Widow's front door.

"What, sir, is going on?" William Dell roared as he entered the kitchen. "Another death? How pray that be, sir? You're a fool. I knew it from the moment I saw you. Never has this village suffered so much death. And I demand an answer, Mr Devereux."

John was at a loss. He glanced at his donkey. The donkey put on a stern face and John understood immediately what his donkey's new demeanour was telling him.

"Mr Dell," John started, "this is a crime scene and as High Constable I can tell you, advisedly, that until this scene has been thoroughly investigated you can go forth and multiply, taking the route into this place as you did follow."

"What? Sir? How dare you address me like that," William Dell said fuming.

"If you would prefer the charge of obstructing the investigation not to be bestowed upon you, I would advise you take your leave faster than a tick in a sheep dip. And as our Scottish foes may say, 'You ken?'"

"How impertin..."

John interjected. "No, sir, *how appropriate*, is what I think you mean. And if you'd leave now I will think nothing more of it."

William Dell, with his face now glowing a bright red, turned to leave. "Devereux, you better make this right or I'll 'ave you out of this village faster than you can say..., say..., a really long word. You get me?"

John bowed doffing his hat. "Of course, Mr Dell, I am your servant."

Before William Dell got out of the door John Devereux called to him. "Sir, with respect, what pray be your interest?"

"Nothing, Devereux, but my duty to ensure this community is justly treated by people such as yourself," William Dell said, lying through his teeth. The last thing he wanted was for Devereux to discover the village was using Butley River to smuggle spirits from France.

John nodded. "Naturally, Mr Dell, I would think nothing more."

The door to The Merry Widow slammed behind William Dell's flustered rear.

"What do you make of that donkey?"

The donkey shook its head.

Chapter 13

Taking one last glance around the kitchen John Devereux was about to leave when he noticed the open window. *That's unusual*, he thought. It was autumn and most people he knew would never leave a window open overnight. He walked over to the sink and smiled to himself. Could he have actually discovered a clue himself without any aid from his annoying donkey?

He looked at his donkey. "Donkey, you ass, did you not notice this window?"

The donkey stood motionless.

"I thought so," John said.

He leant over the sink and looked out of the window. Marked in the ground below he spotted, amongst the donkey's hoof prints, imprints of shoes that could only have been made the previous night when the rain had been falling.

Turning to his donkey still smiling, and raising an eyebrow, John said, "I think we have another clue."

The donkey tried to shrug to convey the idea it didn't give a toss about the footprints outside because it had already dismissed them; there were no muddy footprints in the kitchen. But it gave up quickly knowing, from previous experience, a shrug was impossible. The donkey made a mental note to teach itself shrugging; it was sure to be a boon for the future. Facetiousness and sarcasm would be even better.

John opened the kitchen door and stepped down into the garden. In the flower bed beneath the kitchen window were a multitude of obvious footprints, all of the same shoe size.

***

News had got around East Scythe that Elizabeth Clarke had died the previous evening and it was probably murder that was the reason for her demise. Though the villagers knew they weren't responsible they all developed their alibis, certain that John Devereux would come asking of their whereabouts.
Only Richard Clayton and Bill Gouge were truly worried as they knew they were out and about the previous evening and didn't expect their new High Constable to draw the right conclusions.

***

Although the donkey had thought it the most preposterous idea it had ever heard it still allowed the serving girl to attach the cart to it. When the serving girl had finished she collected the town crier's bell and handed it over to John Devereux along with a list of East Scythe's residents he'd also asked for.

"Thank you, serf," John said as he walked his donkey from the stables into the high street.

Making his way slowly up the high street John rang the bell with aplomb. "Oh yea, oh yea," he cried as loudly as he could.

"Bring out your shoes whether they be boots or clogs… or even shoes."

Windows and shop front doors opened as the villagers looked on astounded. A single thought passed through their minds; what on earth was the High Constable doing now?

"Oh yea, oh yea. No matter whether they be cow hide or wood, sheep skin or… or any other type of skin, bring out your shoes."

***

Richard Clayton heard the bell and as he unlocked and opened the vicarage's door to find out what was going on he heard John Devereux's words. *Oh no*, he thought. He only possessed one pair of shoes and any chance of him getting another pair had been scuppered; John Devereux had stopped outside the cobbler's and was now talking to Mr Forrest, the shoemaker.

"No, that's not what I meant, Mr Forrest," John said surveying the pile of footwear the cobbler had placed in front of his shop. "Please, I only meant the shoes you were wearing last night."

"Mr 'igh Constable, I distinctly 'eard you calling for shoes and nothing else."

"Just the shoes you used yesterday, Mr Forrest, if you please."

"But…"

"Yesterday's shoes. That's all. I'll come back when you're ready."

John continued up the high street and started ringing the bell once more. "Oh yea, oh yea, an update. Bring out your shoes, whether they be boots or clogs… or even shoes, THAT YOU WORE LAST NIGHT. Oh yea, oh yea."

After two hours the cart was full with villagers' shoes, all tagged with the owners' names. John turned to the donkey. "Well donkey, what do you think about that?"

The donkey didn't move.

"Good to see you're learning. That *was* a rhetorical question. Back to The Merry Widow. One thing is for sure, I'll get the person who poisoned Mistress Liz with the Birdsfoot Trefoil, once I've compared the shoes with the footprints outside the kitchen."

The donkey seemed to sneeze.

"Was that a sneeze or a snigger, donkey?" John asked frowning.

The donkey didn't move.

Chapter 14

John Devereux was fuming and striding back and forth along the only bit of the courtyard that wasn't covered in shoes. "Can you believe it donkey? Two hundred and fifty seven pairs of shoes and not a single one matching the footprints."

The donkey had had enough. It wandered down the path and faced a tree. Then it looked up into the bare winter's branches above.

John stopped his agitated pacing, shook his head and frowned at the donkey, trying to fathom out what it was that it was doing.

The donkey took a deep breath and pursing its lips it gruffed out an odd ee-aw sound, like some kind of equine bark. Then it shook its head from side to side and made its way to another tree and stared into that tree's branches, not uttering a single sound this time.

John removed his Capotain and scratched his head. He was now certain that the donkey was past it and its brain had succumbed to whatever the donkey equivalent was to an aged man's mental deterioration.

John spoke very slowly, "Very well donkey. If you would like to come here I can get you some hay. Would you like that?"

In sheer frustration the donkey flopped onto the ground and started banging its head against the tree's exposed roots.

"Very well. Perhaps a bit later then," John said just as slowly. As he spoke the words, inspiration struck him. "But for now I have a crime to solve and with this list of villagers' names, I will find the missing pair of shoes," he said pulling a crumpled list from his coat pocket.

***

From atop the stable's thatched roof a pair of beady eyes watched the scene below unfold. But instead of laughing, the head that contained the eyes and was not swaddled in a cloak of pastel brown feathers that covered the rest of its body, began to twitch in glee, only to suddenly disappear. It had some other business to attend to.

***

"Ah, ha!" John said. "I've got you now, *Mr Richard Clayton*." After an hour's worth of effort John had matched up every pair of shoes with every name on the list bar one – the vicar.

As John strode purposefully out of the stables and towards the high street the donkey got up and, with the apparent seizure seemingly over, the donkey followed John, no after effects to be seen.

John heard the clopping of his donkey's hooves on the cobbled courtyard and turned around. "Are you feeling better now, donkey?"

The donkey nodded solemnly, the developing painful bruises on its head helping it forget the stupidity of its master.

Chapter 15

Bill Gouge was pacing his smithy bare footed; he was worried. Goodness only knows how he would explain to the High Constable what he was doing wandering around Rendlesham forest, at the back of The Merry Widow, just about the same time Mistress Liz was murdered. *Poor, Liz*, he thought.

To calm himself and take his mind off the impending interview, he decided to clear up the mess in the smithy; he'd not done anything since his apprentice's sad demise.

As Bill worked away beneath the hayloft clearing the blood matted straw that had been Tom Stutton's last resting place, the twine securing the scythes attached to the beam above him was gradually being whittled away.

Standing up abruptly, dropping the mucky straw he'd been gathering, Bill was certain he'd heard a strange *twanging* sound.

"That almost sounds like...," he said to himself, getting no further as a sharp driving pain pierced his back and the front of his leather apron achieved a peculiar conical pointy shape. He looked down at his apron. "... like the twine 'olding them scythes has given out. Oh bugg..."

Before he could say any more another of the four scythes swung down, its point entering his open mouth. As his eyes rolled in their sockets he caught a glimpse of a shadow above him in the hayloft. *It's you*, he thought, before finally leaving for the 'iverafter.

***

John opened the gate to the vicarage, walked up the path and knocked hard on the door. "Mr Clayton, if you'd be so kind, I would like a word."

Reluctantly the vicar opened the door. "Ah! It's you, Mr Devereux," he said feigning surprise. "How can I help you today?"

"According to my investigations I'm a pair of shoes short." John glanced at the vicar's bare feet. "You seem not to have any shoes. Is this normal for a person of your standing, Mr Clayton?"

Richard Clayton peered up and down the high street hoping no one was watching, then waved John Devereux in. "Come in, come in, sir. I'm sure this confusion can be sorted out." Richard Clayton shut the door. "Come thro…"

Before he could finish there was a loud thumping at the door. Richard Clayton turned back to the door, "I'm certain I didn't see anyone else," he said.

"And I'm sure you are correct, sir," John said.

"Well who…"

"It's just my donkey and if you would kindly let him in I'd appreciate it."

"Your donkey, Mr Devereux?"

"Yes, what of it?"

"It's a donkey."

"Exactly so, sir."

Richard Clayton gave up and opened the door. With a snort of disdain the donkey entered and made its way to the withdrawing room, carefully selecting the chair it would be most comfortable on.

Richard Clayton walked down the hallway and peered into the withdrawing room not sure to believe his eyes. After a moment he turned to look at the High Constable. "Er, this way, Mr Devereux." Richard Clayton indicated the remaining free chair. All that was left was the chaise longue and Richard Clayton took his place on it.

"What can I do for you, Mr Devereux?"

John got up and walked over to his donkey pulling a sketch pad from the donkey's saddle bag. "If you could hold that pose for a few minutes I would appreciate it."

The vicar frowned, then acquiesced.

Very quickly John had captured a great likeness of the vicar's bare feet. "Thank you, sir," John said replacing the sketch pad before sitting back down. "Now, if you'd be so kind, could you tell me why you have no shoes?"

Richard Clayton squirmed. "They're at the cleaners," he blurted out.

"Ah! And how many Hail Mary's will you have to do for that answer, or whatever it is you have to do, being a man of the cloak or is it cloth? I can't rightly remember."

"It's the cloth."

"If I ask your housekeeper," John took a note pad from his pocket, "Miss Lincolne? Would she be able to verify this?"

Richard Clayton gave up the pretence. "Very well, Mr Devereux, my shoes are in the cupboard over there and I'll admit I was at The Merry Widow this evening just past. But I had nothing to do with the death of that witch… sorry, I mean Elizabeth Clarke."

"That's a very interesting answer, Mr Clayton." John winked at his donkey but it took no notice, it seemed to be asleep. John carried on his questioning, "Because I was asking about your shoes, not Liz Clarke. Do you have anything else you want to tell me?"

Richard Clayton knew he had given too much away. "Very well, I was there. I was there! But she was already dead – I thought she was just lying on the floor because she had possessed one of her familiars. I didn't know she was dead until today. I stood outside the window, saw her on the floor and left."

"You say what you say, sir. But you have told to me in recent days of your dislike of the woman. Why should I believe you?"

"Because it is the truth, Mr Devereux. I swear upon the office I hold."

John eyed the vicar carefully and then looked at his donkey. The donkey nodded.

"For now, Mr Clayton, I will take your word. But believe me when I say – if you attempt to leave East Scythe before my investigations are completed you *will* be chased down like a common murderer."

"I understand, Mr Devereux, I have nothing to hide."

John stood up. "I'll be taking my leave for now."

The vicar led John and his donkey to the door, watching them make their way along the path to the high street.

As John started for his lodgings he turned back to face the vicar. "Mr Clayton, what was your relationship with Tom Stutton?"

Richard Clayton stood slacked jawed in the doorway to the vicarage.

"Don't worry, Mr Clayton, there is plenty of time to discuss that. I bid you farewell." John doffed his hat and started the short trek back to The Merry Widow to go over all the evidence he'd collected.

Chapter 16

"I think we've got our man," John said to his donkey as they walked down the street, "at least for Mistress Liz's murder, if not for Tom Stutton as well."

The donkey sighed heavily and considered its life, wondering what on Earth it had done to deserve being assigned to its master.

"There's certainly a link between Tom and Richard Clayton – in fact Mr Clayton almost admitted as much when we spoke to him just the other day."

The donkey slowed its pace to a crawl as a deep melancholy set in.

"Perhaps for the rest of the day we will take my oils and water colours to the river. And paint, whilst I consider everything I've discovered."

The donkey stopped walking and John was brought to an abrupt halt.

"Are you not well, donkey? Why have you stopped? It's not the onset of another seizure? I pray it's not."

Looking deep inside itself it was all it could do to muster enough enthusiasm to shake its head from side to side.

"I understand, donkey, this case has exacted huge tolls on our very beings. We will have an afternoon by the river, I'm sure this will refresh us."

Moments later John Devereux and his donkey were standing in the courtyard at the back of The Merry Widow. "Serf, serf!" John called out. "Bring my painting accoutrements and load up this donkey. I'm off to the river to do some painting."

"Aye, sir."

"This is going to be fun, donkey, I can assure you."

***

William Dell picked up the last of the blunt meat cleavers and knives. "I'm taking these to Bill for sharpening," he said to his nephew. "I won't be long but please make sure you don't do anything stupid whilst I'm away."

His nephew nodded compliantly.

"Speak up, boy."

"Yes, sir," the nephew responded.

William Dell left the shop and marched the short distance to Bill Gouge's smithy. As he approached he slowed down. Something was amiss; there were no sounds of metal upon metal, there was no smoke pouring out from under the gable at the front of the smithy.

As William Dell turned the corner and entered the smithy he was brought up short by the scene before him; Bill Gouge sagged from the shaft of a scythe that hung vertically down from the beam above, the scythe's blade keeping Bill hanging there by the mouth. The gobbets of matter from the back of Bill's head, stuck to the point of the scythe's blade, gave the impression of the cork one might place on particularly sharp knives and other such utensils for safety.

William Dell left the smithy and grabbed the nearest person likely to know the whereabouts of East Scythe's supposed constable. It was an unfortunate street urchin.

"'onestly, guv, it weren't me t'was the other person, on me muvver's life," the urchin balled.

"You stupid child. What are you talking about?"

"Thems wallets, guv."

"Shut up, I don't care about the wallets. Where's that prat constable?"

"I 'eard 'e was down the river, a paintin' or sommint." The urchin knew exactly who William Dell was talking about.

"A shilling if you fetch him."

"Ta, guv." The urchin held out his hand.

"When he's here."

"Blimey, guv. I gotta make a livin'."

"When he's here," William Dell reiterated.

The urchin eyed the Council's Chairman and decided it would be better for his health not to push the point any further. He left for the river at a pace.

***

John Devereux was making flamboyant strokes across his canvass. "Is this not the life donkey, to be out in the countryside capturing the beauty of nature?" John said, all thought of his responsibilities cast asunder as he immersed himself in his passion.

The donkey huffed. As long as it had to carry the burden its master put upon it, nothing was beautiful, and it was certainly not the life it had planned for itself.

All of a sudden John stopped painting as he glanced up the river. "Look at that donkey, what a wonderful composition that would make. I must capture it. Pray bring me another canvass."

John yelled out to the hay wain's driver. "Sir, stop a moment, if you please."

The driver turned around.

"Three shillings if you stop a moment," John said.

The driver shrugged and loosed the horse's reins, allowing it to drink from the centre of the stream that was Butley River.

Begrudgingly the donkey picked up the canvass in its mouth and dropped it at John's feet.

"Thank you, donkey," John said, picking up the canvass and placing it on his easel.

As John was about to sketch the outline of the horse and cart standing in the river, a high pitched voice interrupted his concentration.

"'ere mister, constable, sir, I 'aves a message from Mr Dell."

John sighed and put his charcoals down. "What pray be that, urchin?"

"Bill Gouge is deaded, sir, and Mr Dell wants you."

Chapter 17

John Devereux slowed as he approached the top of the high street and Bill Gouge's smithy. William Dell's face was completely red and in his hands were a number of meat cleavers and knives.

"Donkey," John whispered, "I've got a bad feeling about this. You go first."

The donkey turned its head and looked at its master for a moment but before it could decide whether to give in and continue or give its master a hefty kick and then continue, William Dell made the choice.

"Devereux," William Dell barked down the high street, "what are you dawdling for you fool? Come here this minute."

"Ah! Mr Dell, felicitations to you, sir," John said attempting to calm the Council Chairman's over wrought demeanour.

"Felicitations? Sir? When my dear and close friend has died? What kind of man are you, if man is the appropriate term to use?"

John realised his tack hadn't worked as well as he'd thought it would.

"What are you going to do about this?" William Dell continued ranting.

"Your dear friend?"

"YES!"

John walked into the smithy then stopped frozen to the spot as he caught sight of Bill Gouge's body hanging like a macabre puppet from the beam above; strings replaced by scythes and rivulets of fresh blood from the fatal wounds that glistened as errant light struck the deep red streaks on the blacksmith's apron.

"Well, Devereux? What are you going to do?"

"I can assure you that I will do everything in my power to uncover the circumstances that led to the death of your dear friend."

"Are you mad constable? Is it not self-apparent to you? The scythes you fool, the scythes. You are a twat of the highest degree, Devereux."

"Please, sir, pray be calm. I only meant how it came to pass that Mr Gouge met his demise by those farming tools."

William Dell took a deep breath. "I suppose I have no choice but to leave it to you, Devereux. I pray that this wasn't so, but my prayers have not yet been answered."

"As a matter of procedure it is beholden to me to ask of your whereabouts for the last few hours, Mr Dell," John said recalling an entry from the Manual of Justice and Law he'd been handed by his uncle before receiving the title of High Constable.

At that point William Dell lost any composure he had and threw one of the meat cleavers directly at John Devereux. John ducked just in time, but not enough to save his Capotain which became pinned to the wall of the smithy behind him.

"WHAT?" William Dell roared.

"Er, nothing, Mr Dell. Just a slip of the tongue. You may go."

"Can I now?" William Dell barked over his shoulder, already half way out of the smithy.

John waited until William Dell was out of sight before turning to his donkey. "That didn't go quite as well as I expected."

The donkey gazed at its master nonplussed.

"However, time to move on and investigate this incident," John said as he walked towards Bill Gouge's slowly cooling body.

Following other entries he'd read in the Manual of Justice and Law, John examined the blacksmith's body starting from the feet. He lifted one of Bill's hands, noting the dirt. "I can gather, by my examination of this man's hands, he was obviously a labourer."

The donkey's mouth dropped open.

"Donkey, bring me my pad. I need to capture this as it is an important point. The background of this man may have some bearing on the case; if this is nothing more than an awful accident."

John dropped to the floor as both legs gave way; his donkey making it plain its thoughts on the matter.

Struggling to his feet John said, "What did you do that for? You're not going to tell me this is anything but a tragic accident?"

The donkey nodded and trotting over to the body it snorted at Bill's face, careful not to cut itself on the scythe.

Bill Gouge's eyes were still open and after the donkey moved away John could see that they were staring towards the hayloft.

Step by step John climbed the ladder into the hayloft. "Now what do you want me to do?" he called down to his donkey.

The donkey started to push some straw around with its nose.

"God's teeth, donkey! You want me to search the straw?" John shook his head. "Stupid damned animal," he muttered under his breath. "Very well," he called down, "if that's what you feel is needed, I'll do it just this once."

Whilst its master was sifting the straw the donkey had a closer look at the twine that had held the scythes in place. It recognised the pattern of wearing that had rendered the twine weak enough to break.

After half an hour of rooting around in the straw John gave up and made his way back down the ladder.

"Well donkey that was a most pointless exercise. There was nothing up there apart from the straw and a few pastel feathers. Absolutely nothing, no clues, not a thing, donkey."

The donkey smiled to itself – the case was solved. The only question that remained was how to apprehend the canny murderer.

Chapter 18

John Devereux's dreams had been a mishmash of names and horrific scenes, huge red faced heads with impossibly sized mouths, images of serene river flows and hay wains.

He awoke with a start and leapt out of bed; a smile beginning to crease his cheeks. "I've got it," he yelled at no one in particular.

John finished his ablutions, got dressed and bounded over to his door pulling it open. "Serf, breakfast if you please, and make it a large one. For today is the day that John Devereux, High Constable of East Scythe, solves the case of the murders most foul."

"Aye, sir," came Serf's timid voice wafting up the stairs.

"Oh! And one more thing, serf."

"Yes, Mr Devereux."

"Please send out a runner to Miss Lincolne, Mr Richard Clayton and Mr William Dell requesting their presence at my newly refurbished office, by three o'clock this afternoon. By order of the High Constable."

"Yes, Mr Devereux."

"Oh! One more thing serf."

"What is it now?"

"Please arrange for tea and cakes to be served."

"Very well, Mr Devereux."

Whilst John waited for his breakfast he scrawled notes on scraps of paper capturing the revelation that had occurred to him during his sleep. After half an hour there was a knocking at his door.

"Come," he said.

Serf walked in with a large tray which held the largest breakfast John had ever seen. "You have done me proud, serf and I will..."

"My name is Mary, sir," the serving girl interjected.

"Right you are serf Mary. As I was saying; you have done me proud and for your, not so small endeavours, I thank you most heartily."

"And?"

"And that is all. You may go, serf."

"Git," Mary muttered as she turned to leave.

"Sorry, serf, I didn't quite hear that."

"I said; I've got to *git* on, there's so much more work to do now that Miss Clarke has gone."

"Of course, of course, serf. I understand."

Mary shut the door a little more forcedly than was required and made her way down the stairs to carry out the other tasks she now had since Elizabeth Clarke's demise.

Despondent she decided to muck out the stables as it was something she knew how to do and enjoyed. Being with the animals, or animal as it was at the moment, was her passion particularly because they didn't order her around; for her it was a release.

Opening the door onto the courtyard she heard the High Constable's donkey braying and rushed over to the stables to check on the poor animal. As soon as she pulled open the door the donkey stopped.

"You seem well, donkey. Is there anything bothering you?"

The donkey shook its head.

"That's good," she said, then poured her heart out. "Your master wants everything done at once; runners to be sent out with messages for meetings at the refurbished office…"

The donkey nodded in sympathy. It certainly knew how demanding its master could be.

"Tea and cakes as well. Can you believe it? The Vicar and Miss Lincolne, Mr Dell – I don't think he's going to like that – they're all invited you know," Mary said as she patted the donkey's neck.

That was all the donkey needed to know. Its master had decided he knew who had committed the crimes and was arranging a meeting. The donkey started to tug at the rope that bound it to the stables; then rubbed its neck against Mary's side.

"You want a bit of freedom don't you, donkey? I understand that," Mary said.

The donkey nodded and Mary untied the knot binding it to the stables. The donkey made a break for it.

"Donkey, come back. You're going to get me into such trouble. Please."

The donkey stopped in the middle of the courtyard and flicked its head in a *come-this-way* manner.

After a couple of hours Mary and the donkey were stood outside the refurbished office of the High Constable. There was not much to the building; it was square, had a door in the front and a small window on one side. The donkey led Mary around the side of the building that housed the small window.

Chapter 19

It was almost three o'clock and the sky had become leaden. John Devereux rushed around his new office lighting the few oil lamps he'd been provided. Suddenly the door to the office flew open and William Dell entered.

"This better be good, Devereux, I've had to leave my shop in the care of that good-for-nothing nephew of mine." William Dell was still wearing the clothes of his trade and around his waist was a leather belt tucked into which were a few of his tools; most notably his trademark meat cleaver.

"Mr Dell, I can assure you that I would not have requested your presence here without good reason. Please take a seat, sir."

Next there was a dainty tap on the door. "Come," John said. Richard Clayton entered followed by his housekeeper, Miss Marie Lincolne. "Please find your selves a seat," John said.

"What are we doing here, Devereux?" William Dell bellowed.

"All will be revealed in good time, Mr Dell."

From the room at the back of the office entered John Devereux's donkey. It looked at the gathered crowd and then sidled over to the room's only window careful to make sure its hoof was in the centre of a loop of thread that lay on the floor.

Once everyone had settled, John Devereux began after taking his place behind his desk. "Sirs, lady, you may be wondering why I have gathered you all here this afternoon and..."

Marie Lincolne put her hand up.

"Yes, Miss Lincolne?"

"Is it because of the murders?"

"Exactly so, Miss. Exactly so. Now if I can continue; as I was saying, and I can announce to you that I know the identity of the murderer."

"Do you now, Devereux? Because from what I've seen of your outlandish methods all you could possibly know is the correct shade of pink to use when rendering the dead to canvass."

"Mr Dell, if you please, pray let me continue."

"Very well."

"Thank you, sir. And may I politely request that you refrain from interrupting."

William Dell harrumphed as he crossed his arms, not adding any further comment.

John Devereux continued. "I will start with the murder of Bill Gouge's apprentice, Tom Stutton." John reached behind his desk and pulled out a large canvass. A scream pierced the room followed by blubbing. "Mr Clayton, please try to control yourself."

***

Outside the office of the High Constable a shadow darted down the side of the building.

***

"...and during my investigation I found this." John held up the small piece of cloth he'd found in the smithy. Marie Lincolne covered her mouth to stifle her exclamation of shock.

John pointed at Richard Clayton and then at William Dell. "You and you colluded in the murder of Tom Stutton because both of you were jealous that Tom's affections had been placed elsewhere. Isn't that so, Miss Lincolne?"

Marie Lincolne sunk into her seat.

"What is this nonsense, Devereux? My Marie would not do such a thing," William Dell roared.

"It's not true, I didn't murder him, I loved him," Richard Clayton balled.

Everyone turned to the vicar, even the donkey's mouth dropped open at the vicar's admission. There was a collective intake of breath.

William Dell turned to Marie. "Marie, my betrothed, have you forsaken me for another?"

"No, no, my love," Marie Lincolne said, "it was an accident, I'm sure. I tripped in the hayloft and bashed my delicate head. I don't rightly recall the rest."

"I understand, my dear, my sun in the sky, my brightest sparkling star of the night, my angel from Heaven, my Venus. Accidents will happen."

There was a swooshing sound as everyone's heads turned to face William Dell. It was now his turn to be gawped at by everyone in the room.

Marie Lincolne fluttered her eyelids at her soon to be husband. "Ah! You are my little Billy Willy, I knew you'd understand." She took William Dell's hand in hers gently rubbing the back of it. A smile appeared on William Dell's face, something no one had ever seen before.

"AND," John shouted, breaking up the lover's reconciliation, "it was you, Miss Lincolne, who brutally murdered Bill Gouge to keep him quiet about your amorous liaison with Tom Stutton in the smithy."

John pulled a second canvass from behind his desk.

"What in the name of God has that got to do with anything?" William Dell said, back to his normal self.

John looked at the painting of Bill Gouge's grubby hand. "Ah… This is Bill Gouge's hand and…, anyway, moving on." John quickly replaced the canvass.

The donkey seemed to sneeze and John Devereux gave the animal a stern look, mouthing, *Shut up*.

"Devereux, I warn you, be careful where you're going with this."

"And then we come to the poisoning of Elizabeth Clarke, Mr Clayton; your muddy footprints outside the window, your known hatred of the woman."

"Mr Devereux, please," Richard Clayton pleaded. "Did you find evidence to show I was in the kitchen? I truly wasn't there. Were my footprints cast upon the floor?"

John paused for a long moment. "…er. Ah! You could have easily wiped your shoes before entering The Merry Widow."

"As God is my witness I swear I had nothing to do with the witch's death."

"And there we have it." John began summing up. "A murderous trio all attempting to protect your little secrets using the heinous tool of murder. It's despicable and I will see you hang for every murder."

"Devereux, you are the king of fools. All you have are tenuous links to us at the very best and what about John Ayers?"

John picked the final canvass from the floor and placed it on his desk. He shook his head tutting as he did so, "Probably the most unfortunate accident that could ever befall a man."

The donkey rolled its eyes.

"If you have nothing more to say, Devereux, me and the betrothed will be taking our leave. This meeting has been nothing short of farcical."

As William Dell and Marie Lincolne stood to leave Mary entered the office from the back room carrying a full tray of tea and cakes.

"Tea and cakes anyone?" she suggested.

"Well, seeing you've made the effort..." William Dell took three cakes and sat back down.

***

During the entire charade the shadow outside had managed to climb up the few wooden crates that stood stacked outside the window. It peered in; its beady eyes swaying back and forth in its twitching head, almost unable to keep quiet at the sheer hilarity of the High Constable's so called investigation. It knew now that it had succeeded, with three others being identified for the ingenious murders it had planned.

***

Mary had just finished pouring the sobbing vicar's tea when she caught a movement outside the window. "Now, donkey," she said calmly.

The donkey kicked its hoof and the thread freed the trapped she'd set earlier.

There was a loud crash outside the window and everyone jumped.

"What in the name of God was that?" John said, staring at the window.

"That was the sound," Mary started, "of your murderer being caught, Mr Devereux."

"How so it that, serf?" John said.

"It is Mary Serf if you would care to use my full name, but that does not matter. I will show you; 'how so', Mr Devereux," she sneered. Mary left the room and within a few moments she came back carrying a wooden cage holding an obviously angry one-legged chicken.

"You impertinent wench. What kind of stupidity is this?" William Dell barked at the serving girl.

"I will tell you, Mr Dell, if you will listen."

"Pray, carry on. I am looking forward to this tall tale."

"This·chicken lost its leg because of the knife Tom Stutton had made. And when the opportunity came, in the hayloft, this chicken planned to give young Tom a fright hoping for the fatal consequences it achieved. In this chicken's twisted and cruel mind it saw others that had conspired against it.

"Mr Ayers brought the leg he'd severed to Elizabeth Clarke to have it made into a charm. And so, when Mr Ayers was out setting his traps, again this chicken planned to scare Mr Ayers so severely that he would lose any thought of where he was and fall foul of the very traps he'd set."

Mary stopped for a moment to drink some tea as her mouth had gone dry. She'd expected cries and taunts from those around her but the room remained silent.

She continued. "But, because of the charm this chicken considered Mistress Clarke a co-conspirator in the enterprise and contrived a time when it could exact its revenge. It knew about my Mistress' habits and took the opportunity to knock the Birdsfoot Trefoil into her drink. By this time its confidence had grown and was taunting the High Constable by the very fact of using the poison it did.

"However, there was one person left – the person who'd set in motion the events that would lead to the loss of its leg – Bill Gouge, the blacksmith, the man who had trained Tom Stutton in the art of metalwork."

There was nothing but silence in the room. All those present unable to raise a single point to denigrate the synopsis of events Mary had relayed.

Then from nowhere a deep gravelly voice seemed to leak from the air itself. "Very good, Mary Serf, if I could, *cluck*, clap my hands I would…,"

Everyone's heads swished backwards and forwards trying to identify its source and as they looked at the cage a deeper silence fell in the room. William Dell frowned. He thought he'd recognised the voice.

"It's you," they all chimed.

"Yes, it is me, but that is not the whole, *cluck*, story," Hoppy said. "I was about to arrest…"

"I do recognise that voice," William Dell interjected, "somehow you're Bartholomew Awdy our former High Constable! But you were murdered."

"Obviously not, *cluck*, Dell, now be quiet. As I was saying; *cluck*," the chicken shook its head. "I was about to, *cluck*, arrest Elizabeth Clarke under the suspicion of practicing witchcraft…"

"I knew it," Richard Clayton exclaimed.

"Will you, *cluck*, up. When she cast me into this, *cluck*, form, but I escaped. Only for that, *cluck*, poacher to capture me and, *cluck*, sell me to Miss, *cluck*, Lincolne."

John Devereux stood up. "Hoppy, you are under arrest for the murder of, Tom Stutton, John Ayers, Elizabeth Clarke and Bill Gouge. Anything you…"

"You, *cluck*, Devereux, will never catch me."

John looked at the insane twitching chicken. "I'm sorry to inform you that you are already caught, sir… I mean, chicken."

"Oh! *Cluck*."

The Emaciated Man

The emaciated man had not eaten since his first attempt at a pot roast four weeks previously. He could still remember the sweet taste of the meat. But since then he'd been too afraid to leave the house and now his phone and electricity had been cut off.

He eased back a curtain with his fingertips and gazed out of his dingy lounge. He yearned to walk in the spring sunshine, but feared his neighbours; they were odd and didn't react as he expected most people would. He'd convinced himself, if only for his sanity, it was the neighbourhood he'd had to move to, not so long ago.

He yearned for help; just someone to come to his front door and knock, like they'd done before.

David dropped the curtain and went to his kitchen. He glanced at the bones on the worktop; there wasn't any more he could do with them. They were completely free of meat and he'd already boiled them for stock and soup.

He filled a large saucepan with water and put it on the gas stove to boil. When it was ready he made himself a coffee.

David sat down at his kitchen table and contemplated his options. His head jerked up in response to a loud clack that came from his front door; someone was knocking. He looked along his hallway and smiled. Someone had come to see him, at last.

He opened the door and beckoned the insurance salesman in; stating he already had a coffee on the go. David directed the salesman towards the kitchen.

The salesman entered David's kitchen and suddenly felt the need to vomit – the bones on the worktop not a sight he'd ever expected to see. But he didn't vomit; the mallet that crashed into the back of his head stopped that embarrassment.

David shoved the bones to one side and manoeuvred the salesman's body into place. As he took the carving knife from the drawer he smiled and considered how fortunate he was to already have the water boiling. He looked forward to his next pot roast.

Killing Myself to Live

Quite often I sit in my study,
thinking about the past that has been.
Not a thing I have control over, just my life before,
and its permeating stink.
And I wonder. I wonder why I suffer this trauma;
this thing that's my life before.
And these thoughts are forever present,
bugging me, taunting me, pushing me to the brink;
contemplating the uncontemplatable
and I wonder why I think,
the thoughts I ought not consider,
the thoughts of what should have been.

I try so hard to reconcile my history
with the way things are as they are.
And occasionally I fail this warranted duty unto myself,
but it's the way things are, it is,
— the way my life is as it is.

And when they're foremost in my thoughts,
still pushing me to the brink.

I look at the bottle before me,
after my mind has turned to drink.
And savour every moment,
when my mind has been comfortably numbed.
It's a release from my torment and although
the mantra has been drummed

— into me
— that I'm killing myself,

the path is already laid.
There's nothing I can do to get off it,
there's nothing I can pay,
for my history and my life before,
things started going my way.

Am I forever having to follow this deep and cataclysmic rift?
The borderline between the now and my past that is as it is?
For now — I know the answer,
as it is in my gift,
to follow through with the only option I have,
and that is,
— killing myself to live.

The Suburban Weekend That Wasn't

Chapter 1

It was a suburban life and as such, mundane. Days passed like irrelevant seconds during the week; work all encompassing; and the weekend – nothing more than time to recover ready for Monday's re-entrenchment.

Occasionally, when Saturday dawned, I took the mower to the small grass patch at the back of my house and gave my usual neighbourly wave to Old Mrs Midfich who, peculiarly, was always in her garden tending to her patch of herbs; tilling it, sowing it and weeding it, whenever I decided to cut my lawn to size.

It seemed the herb patch was the only part of her garden that needed constant care; the rest was spick and span and I assumed, during the times I was not mowing, she tended to the rest of her garden, or had someone in to do it for her. But I'd never seen anyone.

If I was to take a guess she must have been in her mid-eighties and although she walked with a stoop and a cane to support her, she scuttled about quickly enough, always hugging a black knitted shawl during the winter, and, come to think of it, during the summer, for that matter.

Friday had come around again and the suburban and mundane dissipated as I pulled into my driveway. Old Mrs

Midfich was being guided, by two police officers, to a waiting car.

The old woman didn't seem too concerned. In fact she was smiling as she was led from her house; as if she knew something more than the police assumed they knew.

The scene being played out I settled back into my usual weekend ritual, or at least attempted to. Though exhausted by my week's trial my head would not stop replaying the incident as I lay in bed waiting for sleep to overtake my wakefulness.

It must have been 2am before I fell asleep, only to be awoken, what felt like a few seconds later, when the letterbox clunked and the local paper dropped to the floor. Giving up my regular rest regime I got up and lifted the usually useless paper from the carpet.

I rubbed the sleep from my eyes not sure that I'd read the headline correctly;

"83 year old woman in custody – On Friday an eighty-three year old woman was taken into custody after witnesses came forward claiming they'd seen the woman with missing teenager Sophie Chadwick, the third such teenager to go missing in as many weeks. Not an unusual circumstance for cities like London, but for Trelevern, on the outskirts of Bodmin, certainly very unusual...."

Although I agreed with the article's sentiment, Old Mrs Midfich a suspect? This couldn't be right.

I have to admit I don't really know my neighbour that well but I couldn't associate the old dear with everything that was being claimed in the paper. However, the police had taken her away and, I suspect, it had more to do with their failure to uncover any truths about the two other missing teenagers.

As I was up earlier than expected I convinced myself it was time to get rid of the old and dead pot plants that festooned my kitchen windowsill and take them to my miniscule garden shed, with the good intention of recycling them at some stage.

Still in my dressing gown I yanked at the kitchen door – something else that needed to be done; I can't for the life of me remember when the damned door had actually worked without major force, but damp autumns always brought the issue to the fore.

It was a sodden blustery morning with leaden skies and the red-golden leaves of the last few weeks now nothing more than black slimy patches to step and slip on.

Committed as I was I pulled the dressing gown's belt tighter and made my way down the short path. As was habit I glanced over the fence at Old Mrs Midfich's herb garden ready to wave, but, of course, she was not there.

I almost turned back without a second's thought but something jarred in my mind. I came to a dead stop. Though the old woman hadn't been gone for much more than sixteen hours, the garden – all of it – was in utter disarray. Foregoing the dead autumnal leaves that littered it, late weeds were scrambling across the raised borders; grass had miraculously grown in between the paving stones of the path that snaked the length of her garden. Even moss had suddenly appeared in places – but that wasn't the weirdest thing, the entire garden was strewn, hither and tither, with apples suffering varying degrees of decomposition; from pristine to completely decayed – no apple tree in sight, not in her garden, mine, nor other neighbours'.

I shook my head trying to fathom what could have possibly occurred during the night – as far as I was aware there hadn't been any major storms – then all thought of the weather left me as my eyes lighted upon the herb patch.

No longer were her different herbs in their soldierly rows, they were fallen, higgledy-piggledy, uprooted from ground level, with random furrows breaking the previously flat black-brown earth of the herb's parade ground.

Before I could consider the peculiarities of Old Mrs Midfich's garden further, measly icy-cold raindrops began to fall from the sky and I rushed the final yards to my garden shed, pulling open its door and slinging the old plants onto the workbench within, noting that sometime in the past I had done the exact same thing, and if I were to do this again, I really would need to consider some serious recycling beforehand.

I shuddered, brought out of my mental soliloquy by a myriad of raindrops hitting home between my neck and the collar of my dressing gown. I closed the shed door, and with my head bowed, I started towards the warmth of my kitchen.

Habit is a beautiful and poisonous thing in equal measure and as such I glanced over the fence, ready to wave, before I knew what I was doing, particularly because it caused me to pause my retreat from the ever increasing downpour.

Through the vertical lines of sheet rain a pale shape, bordering on the mottled colour of the top of a large edible mushroom, could be seen, filling the crevasse made by one of the larger furrows in Old Mrs Midfich's herb garden. And I lingered; hypnotised by the slow reveal the rain created through its dissolving action upon the furrow.

Water was now cascading down my face and every few seconds I cleared each eye with my forefingers so I could watch the birth of the huge mushroom, as it happened in real time.

Anyone looking out over their neighbours' gardens from an upper storey window must have come to the conclusion I'd totally lost it. I was soaked through, but couldn't tear myself away from the scene, even when a cold dread, that had nothing to do with the rain, began to seep into me.

The top of the mushroom was becoming corrupted, no longer circular in shape because the edge closest to me was crenelated in a fashion, with three or four slender protrusions pointing in my direction.

"Holy shit!" The words slipped from my mouth before I could do anything about it as my brain pattern-matched the shape before me.

I moved towards the wooden split between my garden and Old Mrs Midfich's, in order to confirm what my eyes were telling me.

Without thought I covered my mouth with the palm of one hand, my subconscious already reacting, and leant closer to the fence, grasping its top with the other, morbid fascination taking hold.

I stretched my eyes wide in an attempt to compensate for the rain and what my brain was telling me the shape was, sincerely hoping I'd been mistaken.

But there was no getting away from it; the silver ring on the second protrusion told the story: This was not a large mushroom; it was a hand, and a feminine one, if there is such a thing.

I pushed the fence away, its rotten top breaking and falling into Mrs Midfich's garden as I recoiled, not only from the shape, but also from the realisation; all mental constructions I'd made about my next door neighbour crumbled into nothingness, like a carbonised sheaf of paper plucked from the remnants of a recently extinguished fire.

I pulled the kitchen door closed, then twisted the key in its lock, and stared, gazing at nothing, through one of the many small panes of steamed up glass that constituted my back door, creating a puddle where I stood.

My face became slack as I fumbled with the thoughts in my head; had it really been a hand? Each time the thought came to me I reached for the key in the kitchen door, to unlock it, ready to go and check. And each time I reached something within forestalled my action and I dropped my hand to my side.

The entire weekend was turning out to be something less than the recuperative I expected my weekends to be. The time was coming up to a quarter to ten in the morning and I was feeling as stressed, possibly even more so, than I did during the week.

I was certain no one had seen me, standing in the pouring rain, gazing over my fence into Old Mrs Midfich's garden. And for a fact she hadn't been there. Not my problem, I tried to console myself.

But what if she finds out? a thought came from elsewhere; underlining the fact that part of the fence had fallen into her garden.

I took a deep breath and put the kettle on for some coffee; I certainly needed it, being up as early as I was on this Saturday morning. And as I focused on making my coffee the rigours of the previous hours began to dissipate, allowing me to slip into my usual regime of doing extra things I fancied and nothing else besides.

Chapter 2

By late afternoon the early morning's shock had been consigned to the misty – just one of those things – memory pile: An experience that one could either take or leave without consequence.

Saturdays are a day for something light to eat in the evening, washed down with a beer or two. With nothing interesting on the telly I turned it off, wrenched myself from the sofa and made my way into the kitchen wondering what delight I could rustle up. With my culinary expertise being what it was I decided on two poached eggs on toast, flavour enhanced with a lick of Marmite.

As I took the poacher from the cupboard I glanced briefly at my kitchen door, with its steamed up panes of glass, and a shudder crucified the warmth in my body, the vision, a vision I thought I'd forgotten, flashed through my mind's eye; the pale, almost bleached hand that had nestled in the furrow of Old Mrs Midfich's herb garden blazed in the non-Technicolor cinematography of film noir.

I knew then that I needed to distract myself if I wasn't going to cock-up the simplest of dishes, so I turned on the radio and the light and informative banter of BBC Cornwall began its easy listening.

I lifted the lid of the poacher and saw that the eggs were on the cusp of being ready – the majority of the egg white, white, and the translucent film that covered the yoke now opaque.

The radio squawked the pips for six o'clock and the news began by announcing terrible flooding and mudslides around St Austell. I felt sorry for my fellow Cornishmen but was glad that we, on the north coast, had missed such a downpour this time:

It was only a few years ago that floods had almost entirely demolished the small seaside village of Boscastle on our coast.

The toaster ejected the toast and I struggled to stop the caramelised bread falling to the kitchen floor – I had the same problem every time I used sliced bread – the toaster was really designed to toast doorsteps perfectly and nothing else.

I buttered the toast thickly then spread lashings of Marmite onto the butter, mixing both with the tip of my knife. Lifting the lid of the poacher I began the highly skilled task of removing the eggs from the poacher's cups without leaving half of the newly poached egg behind. No matter what anyone says, there is no such thing as a non-stick cup and unless you use the right butter, in the right quantities, the egg will always stick; though there are secret ways, known only to a few, to get around the problem of the ripped poached egg and it is my belief that those who never discover the skill become the most stalwart advocates of the scrambled egg.

As I lifted one of the cups from the poacher BBC Cornwall carried on with its announcements; "In other news today police released the eighty-three year old pensioner, Mrs Midfich. A police spokesperson stating they were happy with what they'd been told and had eliminated Mrs Midfich from their enquiries."

The poacher's cup dropped from my hand and, as I tried to catch it, I knocked the edge of my plate flipping the toast into the air, everything landing face down on the kitchen floor; one piece of toast taking a more circuitous route via the top of my foot.

All my appetite dissolved there and then. The news of my neighbour's release transmuting hunger into fear; I had seen part of what obviously laid beneath the herb garden, and knowing three teenage girls had gone missing I suspected that there were another five similar hands somewhere under that soil.

I looked at the remaining egg sitting in the poacher; it was perfect, but no matter how so, all urge to eat had been crushed out of me.

I turned the radio off, interrupting the weather forecast, and before I knew what I was doing I'd tested the kitchen door to check that it was still locked, and it was.

Chapter 3

I sat in my almost completely dark lounge, only a few table lamps providing light, seeking comfort from the beer I'd intended to have with my tea. I would have laughed at the situation if things had been different; the fact that, although not hungry, time for beer can always be found, but I was not of good humour.

After the announcement on the radio I'd gone about my house switching off the lights in the vain hope that the news had been breaking news and Old Mrs Midfich was on her way home, as opposed to already being there.

I hoped to make out I was away, ensuring the old woman, once she'd gone into her garden and seen what had been revealed, could not come to the conclusion that, somehow or another, her neighbour, i.e. me, had discovered her secret. I prayed she wouldn't notice the rotten part of the fence that was now sitting in her herbaceous border.

I sat in silence listening for the tell-tale clunks, clicks and thumps that would tell me she was home, my house being part of the same semi-detached house, but I heard none.

By the time I'd finished my fifth can of beer, and not hearing any sign of occupancy from next door, I was settled enough to go to bed, my fears about possible retribution being sated.

In an instant my mind was active and my eyes were gazing at the back of their lids. Something, I didn't know what, had roused me. I opened my eyes.

All was dark and I rolled my head to glance at the clock – its red digits told me it was only one forty-three in the morning. *Bloody hell*, I thought as I studied my bedroom's ceiling, knowing that this weekend was really not going to be the recuperative I'd hoped for.

The ceiling was a dark grey plane only interrupted by the lighting fixture. Barring that I couldn't make out any detail because my bedroom was at the back of my house, its windows opening onto my small garden, with little light pollution.

Fully awake and with all chance of regaining the bliss of sleepful nothingness gone, I attempted one of the three tricks I'd discovered, over time, that always resulted in a return to that state; I started my two to the power of two times table – two to the power of one is two, two to the power of two is four, two to the power of three is eight, two to the power of four is sixteen.

Most times I'd reach a result that was five digits long then wake up in the morning to the alarm, but this time no such thing happened. As I was telling myself four thousand and ninety-six, I was brought to a sudden stop and held my breath. There was a noise. I wasn't sure where from, but it sounded like some furniture protesting as it scraped across the floor downstairs. It was all I could do to stop myself from pulling the duvet over my head.

What the hell was that noise? I held my breath as I listened for other noises.

A gasping inhale escaped me as my body burnt through the last vestiges of air my lungs could hold. My heart skipped a beat then thumped twice in succession telling me I ought to start breathing again if I wanted to remain conscious and aware. I acquiesced, fearing whatever fates unconsciousness may bring, and took a long deep breath. Then I exhaled, but before I could finish, my mouth clamped shut as one of the floorboards on the landing outside my bedroom door creaked and a chill swept through my body; hair prickling on my forearms and the nape of my neck. The skin of my forehead tightened as a cold papery sensation crossed it. Blackness encroached upon my vision and my lungs gave out; I took another breath, and another. And as I exhaled for the third time I was sure that, even in the near complete darkness of my room, I could see the result of my breathing form vapour in front of my face.

Then the darkness of my room turned down another notch or two towards a deeper and more impenetrable blackness, one that seemed to have tangible substance.

I looked at my clock; its red digits were dimmer than before, a thin frost covered the clear plastic of its display. The vestigial warmth of my duvet vanished as if pulled by a conjurer whose party piece was to remove a tablecloth from beneath the cutlery and crockery sat upon it. Every part of me started to shiver and my teeth chattered.

I recalled nightmares from my childhood when, in the darkness, in my bedroom, unknowable sounds wrenched at my sanity and I would pull the duvet over my head and pillow, and clamp my head under the pillow, holding it tight, availing some kind of false protection from the dark creator of the unknown sounds.

But this was worse; I couldn't move and my eyes refused to shut. I was being forced to face fears beyond those of my childhood.

The clock stopped; its vague light slowly extinguished as the electricity drained from the capacitors within.

Chapter 4

I don't know how long it was before I dared to move but if I was to guess my estimate would be about an hour. Whatever amount of time it was, I needed to straighten my arms. All sensation in my hands had been lost, the terror of my predicament fixing them clasped to the top of the duvet as I held it under my chin.

I unfurled my grip and lowered my arms to my side; a numb but warm tingling sensation filled my forearms indicating the onset of pins and needles. I opened and closed both hands to get my circulation going once again.

With no further sounds emanating from the other side of my bedroom door the little man inside me, the one with some semblance of courage, decided to make an appearance, and I decided to investigate the source of the noises.

However, I'd been fooled. The hour's lull in events had been nothing more than a deception. As I pulled the bed covers back and dropped my legs over the side of my bed, my feet seeking the slippers that should have been there, a strange movement in the shadows, cast by the little external light making it past the top of my curtains, froze me to the spot.

I stared at the blackness in the corner of my room made by the meeting of walls and ceiling. I was sure I'd seen the ceiling bow, just for a moment, like a huge hand had pushed it down; the ceiling somehow becoming nothing more than a rubberised skin.

I sat on the edge of my bed as still as I could, though my feet, as was habit, still sought my slippers. It was a few seconds before I realised I'd been holding my breath again. Slowly I exhaled and once more vapour formed before me – but something was different this time; I couldn't hear the passage of my breath. Something had stolen the sound. It seemed like time itself had fled.

Before I could test any other movement to confirm what I was sensing the ceiling bowed again and the bulbous dip glided towards the wall opposite me. Instead of stopping there the wall started to bulge as the shape made its way to the floor, disappearing behind my tallboy, making it judder then move towards me; not a single sound breaking the intense silence that encapsulated me.

Then, as if the invisible soundproof glass that had made my noiseless cell had been smashed, I was immersed in full Dolby 5.1 surround sound; my breathing echoed around the room and a *clickering, clattering* noise came at me from behind the tallboy. It sounded like a multitude of Bic biro lids tapping staccato on the wooden floorboards of my bedroom. But it wasn't a random clattering; it had rhythm and purpose.

Although my eyes had adjusted to the dark in my room there was nothing more that I could see than blobs of blackness beneath the line of my bedroom's windowsill. It was at this time my feet gave up searching for my slippers; it was obvious they were no longer where they should be.

I wanted to get out of the room, slippered or otherwise, but the marching *click-clack* rendered any option to move, impotent.

A flash of negative inspiration hit me; what if it's a mutant spider, grotesquely large, coming at me with its shiny, pointed black fangs, beating like a jackhammer, getting ready to sink into my shins?

I continued to stare at the corner of my room, the source of the noise, and the spot where the black bulge from the ceiling had stopped its journey. My eyes blinked furiously in the continuing attempt to resolve the blackness before me into a shape my mind could comprehend. But it didn't work.

I felt naked; without weapon or protection; Jimjams being nothing more than the Emperor's new clothes.

Suddenly my worst fear was crystallised; an amorphous, clattering, black blob started towards me and I could make out its shape.

Whatever entity that had possessed my room had delved into my subconscious and plucked out my greatest fear. Coming at me, in the near total darkness, was the largest deformed form of a spider I could have ever imagined. It didn't have eight legs. It didn't have eight eyes; though it did have only two glistening, shiny fangs.

I couldn't count the number of legs it had; the darkness and their staccato movement stopped that. But I could count the eyes – two; each with lashed lids and the horizontal oblong pupils of gleaming goat's eyes.

Its spikey back pointing fur, on its swollen abdomen, bristled as the points of its legs hit the floorboards. And some kind of glutinous fluid dripped from between its fangs.

The child in me told me to withdraw my legs and pull the duvet over my head,. and I wished I could comply. But even before the grotesque before me could sink its fangs into me and fill me with paralysing venom, I was already paralysed by the fear the monstrous shape conveyed. And I knew that no matter what I tried, neither hand would relinquish its grip on the mattress.

My number was up and I wished I'd never set eyes on Old Mrs Midfich's herb garden with its secret revealed.

A blinding flash stung my eyes, followed by a wrenching crack that threatened to split my house from roof to foundation as an errant thunder storm let lose its pent up energy. And in the after-image that had rendered my eyes temporarily useless in the dark of my room, the reality of the grotesque, revealed by the clarity of light that only lightning could conjure, was the crumpled form of my Parka, fallen from the back of the chair, lumped like an overly large rugby ball with its fur edged hood pointing in my direction; each tooth of its silver zip reflecting light. I shook my head. But before I could finish admonishing myself for my folly, cold fingers wrapped around my ankles like glassy handcuffs, and the certain knowledge as to why my feet couldn't find their slippers, came to me in a sudden blast of icy terror.

My feet were ripped from under me, pulled back beneath the bed; my hands, frozen as they were, refused to release the mattress and my face was flung to the floor. In a split second I managed to turn my head to stop my nose from being crushed, but I knew my head would pay, one way or another, for the force at which it was being thrown at the floor.

I heard a bang and felt shockwaves through my jawbone.

Chapter 5

I don't know what woke me; whether it was the pulsing thump of pain in my head or the violent rattling of my bedroom door, or both. But, as I opened my good eye, the other swollen shut; I was relieved to glimpse daylight.

As I pushed myself up, press-up style, the back of my head quickly made contact with something, and for a short moment the thought that I was in some kind of coffin dominated reason and a cloying panic gripped me.

But there's light, a small voice inside my head told me. I realised I was under my bed. Then I realised *I was under the bed*, memories of the previous night flooded back. I scrambled out, my head's pulsing pain set to one side.

I turned around, sitting on the floor, gazing at the gap; there was nothing there.

I jumped as the door vibrated in its frame once more; my bedroom curtains came at me as a low *whomping* sound filled the room in fits and spurts. And I recognised the sound. It was a sound from the past, one reminiscent of the great storm of '87 and its damaging winds.

I breathed a sigh of relief. My bedroom door rattled again but it didn't bother me – it was just this draughty old house being draughty.

I picked myself up from the floor and cradled my left eye as the pulsating thud behind the damaged skin re-emerged from the thin membrane of panic that had briefly concealed it.

I needed some Paracetamol, which I knew I had in my bathroom cabinet and momentarily considered whether the beef stew for one, ping food, I had in the freezer, would be just as good as a steak at taking down my eye's swelling. Perhaps I would try it; but first a couple of Paracetamol.

In the mirrored doors of my bathroom cabinet I stared at my bruised and swollen eye and wondered whether last night's experience had been nothing more than an intense and violent nightmare, brought about by too much booze and an overactive imagination.

I gulped down the painkillers with a glass of water and brushed my teeth.

Shaken by last night's excursion into an evil version of a Disney Land attraction, more likely than not hosted by my brain, I had no appetite for breakfast but needed a coffee.

I left the bathroom and descended the stairs only to be brought to an abrupt stop five steps from the bottom; my wooden coffee table was not where it should have been. Rather than being somewhere at the centre of my lounge, it was now next to the final banister at the bottom of the stairs: the rucked up rug around its stubby feet spoke volumes.

Then I noticed the dangly thing above it, hanging from some twine that had been pinned to the ceiling. Though crudely shaped, the form was recognisable; it was the effigy of a person, no more than five inches in height, made from dirty wax with ragged squares of material barely dressing it. I looked closer. I recognised the material. I frowned. It had to be from the old plum coloured work shirt I'd chucked out some weeks ago.

Being a Cornishman I knew the myths and what this was; it was a poppet – a vehicle for hexes and curses to do ill-will against those who wished harm to the poppet's creator or for whom the poppet had been created.

I remembered the dragging sound that had interrupted my quest for sleep.

Then, without any conscious thought, my eyes focused on the poppet's shiny, brass coloured, left eye – it was made from a drawing pin, and the stories I'd heard as a child, about how the poppets were used, came back to me with a terrifying force.

My hand went to my half-closed eye. I was beginning to feel that the previous night's nightmare had at least one foot in reality – though the reality, in the cold light of day, was still hard for me to accept, even with my penchant for excessive imagination.

I leant over the coffee table ready to push it back to its place, putting a hand on either side – it was oak and very heavy, but before I could start heaving it across the floor I noticed four or five, probably five, one not being that well-formed, muddy concentric rings, no larger than an old penny piece. They reminded me of the rubberised end of a cane or walking stick. I let go of the table and studied the muddy marks.

Come off it, Dan, I berated myself. *It's myth, fantasy. Not real.* But the marks were there on the table, and Old Mrs Midfich did use a cane.

As soon as the thought came to me my mind was swiftly filled by one word and one word alone – witch.

Chapter 6

It was a few hours before I could hold a cup of coffee without spilling it; the shakes becoming greater as I'd checked the front and back doors, plus all the windows, to see if I could find any signs they'd been forced or even opened without force. But I'd found none.

I sat on my sofa hugging my cup to my chest as I tried to think whether I'd ever been told of ways to stop witches entering one's home.

Garlic garlands sprang to mind. Should I wear one or hang it above my door? The thought was dismissed. Nope, that's vampires – I was fairly certain it was vampires and nothing else.

Silver bullets popped into my head. Possibly right, but an entirely useless idea; I didn't have any bullets, silver or otherwise. And if I did, I didn't have a gun, and the thought of shooting something or someone was completely abhorrent.

What about removing the head? My thoughts continued and again I had to dismiss the notion. All I had was a crappy hedge-trimmer or a pair of secateurs. And I knew a plan based on the hedge-trimmer would surely fail. How would I know where I had to plug it in? What if its lead reached its maximum extension and I was still not close enough?

I wished my mum, bless her heart, had not put me off reading the horror fiction comics I liked as a child. She'd had good reason – my nightmares and overactive imagination.

And now? I was well-read, but purely non-fiction. Biographies, histories, programming languages, and maps, filled my bookcases.

Although only mid-morning I had to put the lights on. The storm was getting worse; the wind more furious and the leaden sky was even more leaded. My front door rattled in its frame as if to underline the fact the storm had plenty more to give.

"Oh God," I sighed, though not a follower of any faith. But in my breathing of the words another idea struck me; Prayer! For a millisecond I felt relief – then the questions came; who would I pray to? Should it be God (if there was one)? But witches surely didn't follow any god of a monotheistic faith. Who was the god of witches?

I had no clue, so it was time to turn on the computer and search the Interwebs.

An hour of clicking and pointing, typing and reading, revealed nothing more than; hanging, burning, drowning, pouring water on them (I got that from the Wizard of Oz), getting a divorce or plain old; asking them to leave. I knew now that I had to figure out something for myself, as the options I'd discovered were mainly impractical or down right impossible or just would not work.

I turned the computer off and returned to the kitchen for another cup of coffee.

As I supped the hot drink, again attempting to gaze out through the steamed up panes of the kitchen door, a new tactic crystallised in my mind.

For a fact I couldn't get rid of her. But I could impede her mobility, and hopefully stop her getting into my property; at least for a short while.

I wiped the condensation from a couple of panes in the kitchen door with a tea towel and looked out. The rain had stopped and over the fence I could see Old Mrs Midfich tending the herb patch; then my cup slipped from my hand as I tried to comprehend what I was seeing – the whole garden was pristine once again; no apples, no weeds and no moss.

All there was was the old lady, wrapped in her black shawl, tending to her herb garden, her cane leaning up against the rods that would support her pea plants when they grew again.

My eyes focused on her cane – this was it. This was my goal. Get her cane and destroy it. And at least for a while, until she was able to get another, she would be incapacitated and I would have the breathing space to concoct another more permanent plan.

I looked at the kitchen clock; it was mid-afternoon. If I was going to do anything it would have to be soon.

Chapter 7

I made my way upstairs to change into a pair of black jeans and a navy top – something more practical and weather resistant than my dressing gown, and as I changed I began to formulate my plan to relieve the old woman of her cane.

For sure, I couldn't use my kitchen door to enter the garden; it was quite likely not to open on the first attempt due to the moisture it had absorbed. The last thing I wanted was to signal Mrs Midfich that I was on my way out; it might prompt her to get up, take her cane, and approach me for a chat or something – no, to get the upper hand I needed a plan that was as covert as it could possibly be. I would go out my front door and then go through my garage whose rear door opened onto my garden and had never had any swelling problems.

I walked back downstairs deep in thought. There were two remaining parts of the plan to devise: one – securing the cane and, two – destroying the cane. Whilst I pondered these final elements I decided to check that all was well with the first part of the plan and left the warmth of my home for my garage.

The garage door opened without issue; I was glad I'd been distracted from parking my car inside that strange Friday afternoon, a day that seemed much more than just the two days ago it had been.

Inside, the solution to part three of my plan glowed in front of me; it didn't actually glow, but in my mind's eye it did. Under a plastic cover, at the back of my garage, was my gas barbeque. I nodded to myself. I knew this was the tool I could use to destroy the cane. Obviously it had some downsides; namely, where I could set it up. The garage would have been ideal, but the old pots of paint, bottles of methylated spirit made it somewhat dangerous. Reluctantly I decided my lounge was the only place – it was large enough to be a little safer than the garage, and I was sure, because it was a gas barbeque, the smoke wouldn't be that bad. I'd bought it on a deal but so far, never had the chance to use it. But now was its time.

I looked at my watch; twenty minutes had passed. I knew time was against me. Everything I had to do, had to be done before another downpour, sending the w… Old Mrs Midfich (I was having trouble using the word, as contemplations of the fact muddled my thoughts; fear usurping any clarity) back indoors.

I dragged the barbeque set out from the garage and into my lounge, shutting the front door behind me.

I moved all my furniture from the middle of the room, to the sides, and replaced it with the barbeque. As fast as I could I got the thing burning, then made my way back into the garage.

I peered out of the garage window over my garden, but it afforded me no view of the old woman's garden and I wondered how, from my side of the fence, I could reach her cane without her noticing. I knew I needed a piece of equipment that had a long reach and had something at the end that could grab. It sounded like a fictitious piece of equipment; a long reach, cane grabber.

I glanced at my watch again; another ten minutes had passed. I needed a solution, and quick. I looked around the garage. There was a long pole, couldn't remember why I had it, but what could I attach to it?

My secateurs came to mind, but they were in my shed, and I'd have to figure out a way to attach them to the pole with a mechanism to close them around the cane. I was good with my hands in as much as I found turning pages in a book pretty straightforward, but making something that wouldn't fall to pieces; that was for other people.

MY SECATEURS. Yes! I thought. Not my secateurs though, that had just been the prompt I needed. In my shed I had a pole tree pruner. A thing I occasionally used to cut the upper branches of the fir trees at the end of my garden. The snipping curved blades at its end would be just the thing to capture and trap the cane. But that tool was also in my shed and left me with only one option; I had to sneak down my garden, get into my shed and retrieve the gangly piece of garden equipment, all without being noticed.

Time was running out and I had no other choice.

Chapter 8

As quiet as I could I opened the rear door of my garage, stepped through and closed it behind me. Now came the difficult bit.

I really didn't want to crawl down the garden on my stomach SAS style. The ground was wet and muddy and the last thing I wanted was to stymy any grip I had on my cane grabbing tool, though the thought of getting mucky played a part. I decided to risk a crouched run. If I kept my head down there was no way she would notice me.

Half way down the garden I thought it prudent to take a look through one of the many holes in the garden fence to check whether my quarry was still there leaning against the upright struts of the pea plant guide, although on second thoughts the struts might have had something to do with tomatoes; I couldn't be sure.

I took a deep breath and left the path and slowly made my way across the grass towards the fence. I looked through one of the many empty knots in the fencing and nearly choked. Yes, she was still there, her cane against the poles, but the hand I'd seen the other day was a hand no longer; it had an arm attached to it and I could hear the old woman muttering in a language unknown to me as she poured a strange effervescent fluid over it; then I saw one of the fingers twitch.

I reversed direction and again started towards my shed, only taking a breath once I'd reached its door. What the hell was going on? What the hell was she growing?

No time for those thoughts though. I had to get my tree pruner and put my plan into action.

On my knees I reached up and opened the latch that kept the shed's door closed. The door opened without a sound and I entered.

The storm reasserted itself and the wind picked up, catching the door. I swivelled on point just in time to put my hand on the door jamb. The door wobbled as it smashed into my knuckles. I covered my mouth with my other hand and hissed through my fingers in response to the sudden pain. But it was enough; my hand had muted the door's slam.

I stepped backwards one pace and placed a foot on the ground outside the shed to block any further efforts the wind made to shut the door. I reached for the tree pruner, which was hanging on hooks attached to the wall of my shed.

With tree pruner in hand I backed out of the shed, but there was a problem; the pole was long and to control it I need both my hands, and my legs weren't long enough to stop the wavering door from slamming again. I placed the pruner's end on the sill of the door jamb, grasped the door, and eased the pole out of the shed, then closed the latch.

The obstacle dealt with, I made my way back up the garden, still crouched, wobbling tree pruner held out in front of me, to the point in the fence where I could slip the pruner through.

I peered through the hole. Mrs Midfich was turned away from me; if she had not her shawl I would surely be able to see the back of her left ear, and, partially, the hole that led into her head.

To her left, just behind her, but within reach of her left arm was the cane and the pea stands. She had moved a bit since I last looked and I could no longer see that mushroom-white hand and arm. But I could still hear her mumblings and they were more rhythmic now. I suppose I ought to be calling them incantations.

Now it was time for the really difficult bit.

I knelt on my left leg and placed my right sole firmly on the sticky mud that was my border, lifted the cutting end of my tree pruner, and started to slide it through the hole. Inch by inch my end of the pole shortened. Inch by inch, my long reach cane grabber sought its prey.

I placed my right elbow on my right knee aiming to retain control over the extension that was now reaching out over Mrs Midfich's garden towards her cane.

I prayed the wind would keep its lull at least until I had my hands on Mrs Midfich's mobility. Then my right elbow slipped and I knew that I should not have dismissed wearing my best black corduroys when choosing the clothes for this mission.

The end of the pole flicked to the right as my face crashed into the fence, and the pole struck something hard. I peeked through another empty knot in the fence; fortunately it was next to my right eye which, in my awkward position, was now pressed to the fence. I saw her attempt to raise her hand to her temple, but she collapsed to the floor without succeeding.

"Sorry," I hissed through the fence, before I realised what I was doing; habit being a poisonous and beautiful thing in equal measure.

I re-focused on the job at hand, pulled the lever on my end of the pole, opened the metal beak at the other end, moved the pole to the left and sunk my cane grabber's two blades into the cane.

As fast as I could I pulled the cane back to the fence then placed my end of the pole on the ground and stood on it. The hole through which it was poked acted as a pivot and I grabbed the cane over the top of the fence.

"Yesss! I've got it," I said to myself. But my feelings of victory dissipated in an instant as my gaze lighted upon the recumbent body of the old woman.

Chapter 9

I stood transfixed. Although the old woman was lying on the ground, as still as a still thing, her arm wasn't. It dipped beneath her shawl and pulled out, what looked like a twig.

I like to think I'm a quick learner and when the end of the twig began to glow a putrescent green, I knew exactly what it wasn't, and that was a twig.

The air crackled and the small ball of green light leapt into the furrow in the herb patch. As soon as it had disappeared another hand and arm drove itself from beneath the soil; each hand placed itself palm down on either side of the furrow. Then the arms heaved and a head pushed itself from beneath.

I felt my breath had been snatched from my lungs. Before me was a cadaverous white mottled oval, outlined by long lank hair, caked with mud, two oil-slick black eyes, all pupil, and a silent screaming black-hole of a mouth, surrounded by small serrated teeth.

Luck smiled upon me and I fell to the ground as my legs gave out, fear getting the better of them – this broke the evil spell of transfixion that had kept me there, staring at the unknowable.

Schlupping noises came from the other side of the fence and I willed my legs to work. It sounded like the wet mud of the herb patch protesting at its loss of grip on something it wished to retain.

I got up and was half way to the kitchen when my fence caved in. I glanced back over my shoulder and hunched on its ruins was the lithe body of a teenage girl, the colour of a freshly picked mushroom. My stomach rumbled as I realised I hadn't had any breakfast, thoughts of a full English crossing my mind. Then the teen-creature started towards me, teeth snapping shut every now and again, and in between times an impossibly long rotten-green tongue licking its lips. It raised its arms in my direction and it was all I could do to stop myself dry-heaving there and then; the ravages of its sub-soil incarceration being more than apparent as black slimy creatures slithered in and out of tears in its throat and breasts.

I re-doubled my efforts and ran for the kitchen door at full pace. I reached out with my free hand slamming the door handle down and broke my nose on the unmoving entrance. The bloody door was locked.

The she-thing stumbled on, gaining ground. I think it had forgotten how to walk and I realised luck was still with me.

I darted around the back of my house, then through the garage into my front garden. I was almost home and dry.

I yanked open my front door and was greeted by a wall of thick and pleasantly smelling nothingness. It reminded me of the summer and times when my father, bless his heart, had cooked burgers on an open fire.

"Oh shit!"

I clawed at the smoke, trying to create a path to the gas barbeque, which hadn't been as smokeless as I'd been led to believe by the salesman. My eyes stung, but I knew I had to find it and destroy this cane. I stepped inside and locked my heavy front door.

With one outstretched hand I tried to detect the heat of the barbeque, and found it. Through scrunched up eyes I located the burger machine, snapped the cane across my shin. Cursed more than a few times as the cane failed to break, but won in the end, and dumped the damned pieces into the searing heat of the charcoal.

Through the burger-fog I could hear incessant thuds against my door. I looked at the barbeque, praying that something would happen and it did. The cane started to smoulder, but not as normal wood would; green and purple vapour eased itself from the cane and dissolved in the heat of the barbeque. It was only then that I noticed the intricately carved handle, reminiscent of the head and forelegs of a rat, but soon those details disappeared as the defining edges began to glow and reduce in the barbeque's heat.

Not being able to stand the smog any longer I felt my way to the kitchen, opened the door and stepped into a space more conducive to sustaining human life.

I shut the door behind me and pressed kitchen towel into the gaps around the door, then opened the kitchen's fan-light windows to let in some less polluted air. With the remnants of the kitchen towel I dabbed my sore and bleeding nose.

Chapter 10

Now I had some time to think, forgoing the thumps at my front door, and I wondered whether my plan had been effective in its goal to stymie the old woman's mobility.

The only way to ascertain this was to see whether Mrs Midfich had recovered from the accidental brain bashing; I needed to open the kitchen door.

I must admit I was reluctant, but as I knew she was dependent on her cane for movement, and the fact the strange, naked, mushroom coloured teenager, with muddy hair, was still thumping my front door, it wasn't beyond the bounds of reality that I could open my kitchen door, and check the situation, without incurring any further trouble.

I slid the key into the door, pulled at it sharply a couple of times, and opened it.

Near the bottom of my garden I spied the shawled woman standing in the gap the weird teenager had made. Mrs Midfich was waving a clenched fist at me and in her crackled voice, was screaming.

"My staff, you idiot, give me back my staff. I'll turn you into..."

A gust of wind took her last words away. "Pardon," I said, cupping an ear. "Can you say that again? I didn't quite hear."

Suffice it to say she didn't repeat whatever it was she was saying. Instead she pointed the twig/wand at me and another flash of light formed at its end. She raised her arm and flicked it in a motion similar to a person cracking a whip; the yucky-green orb headed in my direction.

Though dazed from my nose incident, I managed to close the kitchen door in time for orb to smash against it. It fractured, many pieces glittering peculiar colours as they *twinked* out of existence, falling to the ground.

Hah, hah, I thought, *can't beat Dan the Man. I'm better than you.*

I wiped the condensation from the glass pane level with my eyes, and cupping my hands to my head I peered out into my garden. Then I frowned; Mrs Midfich had gone.

I needed to consider my next steps – obviously I'd annoyed my next door neighbour somewhat – but I knew I was perfectly within my rights; a Cornishman's castle was his home, etc., and I had every...

I turned to my kitchen door – the muffled sounds of the thumping from my front door seemed clearer. It was then I noticed my kitchen door rattling in its frame in time with the thumps.

I looked around my kitchen, knowing I needed protection from the mushroom-woman with breasts and slimy creatures. But what could I use? My thoughts were drawn to the drawer next to me. I pulled it open whilst keeping an eye on the door. I plunged my hand in and my fingers felt for a long steel blade – I couldn't look, and I trusted my hand to grab the most appropriate tool. If I was to turn away from the door I knew, whatever creature it was, that was trying to reach me, it would get the upper-hand, should my concentration be diverted.

I lifted the implement from the drawer and held the palette knife out in front of me. I stared at the long, blunt, and nicely curved steel tool. But before I could berate my hand for selecting the most useless weapon for defence it could have possibly chosen, the door to the kitchen fell from its hinges and crashed to the floor.

It was a kind of unidirectional Mexican standoff; I waved the palette knife in the creature's direction. The creature staggered towards me, arms outstretched – the palette knife having no deterrent effect.

I needed to act quickly before the burger-fog from my lounge eased its way into the kitchen, completely filling it. Still holding the cake-tool in front of me, I moved sideways around my breakfast table at the centre of my kitchen; my plan "B" being to get back into the lounge and leg it out of my front door.

As the creature hissed at me and licked its lips with its strange tongue, I manoeuvred around the table, towards the door to my lounge, and a way out.

Time seemed to go in slo-mo.

Then I reached the door, and in triumph I decided to see what this eight inch long tool could do. I held the blade in my hand and threw it. The palette knife flicked through the air, end over end, and embedded itself in the creature's forehead.

Dan does it again, I thought, but only for a second.

The mushroom-woman staggered back, and frowned! Moving its uncoordinated hands it reached for the steel icing manipulator that was sticking out of its head, and removed it, throwing it to the floor.

I turned and ran into my lounge, aiming to get through the smoke and out into the road. But as I came level with the gas barbeque I had to stop; Mrs Midfich was standing in my doorway.

Chapter 11

Things were getting desperate; I had Mrs Midfich in front of me, and sooner than later mushroom-woman, with her big tongue, pert but creature infested breasts, would figure a way out of the kitchen.

You know, if I could have worked out a way to die on the spot, I would have done – but nothing came to mind.

Through the smoke I could see Mrs Midfich's cane, something she'd called her staff, still sitting in the charcoals, smouldering, but not destroyed.

Even though the old woman was at my front door, obviously more mobile than I'd realised, I'd only one other plan, one option, and I had to follow through, though the likelihood of it working was moot. But being a man of his word, I went ahead anyway.

I grabbed a bottle of liquid firelighter, from the base of the barbeque, opened the lid, and sprayed the contents on the remains of Mrs Midfich's staff, as she'd called it.

The old woman screamed at me, uttering more strange words and I knew I had to accelerate the combustion of the old woman's staff – her demeanour indicating this was probably the best tack.

What could I use? I looked around my room, then I saw it; Ordinance Survey map, sheet 431, Glen Urquhart & Strathglass – I was certain it was a place I was unlikely to visit in the near future, but was there another of my maps I could use? Was this really the least used one?

I heard something bump into my kitchen table and knew I had to make the decision.

I pulled map 431 from my bookcase and started to fan the flames of the barbeque; with each flap the charcoals glowed and the staff became bright.

I looked at Mrs Midfich, for some reason she hadn't come any further than the threshold, but she was reaching for her twig/wand once again.

I fanned harder than I'd fanned any fire in my life and Mrs Midfich pointed the wand in my direction – its end beginning to glow the putrid green once more. Then, as the staff began to burn more thoroughly, she staggered and the glow at the end of her wand vanished as she collapsed to the ground.

Icy hands grabbed at my neck, sharp finger nails strived to break the skin. I let go of the map with one hand so I could turn to see the thing that would ultimately be the architect of my demise.

The teen-mushroom was right behind me, but seemed weaker. As I stared I felt a burning sensation in my hand that still had hold of the map. Was this another dark power it had? I wondered. I turned back to the barbeque and knew luck was on my side once more. The map was alight and the flames licked my fingertips. I twisted as fast as I could and thrust the flame engorged map into the wretched face of the living mushroom. It didn't scream but its pale skin sizzled; whisps of steam produced where the flames touched, melding with my smog filled room.

I shoved the flaming map into its mouth and pushed it back towards the kitchen. There was no resistance. The she-creature fell back and crashed to the floor.

I turned back to face Old Mrs Midfich, hoping beyond hope, that she'd been incapacitated somehow. But there was nothing to be seen of her, barring her shawl that was now on the ground just outside my front door.

The barbeque crackled and the staff puffed its strange colours, then vanished. The shawl vanished. I looked into the kitchen but there was no sign to be seen of the teen-creature, except the smouldering remnants of OS map 431.

Then the street was filled with a wailing sound and I recognised it. I was something I'd heard before. It was the fire brigade.

Chapter 12

"Mr Rogers," the fire officer started. "What on earth possessed you to use you barbeque in your lounge?"

I was having great difficulty explaining the events of the past few days and the last thing I wanted to mention was the attack on my property by an eighty-three year old woman and her deceased victim.

"I've never used it before," I said, by way of an explanation.

"And this is why you decided to try it in your living room?"

"To be quite honest, sir, the garage was too dangerous. There were pots of paint and methylated spirits in there."

The officer rolled his eyes. "Sir, barbeques are meant for the garden and you're damned lucky your house wasn't burnt down."

I tried to offer a reason. "You must admit, at this time of year, the weather isn't conducive to having a barbeque in the garden. Surely you can see this. And there was a storm."

I got the impression that the fire officer wasn't too pleased with my answer, he said; "If I have any advice I can give to you, it is this; never have a barbeque in your house unless you use your oven. Is this clear Mr Rogers?"

"But..."

"No buts, Mr Rogers."

I conceded his point and after he'd checked the house to make sure there were no secondary fires he left, along with his fire crew.

***

Suffice it to say, my weekends have now become, once again, the recuperative I expect from them. I've never seen Old Mrs Midfich again and her garden has become completely overgrown.

I quite like my new open plan lounge-dinner, though I still have to knock down the wall to match its doorless entry. And to save future problems I have decided to sell my gas barbeque on eBay.

Life is suburban and mundane once more and I know, now, this is the way I like it. And because the house still stinks, I will continue to do my best to erase this toxic legacy from the carpets, the walls and my memory.

The Moon-Shadow Dead

The window in the shed at the end of the garden glinted sporadically as the moon shone out from behind fast flowing clouds. The shadows of the willow's long branches moved in time with the passing clouds making the tree seem to jerk; attempting to grasp at the shed's door. The door snapped open, crashing back against the shed as it was caught by a gust of wind. And the uncut lawn shimmered silvery grey, its frost tinted blades washing back and forth like waves on a calm tide.

The forlorn house stared from its black empty windows watching the night-dance, its soul dissipated six months previously when the very last owner had died.

Dark corners at the junction between the kitchen extension and the house's back wall grew and receded with the moon light's ebb and flow.

In the deepest blackness little crackling rustles could be heard as old leaves jostled for position, driven by the gusts. And a darker shadow sought solace amongst the jigging companions.

Tall fronds of long dead water plants clacked together chattering as their still feet plunged below the cold surface of their pond.

A wooden panelled fence cracked a loud retort as a heavy mass crashed against it; no movement to be seen, the panel obscured by the shrub in the border.

The wind grew in strength and harried the ancient oak at the centre of the garden, threatening to rip its boughs from its trunk and cast them to the ground as the autumn had done to its leaves.

Then all was blackness as the moon disappeared for the final time and the shadow nodded, acknowledging its time was now. And as it screeched, scything the noise of the wind from the air, it opened its blood-red eyes and yawned a drooling yawn, exposing its mustard-yellow fangs. Then it stood and walked into the darkness, merging with its shadow brethren; it was time to feed.

Who's Watching You?

I saw the eyes behind the curtain,
Before they disappeared,
And a voice whispered to my mind;
Who's watching you?

I saw the ephemeral shadows vanish from my gaze,
When I turned to stare,
And something whispered from behind;
Who's watching you?

I walked the dark alley all alone,
Where shadows flinched and crumbled,
And a breeze chilled my neck hissing;
Who's watching you?

Then the black form coalesced,
Blocking my way through.
And two red eyes opened in its head
And its mouth said;
I'm having you!

I stood frozen in the spot,
Where I'd been addressed.
Then the form reached out and grabbed my heart…
Saying;
Now… you're mine too.
It's time to accept your death,
And the people you leave behind.
For I'm the reaper of one's life,
The extinguisher of your kind.

You, Shaun, have had your time,
There's nothing you can do.
No appeal to a higher one,
Or judgement to be changed.
It's very simple, Shaun, your time is done,
There's no one to be blamed.
And I take your soul with me now,
As your body drops to the floor.
Don't worry, you will be discovered,
But a person
– you're never more.

The Road to NeverEver Land

The Road

Dave Johnson had been given his annual ultimatum by his boss; use it or lose it. The way his company functioned meant that he was rewarded for working dawn 'til dusk, Monday through Friday but whenever the annual holiday request slip was put through his boss's office, invariably, his boss would come storming out shouting, "You really want a holiday during that week?" the emphasis being on the words 'really' and 'that'.

And now, as the carry-over time for his leave was ebbing towards a close, his boss uttered the quintessentially paradoxical statement: "*Use it or lose it Johnson, your choice.*"

Dave felt he'd always worked hard and never gave up his entitlement to a little R 'n' R and, though still only February, he'd been keeping his eye on the weather reports, just in case his boss would make his annual clarion call.

It seemed to Dave that the following week would be just the right time to take the winter dust covers off his classic British Racing Green Triumph Spitfire mark IV, to take it for a run down to Bournemouth on England's south coast and pay his favourite great aunt a surprise visit; an aunt who would later bemoan the fact, in her utter grief, that she hadn't seen her nephew since December last.

If he took the scenic route through Hampshire's New Forest then the two hundred mile trip would take about three and a half hours – so no need for an early start, just get up, make a snack for the journey, and go.

***

Monday morning arrived and for a change the weathermen had been right; the sky was a spotless blue veneer and the sun was brightly crisp and low over the horizon following its winter path.

By the time Dave was ready to leave his bachelor pad he'd lost most of the morning, and the time was fast approaching one thirty in the afternoon. If he didn't leave soon there'd be no point in taking the scenic route – it would be too dark to see anything of the New Forest.

Dave packed his rucksack but, before going to his car, he quickly popped into his bathroom for a final brush up. He looked at his features in the mirror, his black haired goatee and thin moustache were pristine, but his eyes said it all – he really needed this break. Adjusting his moss green cotton drill jacket as he faced the mirror he decided he was ready to go and left the flat, looking forward to the time he could spend in one of England's unspoilt forests before arriving at his great aunt's house.

***

After almost three solid hours of driving he was ready to take a break, pull up somewhere, take his sandwiches out and pour himself a coffee from the stainless steel flask he'd brought with him.

He had just entered the beginnings of the road through the New Forest and kept his eyes peeled for a small sign that would indicate a track-way to one of the forest's many picnic areas. He was not disappointed; five minutes after looking, he had spotted one and indicated right to turn into the small woodland clearing; not that he'd needed to indicate, this part of the road had been almost devoid of any type of traffic since he'd been on it.

His car crunched up the small gravel entrance into the picnic area and he stopped the Triumph alongside one of the ten or so picnic benches. Turning his car's engine off, he got out and stretched, raising his arms above his head, fingers interlocked.

Although he loved his car it was a bit of a squeeze for his 6'2" stature and about three hours was all he could manage before having to find somewhere for a pit stop.

Dave walked slowly around the perimeter of the forest enclosed clearing, hoping for little glimpses of the wildlife he knew to inhabit these parts. But the forest was dense and he guessed he could only see about twenty feet into it, perhaps thirty in places, if he was lucky.

The forest was a mixture of pine trees, irregularly interspersed by the odd silver birch here and there, its white bark seemingly glinting out of the darkness as errant light from the sun caught the trees when the wind blew the forest's pine canopy to one side or another.

His stomach grumbled and Dave walked across the clearing to the rear of his car and opened up the boot removing his lunch box and flask. Sitting down on the bench he'd parked next to, he unpacked his sandwiches and filled a cup with coffee from his flask.

As he ate and drank, he started to truly unwind, glad that there'd be another six full days before he would have to return to the manically busy office, continuing his work as the logistics manager for International Global Holdings – one of the only companies left, still supposedly able to ship logged trees from the Brazilian Amazon, legally, something that was in his remit to organise.

Biting into his hastily made Cheddar cheese sandwich his gaze continually flicked across the tree line circling the picnic area, ever hopeful of at least spotting one of the Roe deer the forest was famous for.

As he wondered about the lack of deer he began to realise he could not hear any of the other wildlife that should be bringing the pristine woodland to life; there were no birds chattering and he hadn't seen any squirrels darting from tree to tree either.

Dave shivered. The sun had dipped further towards the horizon and the air had taken on the early evening chill of an oncoming winter's night. He looked at his watch, it was four forty five, and dusk had settled.

Time to get going, he thought to himself as the breeze stepped up a notch or two, making the occasional shushing in the trees a constant refrain upon the general background of silence. Dave paused for a moment marvelling at how similar the breeze in the tree tops was to the sound of waves breaking upon a pebble strewn beach.

Standing up from the bench, he put the lid back on his lunch box and screwed his cup back on to the top of his flask. It was very dark now, the trees surrounding the picnic area blocking out what remained of the vestigial sunlight. Just as he was about to slam the car's boot shut a loud clacking started up somewhere deep within the forest.

Rut-tah-tuh-tuh-tuh. It continued; a staccato sound, not quite branch upon branch as if the wind had blown bough against bough, the sound had a lower resonance than that, more-like stick against a hollow wooden bole; not as melodic as a glockenspiel but a duller, flatter tone – one without rhythm or timbre.

Dave felt the backs of his forearms prickle as the hairs stood on end. He shivered again, but not against the cold this time, it was a much deeper type of chill, one touching sensations humanity had not felt for thousands of years.

He quickly returned the remnants of his snack to the boot and closed it, then got into his car shaking his head, berating himself for the foolish reaction to the alien-but-not sound. Before starting his car he wound down his window to see if he could hear the noise again, attempting to justify his reaction. But all he could hear was the sound of the wind rustling the treetops that overshadowed the picnic area.

He breathed out slowly, suddenly aware he had been holding his breath. Dave tutted at himself.

As he reached for the handle to wind the window back up, the sound was there again; a succession of mournful clacks.

Rut-tah-tuh-tuh-tuh. His neck prickled as a sensation of icy air played upon it; the skin on his cheeks and across his forehead tightened as the unknowable sound continued its thousand year old threat.

Dave made a grab for the handle to close the window, but his hand slipped straight off – his grip unable to do anything, as his whole hand was now covered by the clammy sweat of fear.

Wiping his hand on his jeans, he reached for the handle again, this time managing to turn it. The window shut as fast as he could make it.

"Jesus Christ, you stupid shit," he said to himself as he turned his key in the ignition. "How old are you? Ten?" He continued his self-admonishment.

The engine turned over under the power of the starter motor but failed to fire.

"Oh. For God's sake," he shouted aloud, hitting the car's steering wheel, frustrated by the situation and panicked by the noise in the forest.

He looked out of the Spitfire's small side window and saw the dimly lit reflection of his panic-stricken face staring back at him, eyes wide and mouth turned down.

The sun had almost finished its journey below the horizon rendering the spaces between the pine and silver birch an impenetrable black void.

"Come on you bugger," he said to his car, twisting the key once again. This time, the engine revved into life and he flicked on his headlights as dusk was no more and the early February night had arrived.

Turning the wheel in the direction of the picnic area's exit, he nudged his car to the junction with the main road. Seeing no illumination from car headlights in either direction Dave pulled out and continued on his journey.

He glanced at the clock in his car, it was still only five thirty and it would only be another half hour or so before he would be pulling up outside his aunt's house.

Dave carried on down the road that skirted the great forest and the further away from his pit stop he got, the calmer he felt. As he drove the road steepened, following a line up one of the undulating hills that defined the area of England his aunt lived in.

NeverEver Land

Occasionally he glanced to his left getting a feel for the hill that gently sloped into the shallow valley below; certain aspects being picked out by the intermittent moonlight as it shone out between the fast flowing, dark grey clouds above. Other times he looked into the forest on his right, and saw nothing but the bark of the tree line which separated the forest from the road, flickering in his headlights, as if seen through a zoetrope.

As he considered the view of the valley, being delivered by the gaps in the roadside hedgerow, when the moon was out, his attention was suddenly drawn back to the forest, when he noticed a bright light coming from somewhere within its depths.

"Those posh bastards," he thought to himself, "those posh and lucky bastards," he continued his musings, thinking about how nice it would be if he could afford such a place with so many acres, to call his own.

Luminous, nearly white chevrons, separated by black ones, interrupted his thoughts as the sign in front of him played upon his vision. He slowed the car and gently steered it to the right, the signalled bend in the road being pretty severe.

As he pulled out of the curve his Spitfire's engine coughed, misfiring, then corrected itself. Dave sighed a thanks to the engine's manufacturers. His car wouldn't have been a classic if its engine had been as temperamental when it had originally rolled off the factory line.

He looked at his milometer again and saw there were only another seven miles to go and, as he looked up, the engine failed, becoming silent.

Dave managed to guide the car into a lay-by as it gradually cruised to a halt. After trying the engine again, in the vain hope it would start and without success, he was glad he could still see the light from the obviously posh house, blinking between the wind agitated trees.

By his reckoning, the house could only be half a mile away, possibly further, but, perhaps, potentially nearer and hoped it was the latter. He could knock on the owner's door and ask to use their phone. He cursed himself for leaving his company provided mobile phone back at his flat; but it was a ritual of his – if he was going to have a holiday then there'd be no way his company could contact him during his time away. This time though, he regretted his decision. He got out of his car and locked it, then slapped it very hard.

"You stupid car. I don't even know why I keep you going. This was going to be a very simple day out and now you've ruined it," he said. The car didn't respond.

Dave opened the car's boot and pulled out his Berghaus over jacket and putting it on he zipped it up against the evening's cold, then thought about his trek through the forest to the house in the distance.

***

Next to the lay-by there was, what seemed to be, a path, and with no other choice for him to take, he followed it. Walking past the ferns and bracken that defined its beginnings, he entered the depths of the woodland proper; always making sure the light from the house was visible, it being his only comfort on this forced trek.

As he continued along the loamy track, deeper into the forest's unforgiving darkness, the only sound he could pick out was that of the wind in the trees' branches above, shushing them in gleeful caresses.

Dave was glad that the barely broken overcast sky of earlier had now given way to sparse patchy clouds that allowed the moon to cast its brightness upon the track more often than not. And although he was glad, it was not a light that comforted; there was something ancient and otherworldly about it – and the pitched black shadows it summoned.

To distract his growing overactive imagination, he turned his thoughts to his job and work, fighting to stop his mind drifting back to his time in the picnic area.

After what felt to him to be at least half an hour, the path finally led him into a small clearing within the depths of the forest. At its centre was a stump of three trunks, the trees having been cut down by a warder or some other kind of forest manager, he assumed.

In front of him and to his left, the light from the house could still be seen, twinkling between the trees. At the furthermost edge of the clearing the path he'd been following seemingly continued. Dave rubbed his arms attempting to thwart the coldness of the February evening, making a mental note of the clearing he'd stumbled upon. His car lay directly behind him, some distance away, and the house was almost directly in front of him; though how many more feet or yards he had to go, he had no way to ascertain, the darkness precluding any possibility of judging the distance with accuracy.

He followed the path deeper into the forest, leaving the occasionally moonlit clearing behind. And as he walked an overwhelming impression that the trees lining the path were about to take on a life of their own, somehow animated by the ancient moonlight, overcame him.

Upthrust bulks, almost arms of buried entities with a myriad of fingers pointing in consternation at the night's sky, seemed to be struggling to break free from their subterranean coffins. Each tree alive with its own individuality, moving, communicating with one another – the path he'd taken rippling with the tree-beings' struggle to attain an earth-side presence. But, perhaps, it was just an uneven track of a path not often travelled.

He quickened his pace, shaking his head, trying to rid his imagination of the cloying images that impinged on his sanity. He pushed back at the blocking branches of the undergrowth; the blocking branches that had never ever been there before, as he made his way, desperate, so very desperate, to get to the house, before something happened.

***

The moon slid behind another cloud and Dave had to slow. The path he'd been following wasn't particularly path-like anymore and, if he was going to avoid injuring himself, he would have to pick his footing carefully. He stared intently at the ground, trying to make sure that no twig, nor bramble, would folly him in his task.

As the cloud receded, allowing the white moon to play its light through the canopy of the forest onto Dave's path, he looked up from his feet and saw he was now way off course; the light from the house being directly to his left, instead of in front of him, where he had expected it to be.

The path through the forest was not as it had seemed. He had assumed it would cut straight through the woodland to the house, but now he was more than aware it was likely to be a run the forest animals followed. Looking to his left he now understood that he had to traipse through bush and thickets, and, in order to achieve his goal, he was going to have to make the path, following the direction the light from the house indicated. *If it is a light in a house*, his imagination taunted.

Dave pushed on, brushing aside the shrubs that blocked his path and making his way around the bushes, where they were too thick to go through. Eventually he stopped, needing a break, his journey towards the house being much harder than he had imagined. As he rested he heard the sound of his laboured breathing, then without warning his self-centred focus was abruptly interrupted. He held his breath.

Sharp snaps rang out in the forest; the sound of grounded branches shattering under the weight of unseen entities forcing them to splinter. Then more noises, noises of leaf laden shrub limbs swooshing as they were parted.

Dave mopped his brow with the cuff of his jacket, looking around, peering into the blackness of the forest's depths, listening intently, attempting to locate the direction the sounds had come from, but the noises had stopped... again – and he was alone.

Keeping his breath to a minimum he strained his ears, certain there would be something else, but the forest remained quiet. Even the wind's constant shushing had stopped: there was nothing else to be heard.

Dave pulled a hand down his face wishing that he'd never ever come across this place, this land, he now found himself in.

As the pure silence continued, Dave only just managed to overcome the paralysis his fear had wrought upon him. His heart palpitated and, with the cold and brutal fear still chilling him to his core, he staggered forward seeking the light, and hopefully an end to the nightmare he now found himself a part of.

Within a few short steps the wind came back with a force making the tree tops above him smash together, their branches clacking in unison under Nature's power. He picked up his pace, breaking into a run, accepting the slashes his face took from the unseen small branches of the bushes in his way. Blood trickled down his cheeks in many places from the vegetation inflicted cuts. No matter how he held his arms out in front of him the twigs and branches of the undergrowth always found a way to inflict more injuries.

Without warning, a low ululating moan came from behind him, shifting his focus from the lacerating foliage. It was quickly followed by a succession of cracks as hardier ground bourn branches and ones still attached to their hosts snapped; an unknown force breaking them as if they were nothing but balsa wood.

"Oh my God, oh my God, oh my God," he heard his voice whisper above his panting and the thumping of his heart in his ears. Dave continued thrashing through the forest knowing there was something close behind, following him; ready to take him. The nape of his neck prickled as the chill of the unknown passed down his spine.

Without looking back he started waving an arm behind him, back and forth, in a futile attempt to ward off the forest's predator he believed was now very close. Occasionally his hand felt blasts of icy breath across its back, even though the noise of the breaking undergrowth was much further behind him, or so he convinced his mind to believe.

Then he saw it, it was there, in front of him in the distance, once again, glinting through the pitched darkness of the forest the light shone and he started towards it, pushing at the shrubs and bracken, struggling against the bushes and suddenly he was through; he had entered another clearing.

His initial relief immediately collapsed into despondency as he recognised the three pronged stump at the clearing's centre, and although he was back to where he'd started from he had no idea, now, as to the direction of his car. Everywhere was dark and, each way he looked, the view was the same.

Dave sat down on the stump, head in hands with fingers in ears, to apprise himself of his situation and how he could get out of it. But he could barely think as he wondered how long it would be before his tormentor broke through into the clearing to join him.

After some moments he looked up, afraid, scared for his life with still no idea of what to do, the fear he felt making rational decisions impossible. And as he looked around the light from the house twinkled in the distance between the trees, as if taunting him, '*bet you can't get me.*'

Rut-tah-tuh-tuh-tuh. The sound from many miles ago started up again, echoing, coming from no definite direction. Or was it coming from behind him? He turned his head quickly, attempting to seek its source, then turned back to see if it was now behind him.

"Oh shit," Dave breathed, all his nerves more on edge than they'd been before, but the clacking had stopped. Had he imagined it? He was not sure. Then there was another crack, this time to his right, he turned to look – again nothing to be seen.

Dave peered around the clearing, tenuously keeping hold of his sanity, not seeing any movement, but somehow the trees, that defined the area he sat in, seemed to be closer, a lot nearer to him, the circumference of the clearing reduced, their branches almost but not quite able to reach him. GRAB HOLD.

No, stop it, he told his mind.

He studied the circling trees again, attempting to see their movement towards him, but in the moonlight he could not tell if they really had moved any closer at all. There was only the feeling that the circle's edge was ten steps away from him rather than the twenty his mind insisted they were before.

As he watched the trees he caught a movement in the periphery of his vision, enhanced by the noise of cracking twigs. He turned to face the movement and as he did the dark gap between the pine trees, he now stared at, coalesced into a black, almost recognisable, amorphous shape. In turn, it disappeared behind one trunk of the circling trees only to appear in the gap between the trees further around the clearing's circle: Nature parodying mankind's form in the air, within her own breath.

Dave stood up on shaking legs watching the apparition's dance around the circle. All he could do was follow its movements, turning on point, as the dark thing made a complete circle, his ability to flee being sucked from him by the brutal terror of his situation. As he completed the 360 degree turn of its path around him, the entity, whatever it was, melded back into the forest's darkness and the hex that had riveted him to the spot eased its vice like grip upon him. Dave shivered, his body feeling as if iced water had replaced the blood that had once flowed through his veins.

Rut-tah-tuh-tuh-tuh, came the ancient and evil sound again. Dave felt like he was going to be sick and as he turned to throw up he saw blue and red flashing lights, flickering around and around, obviously from a patrol vehicle, piercing the forest. And as he recognised their source he saw the juddering beam of a flashlight that could only be carried by a person.

A way out, he thought. With what little commandable energy he had left, Dave started to stumble towards the blue and red light and the path back to his car and he prayed for some help.

Picking up his pace, energy coming from reserves he didn't realise he had, he made for the trail out of the clearing.

As he attempted his first step onto the path that led to the road a tree root leapt from beneath the ground's surface under its own power, throwing the path's loamy soil up, out of its way, tripping him. He fell flat on his stomach, right arm out in front of him, and left wrist under his body, snapping as his full weight landed upon its awkward angle. With his neck stretched forward, his eyes focused again on the police officer investigating his empty car. Dave took a breath to call for help, but before he could finish large red capped mushrooms smashed their way out of the earth entering his open mouth, cutting off any sound he was about to make. He breathed heavily through his nose as his lungs continued their heaving cycle.

Other roots broke free from the forest's floor encircling his ankles and his shins, retracting, pulling him back towards the clearing; taking him away from his only escape route.

He tried clawing the ground with his good arm, to halt the forest's claim upon his body, but the forest's strength was greater than his and he continued to be dragged, backwards, on his front, feet first, by the forest's living tendrils; back into the clearing's centre. *The forest's mouth*, a thought flitted through his head.

Struggling to keep conscious he saw the police car's lights stop flashing and heard a car's engine start, then gradually fade away. More chills racked his body as the February night's iciness sought to claim every part of him.

Brambles that were used to travelling the forest floor wrapped themselves around his arms turning him over, their thorns cutting through his clothing, digging deep into his upper arms.

Dave managed to cough out the Fly Garret in his mouth as bushes he hadn't noticed in the clearing before, leant over him, rustling angrily. Then the moon was obscured by a cloud for a moment and, as it appeared again, the rustling became sibilant words.

No more. The bushes rustled in quiet unison. *No more will you take us limb from limb. No more will you kill us. We are one throughout Gaia and we have started the end.*

Dave did not understand and Nature's call to arms sounded again, *rut-tah-tuh-tuh-tuh*, as if to underline the bushes' mutterings.

You cannot live with us and we cannot live with you. The sibilant voice of the bushes threatened.

More tree roots heaved themselves from the ground, rearing above him, and then plunged downwards through his thighs, smashing his femurs as they sought the soil beneath him. He screamed at the pain and continued screaming as the length of the roots' uneven surface travelled through the meat of his legs, snagging tendons, nerves and arteries; but his scream was soon silenced when ivy crept out from the edge of the clearing and wrapped itself around his neck cutting him off, but only just enough to silence his voice. It was as if the forest had decided to torture him. But for what, he could not imagine.

The bushes rustled again: *Know what you do, feel what you do. You take more than you should and the gift to us, of your ones without life, put deep in our body beneath our skin, for our sustenance, is not enough. We follow you now and we take what we want, as you do to us. This is our beginning born in humankind's way.*

Rhododendrons joined the roots and brambles that had already pinned Dave to the ground, wrapping their thin branches around his arms, beginning to pull, and, as he tried to free himself, the grass of the clearing grew, sliding over his chest, weaving itself across his sternum in a mat pulling him tight to the ground, ceasing his struggles.

Dave attempted to scream again as his arms were dislocated by the plants, but he couldn't, the vines around his neck had put paid to that. He attempted to struggle once more, this time without movement and became still as his arms were finally wrenched from his body, skin tearing at the armpits, shock paralysing any further effort he could muster. The shrubs lifted his ragged, partially clothed arms into the air, flicking them around, back and forth, in noiseless triumph.

With his blood pumping into the earth from his pulverised legs and the red fluid spurting from his shoulder sockets in arcs, Dave, in his last living thoughts, almost grasped what he had been told by the plants. But before he was able to scream at the forest, that it wasn't his fault, the vines that had encircled his throat tightened, squeezing his head from his neck.

***

And so it began – Nature's final retaliation. Humankind had ignored her warnings; the tsunamis, the earthquakes, firestorms and floods. She had ceased to accept ignorance as an excuse for innocence. Scorned as she felt she was, the war had to start somewhere – and so it had.

The Time Traveller

Dr Mallory Johnson smiled, because he was the first. He'd shunned the received wisdom time travel was only possible between the time the machine was invented and any other time prior to its creation.

His time travel would take him forward, requiring no huge machines. In fact his time machine existed in the conical beaker he held in his hand. He sloshed the luminescent liquid around and a white vapour cascaded over its brim.

There was a downside to his time travel, but it was only minor; if the historical time machine was not invented by the year he arrived there would be no way back – but was this a bad thing he wondered?

His dilemma was how strong he should make the liquid; its strength determining how far into the future he would travel. Johnson settled for 200 years and mixed the liquid appropriately.

He was certain most of mankind's stupidity would be eliminated by then; famine and war eradicated and the use of fuels that contaminated, finished with; renewable energy through nuclear fusion, turning atoms of hydrogen into helium, would be the future's energy source.

Removing his clothes and stepped into his time tube, a tank of clear gel, attaching the cannula in his wrist to the pump, then closed the tank's lid. Taking a deep breath he turned the cannula's tap to open. Searing pain shot through his veins but before he could do anything about it darkness descended.

***

A hiss sounded as Johnson came round, the tank's lid springing open. He climbed out feeling no ill effects, wondering whether he'd travelled at all. Then he saw his rotted clothes; then a myriad of spider's webs; but no spiders.

He took a deep breath and the air seemed clean, almost pure, re-enforcing his belief mankind had left its stupidity behind. But then a cloying weakness struck him and he staggered to a chair. As he sat hair dropped from his head and his skin began to peel, falling to the floor.

He sighed recognising the symptoms of severe radiation poisoning, and knew what mankind had done to itself since he'd decided to travel to the future.

A Portrait in Black

Her bipolar shadows, cast across a dim room,
reveal the compulsive/obsessive's veil.

And her ranting and raving of contrary fib tales,
make sparkles of vitriol from the gloom.

She's a shadow of nobody,
rarely acknowledged,
never more than her consonants or vowels.

And her life's mirror,
When observed,
shows nothing looking back.
No beauty, nor solace to be found.

Just a bitter, shrivelled, disconsolate shell of -
what may have been,
that basks in a bile of its own.

Reason - her anathema - fathered by troubles
from her far and recent past,

make her alone and a long time blind;
inhabiting dimensions that are dark,
as she forsakes the problems of the self,
to indulge her twisted joy.

To her, there is only her.
No one else,
that is cognizant of the world.

And in the room she never leaves,
she smiles as she pulls a blade from its clasp.
To meld it with the skin on her neck,
– drawing a line that is her own.

Then slowly her giggles turn into a rasp,
the lights in her eyes – going out,
as her vision of her inner world
becomes nothing more than a wretched dark;
her mouth with near lifeless pout.

Finally – crystal sounds – she once heard,
change into a bleak and fading drone.
As she hopes, once again,
she will be found,
lying there,
in the place she has to call a home.

A Quiz Night in the Sticks

"Are you sure we're on the right road?" Paul asked his wife, after what had already been two miles travelling along something that was hardly a road, and more like a rarely used track only wide enough for a car. The scraggy tufts of grass along its centre and high hedgerows on either side were telling him they must be off the usual tourist routes.

Jane didn't answer and after quickly glancing at his wife, and seeing the look on her face, Paul decided not to push the point any further. She'd always been an excellent navigator and because the road wasn't what he'd expected, he should have known better than to question her skills. Jane ran a hand through her thin blonde bob, as if conscious her husband had been observing her.

They'd left booking their holiday, for the New Year, too late to get a place on the coast of Cornwall. So they'd accepted the fact that the Swedish style lodges they'd found advertised on the Internet, in the grounds of Eastcutt Farm, well away from the coast, was where they would have to stay if they were going to carry on with their Cornish breaks over the festive period.

Moments after Paul's comment, a large beige sign attached to an oak tree, loomed out of the hedgerow. "Eastcutt Farm & Lodges" it indicated in very visible maroon lettering; a small black arrow pointed to a concealed entrance on the left. Paul indicated and turned the car into the lane that was somewhat smaller than the vestigial road they'd been travelling. He shook his head wondering where they would end up. Jane didn't notice, the views of the frosted countryside outside the car keeping her attention.

A quarter of a mile further on, another sign appeared; "Reception" it declared. No matter how much faith Paul had in Jane's incredible navigation skills, he was always stunned when they ended up where they ought to be and he was envious, though he could never admit it. He pulled up on the gravel laid parking area, crunching to a halt next to a wooden planked reception building.

Paul and Jane got out of the car and stretched their legs; the four hour drive from their breakfast stop at Stonehenge, taking its toll.

As Jane pulled her blue and grey Berghaus jacket tighter, to fend off the cold, she gave Paul an "I told you so" look across the car's bonnet. Paul shrugged knowing he shouldn't have questioned the route his wife had chosen.

Though there was a sign hanging on the glass panelled door to the reception stating it was open, the only light inside was seeping from another room behind the reception's desk, its door slightly ajar.

Paul was about to comment that the reception looked deserted when a small head, with long lank mousy brown hair, quickly peeked out and disappeared again.

"Looks like there's someone in," Paul said to his wife and the couple walked the short distance from their car and entered the bare reception area.

As per the outside, the interior walls were of thin pine planks; the flooring was the same. On one of the walls hung a cork notice board, bereft of any notices. The reception's counter was surfaced in nondescript Formica.

Paul and Jane looked around, trying to find something to summon someone so they could book in for their short break, but there was nothing.

Jane called out. "Hello?"

The door behind the counter opened slowly and a woman in her late thirties, wearing an obviously old, baggy brown woollen knitted jumper, entered the reception. Paul recognised the lank hair.

"Ah. Good," the woman said. Paul noted a peculiar reluctance in the woman's few words. "Mr. and Mrs. Johnston?" the woman asked.

"Yes," Paul said.

The woman began to explain the general rules of the holiday site and what should be done in case of any problems. Once she'd finished her spiel she reached under the counter and retrieved a set of keys. Without meeting Jane's gaze the woman handed the keys over, her hand trembling almost imperceptibly.

"If you would like to take your car to the cabin, to unload, then there's a small gap between the trees over there," the woman said pointing to a gap that wasn't visible from where they were standing. "You can only take the car when loading and unloading. The rest of the time you must park where you are now."

"Thank you very much," Jane said.

Jane and Paul left the woman in the reception and got into their car. Paul didn't mention the peculiar demeanour of the woman as Jane hadn't indicated she'd picked up on anything out of the ordinary.

As soon as Paul had reversed their car a little way out of the parking area, he spotted the gap the woman had spoken of. "Ah! There it is," he said and drove the car through the gap, then down the gravelled slope that had been cut through the thirty foot wide strip of fir trees. Exiting the manmade track way Jane and Paul saw the woman from the reception beckoning them, insistently, toward a log cabin that was raised from the ground on breeze block stilts. It was almost as if the woman's life depended on them reaching their cabin, and no other by accident or folly.

Paul frowned as he pulled up next to the wooden cabin. He couldn't imagine how the woman had got there before them.

Turning off the engine he looked at his wife and could just make out the smile on her slightly round face, hidden beneath the hair of her blonde bob, as she looked out of the passenger window at the lodge. He smiled too, happy that she was happy. They got out of the car.

The woman from reception stood on the veranda that fronted the lodge and opened the cabin's wooden framed glass panel door, as the couple walked up its few steps, and showed them in.

The inside was impressive and had all mod-cons. Apart from the huge expanses of glass making up the front; the cabin was entirely of wood, planks for the interior and logs for its exterior.

Before leaving Jane and Paul to unpack, the woman said, "John, the farmer who owns this site, is having a quiz tonight in the pub about three hundred yards further on from the reception." Again Paul felt the woman was giving information against her wishes.

"Thanks," Jane said. "That'll be nice." The woman left.

"Well. Wasn't that strange?" Paul said.

"Strange?"

"Oh. Nothing," Paul said. "Shall we get the stuff in?"

"That'll be a good idea."

Before going back to the car to unload Paul and Jane stopped on the veranda and looked around. The place felt isolated and calm. The iciness of the last few days had glazed the surrounding vegetation and the small fifteen foot wide strip of grass that separated cabins from the line of fir trees hiding the entrance to the site. It was ideal.

As they made their way down the frost covered steps to the path and their car, a voice called out, "Hello?"

They both looked up. A man in grubby overalls, who had seemingly appeared from nowhere, was striding quickly towards them across the crystal sparkling grass in front of the lodge next to theirs.

"Hello. It's Paul and Jane I take it?" the man said.

Jane nodded.

"I'm John and this is my farm. It's great to have you here. I hope the cabin is to your liking."

Paul was dumbstruck. Where had this guy appeared from and how did he know their names? How had he known they'd arrived? It was only a mere few minutes since the woman had left them and Paul hadn't noticed a mobile phone on her belt or any tell-tale bulges in her pockets. He was certain she hadn't had enough time to let the farmer know they were here.

Jane said, "Hello."

As the man got closer Paul saw how grubby his overalls were. Little pieces of straw covered the navy blue dungarees and dotted amongst them were spatters of something deep red in colour.

As if reading Paul's mind, John said, "Sorry about my clothes," the farmer made a sweeping gesture down his front, "but I've just been feeding the sheep."

Paul thought, *Feeding the sheep to what?*

Jane said, "That's all right."

"Anyways," John said, "I was wondering whether you'll be popping into my pub a bit later, for the quiz night. It starts at eightpm You *will* be there?"

"Of course we will," Jane said. She enjoyed her quiz nights.

"Good. Use your torch on the way. The path to the pub is very dark this time of year."

Paul pressed the button on his car's key fob to open the boot, the boot unlocked and as Paul was about to echo his wife's acceptance of the invitation, the words stopped in his mouth. John was gone. Paul froze for a moment, attempting to work out what had happened to the man.

After half an hour they'd finished unloading and Paul stood on the veranda to have a cigarette. Although it was now only five thirty and early evening, the site was utterly silent – no wildlife could be heard clucking, tweeting or cawing. Nothing rustled in the bushes and nothing scampered across the grass strip in front of the twelve or so Swedish cabins on the site. It seemed, at this moment, the world had become devoid of sound.

Paul shuddered. He couldn't understand how something that seemed so idyllic could also seem so ominous. Shrugging the thoughts off, he finished his cigarette and went back into the cabin to help Jane finish setting up their temporary home, unpacking the food and loading up the pine cupboard in their bedroom with their clothes for the next few days. Paul then made his way to the kitchen and pumped all the coins he could find in his pockets into the electricity meter. The place would need a lot of heating if they weren't going to freeze overnight.

After a snack of cheese on toast and the time now six forty five, the couple got ready for the quiz night. Paul and Jane left their cabin and walked up the short path between the trees, to the lane that led to the site's pub. Paul now knew why John had mentioned the use of a torch; it was unfortunate they hadn't brought one with them. There was no moon and no light pollution; the site was truly out in the "sticks" and as still and as silent as a… Paul didn't finish the thought. Jane hugged her husband a little closer in the darkness, as if she'd been infected by the notion that had passed through his mind.

Turning a corner in the lane the festive New Year lights of the pub came into view and at last they could see the path they had been tentatively following. Like moths to a flame Paul and Jane made their way the final hundred yards to its entrance and entered the pub.

The converted barn had a low ceiling and Paul had to stoop as he entered, his six foot two stature not allowing him to stand upright. However Jane was okay, being almost a foot shorter than he.

To Paul's mind the pub's décor was eccentric, if not damned weird. Although the walls were whitewashed and its ancient wooden beams painted black, the two goats' skulls and a single sheep's fleece pinned to its walls, gave the place an otherworldly feel.

As the couple walked further into the warm pub, towards the bar, the ceiling got higher and Paul was able to stand. Everyone there welcomed the couple as they walked in, saying such things as; "*Good to see you, Jane*", "*Nice to see you, Paul. Hope you like the place*", and "*Glad you could make it*." Paul and Jane nodded their acknowledgments.

A wood burning stove halfway between the door and the bar against the left hand wall provided the heat. Jane sat down at an empty table against the wall opposite the burner.

Next to the stove sat a large bellied man who leant back against the pub wall behind a small mahogany table, not a single hair covering his head. At the same table, two teenage girls and an older woman sat, the trio still wearing their outside coats, the girls' ones more fashionable than the one the other woman, presumably their mother, was wearing.

At the bar on a stool was another man, also in an outside jacket, a dark blue one this time, compared to the light colours the teenagers wore, with a woollen hat pulled down to his brows and a beard that covered his face in its entirety.

On the surface everything *seemed* right to Paul; the amicable introductions, the lack of prejudice from the locals and a general feeling of "rightness" – a happy atmosphere all in all. But no matter what his perception, the whole circumstance had an edginess lurking somewhere beneath the good-humour, and Paul couldn't figure out why. Possibly it had something to do with the fact it wasn't New Year's Eve – a time when people might behave like this; it was the day before. And the more he thought about it the more he couldn't shake the feeling the whole situation had an overtly embracing wrongness about it.

Paul continued to the bar and ordered himself a pint of the local cider and a Bacardi and Coke for his wife. Then made his way to the table Jane had sat at.

"Isn't this lovely?" Jane said quietly. The room was small and didn't lend itself well to private conversations.

"I suppose, but don't you find this all a bit peculiar?"

"Peculiar?"

"Well… you know… the décor? The way everyone knows our names, for instance."

"Don't be silly, Paul. It's their way of making us feel welcome. I'm sure the woman from reception let them know."

Paul wasn't so sure. The woman from reception wasn't even in the bar. He might concede the point, later, if she ever turned up. He supped his pint and looked around. Everyone seemed genuine enough though, sitting in their small groups, around the other five tables, all chatting happily to one another. The bearded man chatted to John whilst he pulled a pint for himself.

After half an hour the quiet background music got even quieter and John picked up some sheets of paper. "Okay," John said, and the conversations hushed. "Right. Round one of tonight's quiz will be the general knowledge round."

John made his way from behind the bar and walked over to where Paul and Jane were sitting, past the tables that were nearest to the bar, the people sitting at them not even noticing they'd been overlooked in favour of the newcomers.

John winked at the couple. "Don't worry if you lose, we've got a professional quiz team in tonight." He handed Jane one of the sheets of paper, there were lines on it numbered one to twenty. "Do you need a pencil or pen?"

"No thanks," Jane said as she took a pen from her handbag.

John smiled, and before leaving them he took a tooth pick from the breast pocket of his tweed jacket and began to dig at something stuck between his teeth. Once satisfied he walked away handing out the remaining sheets, then returned to the bar to start the quiz. "Don't forget to write your team name at the top of the sheet. And here we go, question one; which of these continents has the greatest landmass. Is it a) Britain, b) Australia, or c) Antarctica?"

"Oh, that's easy," Jane whispered as she wrote down Antarctica.

After half an hour of delivering questions, John said, "We're half way through round one and time for a little breather I think. If you need a break or a drink now's the time, part two of the general knowledge round will recommence in fifteen minutes."

"Do you want a top up?" Paul asked his wife.

"Yes please."

"Same again?"

Jane nodded and Paul took their empty glasses to the bar to order another round. As he waited for their drinks the man in the woollen hat finished scrutinising his answers, turned his sheet over and started to roll himself a cigarette. Paul glanced at the man out of the corner of his eye; his beard really did cover his whole face. *Weird*, Paul thought.

"That'll be four pounds eighty please," John said.

As Paul took the money from his pocket, the man in the woollen hat and dark blue jacket got up and made his way out of the bar to have his roll-up.

"Thanks," Paul said and went back to his table, putting the drinks down. "I'm just going outside for a cigarette," he told Jane.

"Okay. See you in a minute," she said.

Paul pulled open the door to the pub and stepped outside, then shivered. The temperature had dropped considerably and a mist was beginning to develop. As he shut the door behind him he realised the furry faced man was nowhere to be seen.

Paul took his packet of Marlboro Lights from his coat pocket and placed one in his mouth as he leant back against the railings surrounding the large top step of the bar's entrance. Putting his hand into his coat's pocket, seeking his lighter, he looked around. There were four outhouses of differing sizes, but no sign of the bearded man.

Pulling the lighter from his pocket, he flicked its flint. A flame sparked and, as he craned his neck forward to light his cigarette, a movement in his now diminished night vision stopped him. He looked up, away from the flame, toward the bushes that lined the furthest edge of the lane, and frowned, shaking his head.

"You didn't see that," he told himself, trying to rid the idea that he'd seen someone in a dark coat leap from the ground, over the hedge and into the lower branches of the trees that lay beyond. A sound of snapping branches drifted across the silent "*farmscape*". Paul took a couple of deep puffs. "You're just tired," he tried to reassure himself. "You've been on a long drive and you're just tired." Paul finished his smoke quickly and went back into the pub.

He sat down and finished half of his pint in one go.

"Paul, you okay?"

"I'm just tired. Six hours is a long drive."

"Okay, ladies and gentlemen. And locals of course," John said and quiet laughter broke out. "We're now starting part two. We're still on the general knowledge round and question eleven is; which of the following chemical symbols represents diamond. Is it: a) C, b) Di or c) H_2O?"

Jane looked at Paul. "I don't know this one. What is it?"

"It's C."

"Are you sure?" Jane asked. "I thought H_2O was water."

"No, it's C for carbon."

"Oh! A."

"Yes," said Paul a little too forcedly. He was finding it hard to relax, his thoughts elsewhere.

"Don't get cross."

"I'm not cross. Just tired. That's all," he said.

The questions carried on and Jane continued to fill in the answers.

As John was about to read out question seventeen Paul crashed his pint onto the table as a thought struck him.

"You all right?" Jane asked, concerned, seeing her husband had paled.

"Yeah, of course," Paul said. But he wasn't. Whilst he'd been concentrating on the questions his subconscious had proposed an answer as to why he felt something wasn't quite right. "*They're afraid of scaring us away*," it had posited. Why that should worry him, he didn't know.

"Are you sure, Paul?" Jane pushed.

"Of course I'm sure. Don't worry. Just answer the questions and make sure we win. We can't be beaten by a professional team; especially not on holiday."

***

"Okay. That's the end of the general knowledge round. Please exchange your answer sheets and after you've done that, don't forget the bar is still open for drinks and snacks."

The bald man with the paunch walked towards Paul and Jane's table, answer sheet in hand. He rubbed his stomach in a circular motion as he made his way and mumbled, "Yum, yum, yummy," then winked at Paul.

Paul blinked. "What?" he breathed.

"I said; Jane, here's our answers, how do you think you did?"

Jane looked up from her answer sheet. "Okay, I think," and swapped the sheets. The man nodded and walked away with Team Jane's answers.

Paul thought about asking his wife whether she'd seen what had gone on, but looking at her he realised it would be pointless. He stared into his empty pint. "Do you want another drink? I think I could do with one."

"Yeah, but just a Coke this time."

"Okay." Paul got up, giving the fat man's table a wide birth as he returned their empty glasses to the bar. Whilst he waited to be served he noticed that the furry faced man had not returned; the guy's answer sheet remained face down. Paul glanced around the pub, the man was not there.

John filled Paul's glass and got a fresh one for Jane, topping it up with Coke only.

"How are you doing?"

"I think we're doing quite well," Paul replied.

"Reckon you'll like the next round – it's a little bit different."

Paul handed over the cash for the drinks but didn't respond. *A little bit different*, Paul thought. *This whole place is a little bit different*.

Paul sat down next to Jane. "John thinks the next round is going to be a little bit different. Is that possible with quizzes?"

"I suppose he must mean the subject."

"I can't imagine any subject that hasn't been used in the quizzes we've been to."

"Let's wait and see. You never know."

The large bellied man got up from his table after a short conversation with one of the teenage girls. Picking up a scuttle next to the wood burner he opened the burner's thick glass and metal doors, and using a scoop, he shovelled short chopped logs into its centre. Once satisfied he replaced the scuttle, closing the wood burner's small doors and returned to his seat.

"Right people, the final round," John said.

Paul looked at Jane and whispered, "Final round? I knew it was going to be a bit different but only two rounds in a quiz?"

"It must be the way they do it here."

"Get your pen or pencils ready. The last round in tonight's quiz is… religion."

"Not that different then," Paul said to Jane.

Jane smiled.

"Okay," John said, "the first question of round two is; in the Christian belief system which one of these is said to be present in devil worship?"

Paul gave Jane a quick frown.

"Is it: a) Christ with a thorny crown, b) the donkey from the nativity, or c) an inverted cross?"

Jane wrote "C" on their piece of paper.

"Can you believe this?" Paul asked Jane tersely beneath his breath.

"It's only a quiz on religion."

Paul nodded twice. "Okay, okay. I'll go with that – just until something more weird happens."

"Question two," John said. "Which of the following numbers is said to represent the anti-christ? Is it: a) 999, b) 118, or c) 666?"

Jane scribbled down her answer.

Paul looked sternly at Jane. "This is mental," he hissed. "Can you believe these questions?"

"Paul, it's a quiz. That's all," she whispered back.

Paul conceded. "Okay, it's a quiz. But if this goes on for much longer, I'm out of here. Okay?"

Jane didn't respond, she'd had enough of Paul's wild assertions that there was something untoward going on.

The quiz carried on and Jane, after every question, wrote an answer on the paper.

"Okay, that's the end of round two. Please exchange your answer sheets for marking."

As Jane checked everything she'd written down the fat man from the other table got up and walked across the room to their table.

Smirking as he approached the man said, "Here's Team Reficul's answers." He thrust his sheet towards Jane.

"Thank you. Here's ours," Jane said, swapping the sheets again.

"How d'you think you've fared?" the man asked, resting both hands on the table as he bent over so his head was level with theirs.

"Quite well, I think," Jane said. "I used to be a Catholic, so this round was quite easy."

The fat man stood up abruptly and as he walked back to his table, he shuddered.

Paul studied the back of the receding man, then turned to his wife. "You can't tell me that wasn't weird."

"Paul, he shuddered, that's all. You really must be tired, all these crazy thoughts you're thinking. I'm glad it was a short quiz."

"Ladies and gentlemen, all the sheets have been handed in and the scores have been calculated." John paused for a moment, then said, "I'm very happy to announce that Team Jane, albeit coming second to our professional team, have won, with thirty three points."

All the people in the pub nodded their appreciation of the result, a few clapping as well.

"Well done, Team Jane," John said, leaving his position behind the bar. "Here's your prize."

John walked over to the couple holding out a blue circular tin of chocolates. "Not a lot I know, but it may fatten you up." The farmer smiled.

"Thank you very much," Jane said laughing, accepting the Cadbury tin.

Paul was nonplussed.

"Can I interest you in another drink? One for the road, so to speak."

Before Jane could respond Paul answered. "Sorry, not tonight, John. It's been a long day. Need to get some shut eye if we're going to make the most of tomorrow."

"So be it," John said, his demeanour darkening as he walked away.

Jane and Paul put their coats on and before exiting the pub turned to say their farewells, but no one was looking their way and John was talking quietly to the bald fat man.

Standing on the top of the steps outside the pub's entrance Jane pulled her coat closer. "Wow. The temperature's really dropped." Vapour formed as she spoke.

"Can we hang on here a moment while I have a cigarette in the light?" Paul asked.

"As long as you're not going to be too long. It's really cold," Jane said.

"Just a few moments." Paul retrieved a cigarette and before he lit it he quickly glanced at the bushes across the lane then struck the flame.

Inhaling deeply Paul looked at his wife and breathed out. "You didn't find anything remotely odd about that?"

"Not really."

"What about the second round?"

"It was only a round on religion."

"Pretty specific though."

"It wasn't general knowledge."

"I suppose," Paul said, dropping his cigarette into the water filled, white plastic container on the ground. The cigarette glowed for a moment on the surface ice before going out. "It's cold. Let's get going," he said.

"Good idea."

The couple walked along the lane then Jane stopped and listened. "It's very peaceful isn't it? Listen. You can't hear any cars at all; nothing like it is at home."

"You can't hear any wildlife either," Paul said.

"It's winter. There's probably not a lot of wildlife around."

Paul and Jane started walking again and as they got to the bend, when the lights from the buildings behind would diminish, they all went out. Paul looked back at the pub.

"Looks like the pub's finished for the evening. The only light they've left on is the one above the steps; not a lot of light really." He turned back. "Bloody hell! You can't see a bloody thing. It's pitch black."

Jane was now worried. Her night vision had always been atrocious. "Should we go back to the pub and ask for a torch?"

"Wait a moment, my eyes will adjust." The last thing Paul wanted to do was to go back to that place. He was glad his mother had always insisted he should eat carrots, though he had doubts as to whether that was the real reason for his good night vision. "Okay. I can make out the path," just, he said and thought. "Hold on to me."

Paul started walking and Jane followed with her arm firmly looped through her husband's.

Paul stopped. "I think we're nearly at the cut through the fir trees."

The cold mist wasn't helping any; all Paul could really see was a grey wall surrounding them. If they were near enough to the path through the trees Paul could press his car's key fob and the lights indicating its alarm was off, would flash, giving them a little light to determine exactly where they were.

As he fumbled for his jacket pocket and his car's key a sudden loud cracking, in what could only be the branches around them, rang out in the still and chilled air. All the hairs on his neck and forearms stood on end, the skin across his forehead tighten and he shuddered; goose bumps prickling his skin. Jane seemed to sag, pulling on his arm.

"Paul. What was that?" Jane's voice was feeble.

Paul drew a deep breath trying to calm himself. "Dunno. Probably a badger in the undergrowth or something like that." He was pleased his voice was steady, not giving away the dread he felt inside.

Paul found the key and the car's indicators flashed. He had judged it right; they had stopped in line with the path down to their lodge. Quickly Paul turned to the right and shortly after entering the cut, through the line of fir trees, the outside light of their lodge illuminated the sparse strip of frosted grass in front of their cabin.

The wooden steps to the veranda creaked slightly in the freezing night as they made their way up them, the frost covering the planks hardly affected by their footfalls. On the veranda Jane took the cabin's keys from her handbag and unlocked the door.

Inside Paul said, "I must admit I've never had to walk along a lane that dark, ever before."

"Let's get a torch when we're out tomorrow," Jane said.

"Good idea," Paul said holding out his hand.

"What?"

"Keys please," he said.

Jane handed Paul the keys and he locked the wooden framed glass door.

"At least it's warm in here," Jane said.

"That's because I charged the electric meter and turned on the heating before we went out." Paul pulled the thin curtains across their cabin's front windows and door.

"Time for bed?"

"Yeah. In a minute. Going to have a can."

Now they were in the cabin Paul started to relax. *The holiday begins here*, he thought. Entering the kitchen he checked the meter and seeing it was almost full he went to the fridge and took out a can of cider, then sat down on the sofa in the lounge next to the cabin's front door.

"I'm going to bed, to read," Jane said.

"Okay. See you in a minute."

Jane opened the door to the master bedroom and went in; its entrance was also in the lounge. The wooden bed creaked loudly as she got under the duvet, blankets and the extra blankets they'd taken from the other bedroom.

Paul listened to the nothingness as he supped from his can; the silence only being broken on occasions by Jane turning in their bed. Paul was happy with nothing to think about and no signal for his firm's mobile. The more he relaxed the further the weirdness of the evening and their arrival moved from his immediate thoughts.

Paul finished his can and got ready for bed. In the bedroom, he found Jane already asleep, though she'd left the bedside light on. The bed creaked as he got in, but Jane didn't stir. As he flicked the light off, he smiled. There was something special about the air in Cornwall, and he couldn't wait for its effect to take hold of him.

Thirty minutes later he was still lying there, wide awake, wondering why the sleep he was used to in Cornwall had eluded him. He looked at the clock; twelve thirty, and then succumbed.

Gradually Paul's consciousness came to the fore. What had woken him? Had he heard a noise? He twisted his head and looked at the clock again. Its red digits blazed twelve forty seven. *Oh God*, he thought. *Was that it? Seventeen minutes?* He turned onto his back, the bed creaking, and he listened. Nothing. He turned onto his side facing the clock and the dressing table, but his body was telling him sleep was not the right thing to do.

Paul tried one of the tricks he'd learnt a long time ago that would always bring sleep; he imagined a desert island with a blue sea surrounding it and a beach of soft beige sand, the waves gently crashing upon the shore. He imagined sitting under a palm tree on his idyllic island and he began to drift off.

Then he was wide awake again. This time he'd definitely heard a noise. It was either the creaking of the veranda or the brass handle to the front door being gently twisted to free the catch. He was glad he'd locked it. He turned onto his back and lying still he listened more intently. Nothing. Still he listened and as he did his body began to feel cold, though sweat was now running off it. His body started to buzz, adrenalin coursing through him, and the hairs on his arms prickled to attention. Still he listened, still nothing. He tried to relax. Something cracked lightly. It sounded like the door to the cupboard in the room coming ajar. Paul lay frozen to the bed, cold, with the hair on his scalp bristling. Then no noise, the alertness in him receded. Then nothing and his tension dissipated. And finally, calm. Paul breathed out slowly, chastising himself for the fool he was, and again drifted off to sleep.

***

Paul's eyes flicked open and he glanced at the clock, it was gone threeeam He pulled the duvet down so his head was completely clear. The noise started. This was a real noise; a pointed claw dragging its way along the grain of the wooden panelling. He could imagine the natural swarf curling out of the rut being driven into the logs that made up the walls of the lodge. And the noise continued as it vibrated through the cabin's wall. Then a loud crack of glass, from the lounge, a pane almost giving way, and Jane awoke.

"Paul, what's happening? What's that noise?" she said, the depth of sleep she'd come from not allowing her to form the questions clearly.

Paul remained silent, his fear stonewalling his ability to speak.

"Paul?" Jane implored. He could hear the tears in her voice.

The handle to the front door rattled and clacked as it was forced viciously up and down.

"Don't leave me," she said.

Paul couldn't move, he couldn't do or say anything.

"Paul!" Jane wailed.

The clawing on the logs multiplied. Jane, in her fear, turned to face her husband then slapped his face without holding back. The noise of shattering glass resounded around the lounge and Paul blinked. His left cheek burnt and he looked at Jane. Something within him grew; he couldn't let Jane become a victim of whatever it was that wanted them. He got out of bed and lifted the cupboard, with all its contents, off the floor and placed it against the bedroom's door, then pressed his back against it, arms splayed outward next to his sides, holding the cupboard in its new position. There was a final cracking and crunching before the hammering on the door started. Paul could see in his mind's eye the smashed entrance to the cabin. Using his legs Paul pushed harder against the cupboard.

Heavy thumps threw Paul forward and the gouging of the bedroom's outside wall continued, though it didn't give way like their cabin's front door had.

And on it went, THUD. Paul pushed back. The noise sounded like a shoulder muffled by something. *Hair?* he thought.

Then a rattle – the handle to the bedroom door being tried again.

THUD. This time the force jarred his neck as his head was thrown forward.

A quiet squeak – the bedroom door's handle being tested carefully – THUD, THUD, THUD.

Paul gritted his teeth as he leant against the cupboard with all the force he could muster. Holding back whatever was coming for them; hoping he could, wondering what would happen if the bedroom door caved in, leaving only the cupboard between him and whatever it was that wanted them.

He knew, if it came to it, he would do everything he could to protect his wife for as long as possible. He looked at Jane cowering beneath the duvet she'd pulled up under her chin, as she sat against the headboard, arms around her drawn up knees, and prayed she would not suffer when they got through.

After an eternity the thumping and crashing on the back of the cupboard subsided, then stopped. Paul looked at the clock; only an hour had past, but he knew this respite was no reason to lower his guard. And his fear was confirmed.

BANG. The floor beneath his feet shuddered. The force lifting the floorboards he was standing on. It was now under the cabin, attempting another way in.

Another bang jolted him upward. The bones in his heels felt like they'd been pushed through the flesh of his bare feet. Slowly, ever so slowly, the floorboards lifted, retching their complaints, creaking against their new form, as the nails holding them fast were eased from the beams that held them. Ignoring the pain Paul stamped down hard; once, twice, then three times. The floorboards returned.

***

Jane stopped sobbing and listened. There was silence; another half hour went by; still silence.

It's now or never, Paul thought and moved away from the cupboard, then eased it back from the door. Whatever the reason why the onslaught had stopped, he had to take advantage of the opportunity; it may be the only chance they had. He waited for a moment. Nothing tried to push the door open. Paul reached for the handle and pulling it down he opened the door slightly. After a few minutes he peered through the gap between the door and its frame. There was nothing to be seen.

He shut the bedroom door quickly and manoeuvred the cupboard away so he could get out into the lounge. He opened the door fully and looked out. The lounge was as pristine as when they'd arrived. There was no broken glass on the floor and the front door remained invisible behind the curtains he'd closed when they'd got back from the pub. Pulling back the drawn curtain he saw thin cracks in the door's upper most pane. Then he jumped back, shocked, as a flashlight's beam, coming from somewhere in the fir trees, picked out a dead barn owl lying motionless on the veranda. Its beige speckled wings were splayed out, old nails pinning them to their position. Viscous blood pooled beneath its beak and its large eyes were glazed, clouded by death's exclusive privilege. Paul was certain they'd been left some kind of gruesome message and although he didn't understand it entirely, its grimness spoke volumes.

"That's it, Jane, get dressed. Forget about anything else. We're not staying here a moment longer."

Jane dressed. "What's going on?"

"I don't know. I *really* don't know. Are you ready to run? Because we're going to have to run for our lives, I think. Just stay close and don't think."

Paul unlocked the door and waited for the inevitable. Nothing happened. He looked at the tree line – whoever was holding the flashlight was still there, waving it around in sudden jerks.

Good, he thought. "Ready?" he said as he looked at his wife. Jane nodded.

Paul pulled open the door and grabbing his wife's arm dragged her onto the veranda and then onto the path next to the cabin, then started running.

Within moments they were across the grass strip and through the thin strip of fir trees. He pushed the button on his key fob and their car unlocked. Paul got in the driver's side and Jane made her way around the back of the car to get to the passenger door. Time seemed to drag. Paul twisted around in his seat to see where Jane was, but the outside was too dark. *Where the hell are you?* Paul thought, shaking his head. They'd got this far, surely she was about to get in. He was on the verge of getting out when the passenger door was wrenched open. Jane jumped in and quickly closed the door. Paul hit the central locking and started up the car; slammed it into reverse and turned on the headlights. He swung the wheel to the left and steered for the lane, shifting the car into first. In the headlights Paul thought he glimpsed the woman from reception, madly waving a flashlight about as humanesque shadows circled her. Then the flashlight went out.

Paul drove down the lane as fast as he could, but if he was to avoid crashing the car in this miniscule lane, he had to take it easy. The last thing he wanted was to be marooned and at the mercy of whatever it was this *holiday* site harboured.

The hedgerow had been unmoving in the windless night, but as the car's headlights picked it out, it began to shake violently. Then at the limit of the beams Paul saw man-shapes, leaping over the bushes, flying through the air across the lane.

Light coloured jackets becoming visible. And then he was there, the bald fat man, standing in the middle of the lane – except, somehow, he was less man. Paul's brow furrowed as he tried to make out what it was between the man's out stretched arms and waist. Questions fired through his mind. *What is that? A cloak? Black skin of some kind?*

"Paul. Stop!" Jane screamed. "You're going to hit that man."

Paul glanced at his wife and shook his head. "Whatever that is, it's not a man." Risking all he pushed the accelerator down and before the fat man-thing could get out of the way the car clipped it, throwing it hard into the hedgerow. Momentarily the car lurched.

***

To this day Paul and Jane can't explain what they'd experienced during their curtailed time away and resolved never to go anywhere without checking the details. They would definitely never go to a place one could call "in the sticks" again.

***

A few weeks after their nightmare break, out of morbid curiosity, Jane looked up the place they'd stayed at, but her Internet search failed to return any results.

Buzz Lightyear's Super Blaster

"Jimmy?" his mother called out after looking at the clock – it was gone 8pm and a time all nine year-olds ought to be in bed.

"What, Mum?" Jimmy called from the conservatory-cum-play area as Buzz Lightyear leapt from Mount Zanussi just before the earthquake struck, or spin cycle as his mum called it.

Marjorie ruffled her son's hair. "Go on, up you go, it's bedtime."

Almost defiant, he nodded and ran up the stairs. Marjorie smiled at her little soldier.

After the shock had passed Jimmy had become so grown up since the death of his dad. A tear ran down her cheek and she shook her head; such a terrible scene, gore everywhere; her husband lifeless and eviscerated. No rhyme or reason, and the murderer still at large three years on.

A sudden noise brought Marjorie back to the here and now.

Jimmy stormed down the stairs, "Mum!"

"What's wrong, Jimmy?"

"My Buzz Lightyear Super Blaster; it's gone, I can't find it." Tears were welling up in his eyes.

A quick search of Jimmy's room confirmed the toy was missing.

"I'm sure it will turn up."

"Can't I sleep in your bed tonight, Mum?"

"Big boys don't do that."

"But I can't sleep without my gun."

"Of course you can."

"But the monster will get me."

"There's no such thing as monsters, Jimmy."

"It got Daddy."

"Don't be so stupid, James," Marjorie said too sharply, regretting it in an instant. She hugged her son. "I'll look for it in the morning when you're at school."

***

"Come on down, Jimmy. You'll be late and you won't have time for breakfast."

There was no sound. The house was still. "Jimmy?"

Marjorie started up the stairs. "Jimmy? Come on, Sweetie. It's time to get up." She stopped and listened; nothing.

"Jimmy?" she whispered as she pushed the boy's door open. "Come on, Jimmy," she cajoled, seeing the boy outlined beneath his duvet. "Get up."

She pulled the duvet back and frowned; she couldn't rationalise her son's saucer-wide eyes or the dark red paint he'd covered himself in, nor the empty cavity of his torso.

A Night Crawler Called Ween

Drifting under a moon-bright sky
with shadows shivering as I pass by.
Along the beach I leave my trail.
And in my wake even banshees wail.
For I'm the one of whom no-one speaks.
A nameless entity that raises shrieks;
from all those;
— that come across me.

From the dunes, I am born.
The gaps between grains from which I'm torn
creates the mist from which I'm made.
It's oil-slick black, cold, and made of shade.
But some know the name of which no-one speaks;
still leaving me as nameless freak.
In their world
— some don't know me.

There are the foolish who use my name.
Who summon me and think it's game,
to raise me from my sleep so deep,

but never hang around to make a peep.
Then there's the idiots who stay to look
when I seep out from my little crook.
Then try and hide themselves,
— from me.

When I am summoned they know I'll act.
I don't flit mindlessly like a large winged bat.
I seek my caller to take their breath.
And, with satisfaction, I'll watch their death.
They know not to use my name in vain.
But for some it's still a game.
They say "Hallo Ween!" when I appear.
— then DIE before me.

Displaced

Chapter 1

I was an ordinary soul in our village, just a young twenty-something farm worker, trying to make my way in life. The village I called my own was Trelevern, it was small and just a rural farming community in the South West of England. But we did have our grocery store, and we did have our petrol station, in essence though, that was it. The Cornish town of Trelevern wasn't on the coast and it wasn't next to any of the moors and I suppose this was why we were uninterrupted by holiday makers and truly uninterrupted by the rest of the world: it was a good place to live.

***

After my father died, I was willed the cottage I now live in, attached to Farmer Pengowan's land, a few miles away from the village centre. It was quiet and serene, if you could call nature quiet; but that's the way it felt. There's something peaceful about nature's natural cacophony.

Fortunately for me Mr Pengowan believed in perpetuating the rite of the workers and, although I didn't work for him often, my father had, and that had been enough; I was allowed to call Pengowan's cottage my home.

When the sun came up, I got up also; whether it be 4am in the morning during the summer or 7am during the winter; I followed the sun – this was the way; very rural, but nothing could beat it.

On occasions, Pengowan asked me to perform the odd task; herding the sheep or using the great combine to harvest his crops. It didn't matter to me what he asked, I was pleased to be a part of Earth's natural cycle; sowing, seeding, and reaping: I enjoyed this life.

After finishing my chores, I would collapse in my bed, which overlooked the fields, exhausted and happy; fulfilled; and this was how I had continued for the thirty-six months, three seasonal cycles, since my father's death, until today.

***

This morning I had awoken, feeling groggy, as if sleep had eluded me for most of the previous night and, as I sat on the edge of my bed trying to shake an unusual consuming tiredness from my mind, I recalled strange dreams of dazzling brightness; images of corn fields somehow below me, ones that were moving away becoming smaller until they seemed nothing more than scale models.

For a short while I struggled to grasp the dream-memories, trying to get hold of them, trying to visualise them in the clarity they'd had but, as I did, they slipped away becoming more elusive as my tiredness receded.

Eventually they were nothing more than wisps of a memory I was no longer interested in and I got up as my thoughts turned to my usual routine.

***

Every few days I visited the village store purchasing the bread, milk and eggs Pengowan's farm didn't produce – I was okay for meat, particularly lamb, and sausages were available, intermittently.

But this day, Mrs Cottral, the owner of the store, ignored me. Ignored me is too strong – she didn't recognise me as a regular; she didn't recognise me at all. She also seemed a little afraid by my presence in her shop.

"But Mrs Cottral…", I implored, "I'm Joseph. You know, Joseph Meveres from up the lane."

And, as I indicated my road, pointing in its direction, she stepped back from her side of the counter before answering.

"So you say, but you're not *the* Joseph Meveres I know." Though she was robust in her reply I could tell by her stance fear had taken hold. "You are not entitled to any discounts," she continued. "Now pay me what you owe and get out. Go away and don't come back. I know what you are… changeling."

Though confused and having no clue as to what she was talking about I didn't want to upset her any further, so I purchased the food I could afford at the going price and left; I certainly didn't want to upset the owner of the village shop any more than I had done.

But the situation was strange and I could not figure out why she'd decided not to know me anymore, apart from that peculiar word she'd used – changeling.

I shook my head, nothing clear becoming apparent: I knew she was getting on a bit and dearly hoped that this wasn't the onset of one of those degenerative mental illnesses; she was too nice to have that happen to her.

I left the village centre and made my way back to my cottage trying to reconcile what had just happened with the woman I knew her to be, from past experience.

Just as I approached my front door I was distracted from my thoughts as Farmer Pengowan stepped out in front of me, blocking my way.

"Joseph," he said. "I need to know what you have been doing."

"Nothing," I answered immediately in my defence, then considering what had been said, I asked, "What do you mean?"

"What have you done to my crop?" he said.

I had no idea of what he was talking about. I was just making my way back from the village to my cottage.

"At least seventy per cent of the corn has been irrecoverably damaged," he told me. "You look after it; what have you done?"

"Nothing, sir, honestly," I said. "I haven't even started to harvest it."

"Are you responsible for the field?" Pengowan asked me.

"Of course I am," I replied.

"Then how do you explain the state it is in now?"

"I don't know," I said. "What's wrong with it?"

"Have a look for yourself," he told me. He let me go past him, so I could dump my shopping in the house.

Once I'd put the carrier bags on my kitchen table I stepped back outside my cottage and he spoke to me again.

"Well?" he said.

"Sorry, sir, I still don't understand what you're talking about," I said, shaking my head.

"Come with me," he instructed.

I followed him around the back of the cottage and along the path towards the fields.

He waved his arm across the vista and I looked; I couldn't see anything of a worry: but then he pointed it out.

"See?"

What I saw was a field of corn that had somehow been flattened, in places. My first thought was that there had been a localised storm, some wind or something, perhaps even some heavy rain; but seeing how the corn had been flattened I began to wonder.

There were twirls and circles, lines and more circles, spirals; all interconnected – a very strange pattern. And I began to feel Mr Pengowan was blaming me for the damage.

"I didn't do this," I told him. But he just looked at me. "I didn't ruin the crop, honestly, sir," I affirmed.

Pengowan, and his family, had known my family for a long, long time, and I think he believed me because of this, though his demeanour glinted with an edge of doubt, but, if he didn't, then the reasons were beyond me.

Saying no more he turned for his Land Rover, got in it and left me, driving up the unmade road, which led from the cottage to the farmhouse, some half mile up the hill.

I looked at the crop again and the damage, now that it had been pointed out to me from this vantage point, was obvious.

Between the remaining upright sandy-yellow corn stalks that rocked gently in the slight breeze, around the edges of the field, I could see that the centre of the field had been pressed down into the earth, in some way.

There'd be no harvesting of this field in a few weeks I knew; if anything it would need ploughing straight back into the ground: what a waste of a season.

I left my vantage point next to the low leafy green hedgerow at the rear of my cottage, and made my way back, entering the kitchen and putting the kettle on. Whilst the water was trying to get up to the boil on my gas cylinder driven stove I climbed the short stairway to my bedroom, beneath the cottage's thatched roof, to look out of the window over the field.

I was stunned when I saw the full extent of the geometric designs that had been imprinted on Farmer Pengowan's field, and, although I'd heard of such things, I'd never seen it but, for sure, this was one of those crop circles you read about in the newspapers from time to time.

I began to wonder about who could have done this; who in our village would have such a malicious but artistic bent.

None of the families I knew would; perhaps it was the out-of-towners attempting a laugh at our expense.

At least none of the fields further away from the cottage had been damaged, as far as I could tell from my window.

The kettle began to whistle, summoning me, and I left the view to go back down the stairs to the kitchenette to make my tea.

As I sat there on my chair at the plain wood table in the middle of the kitchen's dusty grey slate floor. I wracked my brains trying to think of anyone who may have something against Mr Pengowan or me, but no-one would come to mind. I decided the destruction of the crop was down to a misguided practical joke by some townies.

As I had an early start the next day I quickly washed up the crockery and cutlery and turned in for the night.

***

Morning broke and I woke up. I didn't need an alarm clock as my bedroom window was without curtains and the early morning light always roused me from my sleep, and if not the light, then nature always had a way.

Gingerly, I got out of bed, my body felt as if I had been stacking straw bales for four hours straight, but I hadn't. That onerous task was to come in the next few weeks. And again, I felt as if my sleep had been poisoned by strange dreams of dazzling lights and the view of fields below me but even these memories had been tainted further, by images of sleek glistening black-walled triangular rooms, illuminated by purplish UV light, and gangly humanesque surgeons.

Everything ached and my head throbbed terribly; each way I turned to look it felt as if my sinuses were filled with fluid. n In my ears I could hear the sounds of light kindling crackling as if in a fire. I hoped I wasn't coming down with a summer flu, but, if I was, it would explain the fevered dreams.

Standing up on my feeble legs I got dressed and made my way downstairs for breakfast, though I didn't feel like eating. Ultimately I opted for a cup of tea and nothing else.

After putting the kettle on I opened the fridge and poured some milk into my cup. The milk trickled out of the bottle sludge-like; it was off. Just to make sure I sniffed at it and recoiled smelling the wet sour smell that indicated it was no good anymore.

I'd bought it only yesterday so I checked the fridge hadn't turned itself off during the night by looking for the frost that always built up in the freezer compartment – it was still there. The milk had not been exposed to a warm summer night and there was no icy caking along the bottom of the freezer box.

I made myself another cup and took my tea neat, swilling down a couple of Paracetamol along with it.

Knowing the chores I had to complete for this morning I checked the clock to see how long I could rest before getting on with them. I hoped there would be enough time to allow the pills to work, but there wasn't.

I rubbed my eyes to make sure they were free from sleep and it wasn't affecting my vision, but it didn't help.

The clock said 8am. Somehow I'd slept through the sunrise at 5:30am and, although the quality of light coming through my kitchen window told me it must be later, I still reached for my wrist watch I always left in the fruit bowl on the sideboard, before I went to bed. Looking at it, it told me the same thing; it was 8am.

Now I knew I wasn't well at all and, for the first time since I'd started working for Mr Pengowan, I picked up the phone to call him, to let him know it was not possible for me to work today.

Dialling his number I waited for the connection to click through and for him to answer but, after the numbers had stopped clicking, all I got was a single pitched tone telling me I'd either rung the wrong number or he'd been disconnected. I tried again, dialling the numbers for his farmhouse, more slowly this time, but the result was the same.

As the painkillers began to ease my bodily aches I decided to go to the village to get some more milk and replace the pint that had gone off.

I picked up my moss green jacket from the back of my battered sofa and, putting it on, I left the cottage: Then stopped abruptly after shutting the door behind me.

I stared at the path which led to my front door; the path I cleared of weeds at least once a week, normally twice. The path I now saw had at least three weeks' growth on it, I assumed, if not more.

If I was going to do anything today I would clear the path. But first I would get some more milk.

I began to walk the two miles into the village down the single track road, which led up to my cottage. It was lined by hedgerow on either side interspersed by the occasional tree and had, in places, the odd tuft of grass poking through the road's surface along its centre-line.

As I made my way I started to notice inconsistencies in my next day's life, all of which were pointing to a wholly different season from the one I went to bed in.

I noticed red holly berries that were beginning to show themselves in the hedgerow, the leaves on some of the trees that lined the lane had started to turn autumn's orange golden-brown. The acorns from the oaks, which grew at random intervals on either side of the road, were scattered across its uncared for tarmac.

If I was perceiving all these signals correctly, then, without a doubt, it was autumn. But I knew for certain I had gone to bed in late August, the summer.

Knowing I was unwell I decided to put these thoughts to the back of my mind; I would get my milk and then I would tackle my path.

***

At the end of the lane was the village petrol station. Arriving here always told me that I was only a few more minutes away from the grocery store.

I nearly walked past the garage without a second's thought but, as I got to the furthest end of its forecourt, something triggered in my head and I stopped.

I turned to look at it. There was a rusty iron chain across its entrance and exit; there were no lights illuminating the inside of the little shop that was a part of it, and there was a sign, which stated it was closed.

In my entire life this petrol station had never been closed during the day, especially at this time of the morning, but today it obviously was. I wondered where the owners were.

I was certain Mrs Cottral would know what was going on. So I stepped up my pace and made my way to the shop, as quickly as I could manage with my aching limbs.

Even if she still didn't know me, she would definitely know what was going on; she was the village's information centre, though this was not an official title or anything, it was just the way the village worked.

Mobile phones were next to useless as the operators had not considered getting a decent signal in Trelevern a priority and, those of us who did need mobile communications, stuck with the trusty walkie-talkie, and this was the way we liked it.

Walking past the small concrete based, tubular open sign on the little bit of pavement that existed in the village, I pushed open the store's olive-green framed door and entered. The brass bell above it announced another customer's interest.

The interior had changed somewhat, since my visit the day before and it took a few moments more than usual before I found the open faced fridge containing the plastic milk cartons. I picked one up, a two pinter this time.

As I didn't need anything else I walked around the new shelving, which filled the centre of the shop, to find the checkout and, finding it, I waited to be served.

There was no bell to push on the counter that I could ring any longer. It seemed that this style of service was no more, so I coughed.

Eventually a woman in her early forties, I must guess, wearing a dowdy brown knitted cardigan, walked up to the counter from the back room, which was still separated from the shop by multi-coloured vertical strips of 1970's plastic.

I didn't recognise her at all.

Seeing the milk carton I had in my hand she asked me; "Will that be all?"

I told her yes and she rang up the cost on the till.

"That'll be £1.15," she said.

Before handing my money over to her I was determined to find out where Mrs Cottral was, so I asked; "Where's Mrs Cottral today?"

I got a blunt reply. "She died two weeks ago," was the answer and, although I thought that would be it, she continued, "I haven't seen you in here before. Did you know her?"

"Of course I knew her. She served me..." I nearly said, yesterday, but quickly changed my tack, "only the other week. I live just up the lane, here." I indicated the direction I had come from. "Was it dementia?" I asked.

"No, no," the woman in the shop started. "My aunt was sound as a bell. It was a heart attack. Though, if you believe what some are saying in the village, she'd been scared to death."

I just blinked at this answer and then Mrs Cottral's niece continued; "Have you heard that Farmer Pengowan has disappeared?"

All I could do was shake my head; my mind was in turmoil, surely only yesterday I'd had a minor confrontation with Mrs Cottral; and Pengowan? That was another question.

Suffice it to say, I handed over the money and left the store.

I now felt very confused – all my timelines were off somehow. I wandered back home trying to figure out what was happening.

As I walked up the lane I saw a grey squirrel grasping at one of the acorns on the road, putting it in its mouth. When it spotted me it leapt into action keeping the acorn in its mouth as it dived through the hedgerow, to wherever it needed to go.

***

Sitting at the table in my cottage I glanced at the clock. It told me that it was only midday.

As I waited for the kettle to boil I looked around my kitchen not knowing what else to do and noticing the heavy cobwebs that had appeared in its corners.

I rubbed my head round and round with my hand trying to get a handle on the situation I found myself in – but it didn't help.

The only conclusion I could draw was that I'd lost some time out of my life, somehow. And, before I could think further about it, the kettle boiled, whistling, so I picked it up and made my tea.

Pouring the warm refreshing liquid down my throat my thoughts turned to the chores Farmer Pengowan expected me to complete; barring the field that had been flattened, there were three others to harvest, but I couldn't do this today – I needed some rest; tomorrow would be the day, I decided. But the thought I was not like this – or I shouldn't be – instilled a sense of guilt I wasn't used to feeling.

As I supped my tea I knew today was not the day I should climb into the great yellow and blue combine to start my task.

Tomorrow. I would do it tomorrow. And that was fact. And that was my decision.

As I sat at my table and looked out of the back window of the kitchen over the hedgerow and into the un-harvested fields that lay beyond, I rested within myself, just being, with no thoughts as to doing.

Gradually the sun continued its path from the day-time sky and started its descent towards the horizon. All the while I watched the colours the sunset created as its light made changes to the contrast and brightness that accentuated the life force the crops seemed to emanate and, not moving from my seat in the kitchen, I sat there watching, somehow being a part of the cycle.

As I did this I attempted to put all the things I now knew into some kind of logical order, some neat little scenario, which would explain everything I'd experienced so far.

***

Darkness enveloped the outside with hedgerows disappearing into blackness beyond the beige corn fields.

I got up from my table; it was time to go back to bed and rest, getting ready for the coming morn and the tasks I would have to complete as a part time employee of Farmer Pengowan, though I wasn't sure I needed to anymore, if he had truly disappeared.

But I had been charged with these duties and, just because he wasn't here at the moment, it didn't really mean I was discharged from them.

Chapter 2

I awoke in my bed suddenly, thrown from another traumatic nightmare, fleeting glimpses of a chilled dark room, which now included too real visions of a three-pronged instrument sizzling as it pushed through my abdomen. I leant over the side of the bed and dry heaved, no contents to expel.

As I sat back up I began to feel a little better. The retching had seemed to purge my illness slightly and, as I recovered, whatever had woken me was gone; and it was morning again.

My body still ached; but, as I looked through my bedroom window, the pains I suffered disappeared to the back of my thoughts.

I now looked out over fields hidden beneath a severe blanket of white; the hedgerows and fences that separated them were now walls of white... something.

As I breathed out I noticed a cloudy vapour and then the penny dropped; I was looking at snow. But snow in August?

I eased myself out of my bed into the bedroom. The cold hit me with a force I was not used to at this time of year.

I got dressed as fast as I could and made my way down the wooden stairs to my kitchenette.

I had to get the heating on. This was my first concern before I could try and tackle, mentally, the un-seasonal weather.

Within a few moments I had the fire burning in the hearth and, although I'd achieved this fairly quickly, I knew it would be a good forty minutes before it began dishing out the required heat to the rest of the cottage.

Wrapping my dark blue cotton dressing gown around me, over my clothes, I sat in front of the fire waiting for it to do its work, wondering why I should have had to take such actions. Perhaps this was just one of the problems supposed climate change wrought.

As the heat permeated the cottage I removed my dressing gown and threw it over the back of my sofa. Very soon I could have a shower, the water in the back boiler being hot enough to do so.

In the meantime I made myself a hot drink; tea seeming the simplest option. I didn't bother with milk this time as I desperately needed to warm up and, as I poured the boiling water onto the tea bag, I began to feel like this drink was all I was living on. But, as they say; starve a fever, feed a cold.

As I supped my drink the wood in the fireplace began to burn low and it was apparent that I ought to top it up, if it was going to continue to heat my home.

I pulled on some Wellington boots and shrugged on a jacket and left the comfortable heat of the kitchen-cum-living room. I crunched through the snow in my small back garden to the shed that housed more fuel for the fire.

After clearing the snow from the shed's entrance I pulled its rickety door open and began removing the logs I would use, placing them on the roped flat piece of hardboard I had for these occasions.

Almost full I picked up three more logs continuing in my automaton style of stacking that I'd developed over the years from tasks such as this. My mind focused on heaving the load back up the garden to the kitchen.

Turning, I pulled the hardboard sled away from the shed's door so that I could close it easily, then, turning back, I placed my hand on the edge of the door, about three quarters of the way up ready to close it and, as I did so, I glanced at the depleted log pile.

I collapsed heavily one the make shift sled, the sight before me draining my strength. Two boots, ones you could call farmer's boots poked from the bottom of the stack.

I blinked my eyes and shook my head in an attempt, I suppose, to clear what I was seeing from my vision.

Within seconds my consciousness began to register the odour of death, but not the usual smell of an abattoir that housed dead pigs or sheep, there was a very subtle difference, a difference I instantly recognised, because I could see the boots.

I had to find out who it was, though my mind was already telling me.

As fast as I could I worked through the remainder of the pile chucking each log to the other side of the shed.

One by one the removed logs began to uncover shins, knees and waist, all still clothed. But after that the torso was bare; but not just bare, it was mutilated: The internal organs, those that still existed, were there to see. Exposed as nature hadn't intended them to be; their covering missing.

I'd done a fair bit of butchery as part of my chores for Farmer Pengowan, and saw immediately that the liver and heart were gone, though the strangest thing of all was the lack of any blood. It was as if this body had been prepared in some way; perhaps, even, for exhibition.

I didn't pause for long contemplating this. I had to know who it was, for definite. I cleared the last of the logs away – then froze.

The dull open eyes that stared back at me belonged to my father's friend and employer: It was Farmer Pengowan. My empty stomach retched.

***

It was only the uncontrollable shivering that brought me round. I'd passed out and fallen into the snow that had enveloped my garden.

With as much control as I could muster I pulled the loaded sled back towards the cottage, not looking back, not wanting to acknowledge that which existed in my shed.

Eventually I pulled the back door closed. The logs were now stacked up appropriately, next to the fire. Although the cottage was warm and cosy I still shivered, deeply, as if my very soul had been chilled to temperatures that only existed in the minds of scientists.

In an attempt to rid myself of these shakes I picked up my kettle and held it, clattering, against the silver nozzle of the tap in my kitchen. As it rattled, so it filled, very slowly; my shivering making the water's flow a hit or miss affair. But I did it and, once completed, I placed the kettle on the stove after which I fell back into my sofa to wait, still riven by the shakes.

The kettle began its whistle and, unsteadily, I got up reaching for the cupboard, taking a single tea bag from the steel container marked 'Tea'.

After pouring the hot water onto the tea bag I open my fridge to get the milk, reaching for it.

I didn't pick it up. This time I knew it was off, the fur on its surface, a very light avocado in colour spoke volumes.

I poured the hot water into my mug and sat down again, ready for yet another cup of neat tea.

I now knew it wasn't August any longer, no more than yesterday had been late August; somehow my life had been skipping weeks at a time and, during these periods, I had slept, but I felt this couldn't be right. The times I'd awoken full of aches and pains surely meant that, during my unconscious moments, I'd been doing something.

As these thoughts went through my mind I finished my tea and, putting the mug down, I made my way to the shower believing that, perhaps, this action would afford me some clarity on the situation I now found myself in.

Stripping off in the bathroom I turned towards the shower reaching in and turning the taps to the positions I knew, from experience, would deliver a comfortable stream.

I then turned to face the full-length mirror. At first, what I saw I believed to be an artefact of the condensation that coated it but, as I rubbed it down with a towel, the illness I had been suffering showed itself in its entirety.

I was looking at an exhausted man whose pallor was that of a person tinged a light grey-green, one who had three open and weeping suppurate welts, two just below the left and right rib cage and one where the belly button should have been, each as raw as they looked.

Logic told me that these wounds on my torso ought to be extremely painful, should be hurting, but there was no sensation at all; no irritation and no feeling. It was almost as if the damage to my body had been anesthetised in some manner.

I looked at my eyes as I now felt that all parts of me ought to come under some kind of self-scrutiny, and saw desperation encapsulated by heavy brows and dark rings.

I closed them to this vision and rubbed the mirror once more, hoping, beyond hope, that all I was seeing was part of some fevered hallucination. But, as I slowly opened my eyes and saw my hand, I stopped.

What was before me, holding the towel against the mirror, wasn't my hand.

Although I'd accepted, sort of, the colour of my skin, the webs between my fingers were plain to see; I dropped the towel and checked my other hand; it was just the same.

Whatever I was suffering was more than just a summer flu. But what it was I couldn't fathom.

One thing was for sure though, I was changing, metamorphosing in some way; I was becoming not me anymore, physically at least.

I turned the shower off knowing in my heart it wouldn't help.

Chapter 3

Everything I'd seen and acknowledged so far was a trauma but one part of me, deep down, was exerting normality. A way to survive this experience, I guess. And, in this vein, I decided to go back to the village to pick up milk once more; it was like a craving – something telling me this was the way I would survive what I was going through.

Perhaps Longlife was what I should choose this time, my mind told me; but not on foot, don't be silly, the snow had put paid to that.

Of course it had. It would be easier to use my mountain bike as I had done in previous years when the snow had fallen. The bike would cut through the snow quite simply.

I would go to the village and stock up on the milk and any other food *he* required.

***

My bike was kept in the outhouse, a flimsily built attachment to the cottage. Well it looked flimsy to me but it had been there as long as I could remember.

Normally I would enter the outhouse from the rear of the cottage but, not wanting to clap eyes on the shed ever again, I went out the front door, traipsed across the snow covered overgrown path, and opened the front of the wooden building, entering.

I saw my bike leaning against the old wooden walls, its tyres deflated through lack of use and care, but this was the norm; I only ever used it when walking was going to be too slow and, strangely, when it snowed, cycling on a mountain bike was a lot easier than walking.

Knowing where the pump was I pulled the canvas covering from the top of the oil and muck stained bench to retrieve it, dumping the canvas on the floor.

Reaching for the pump I nearly picked it up but impossibly gleaming silver tools stopped me. I looked at them and, for some reason, a smile that felt knowing graced my face.

These tools, ones I'd never seen before, were lying on the bench, calling to be held.

They were vaguely similar to a butcher's kit but more perfect in some way. As I looked at them I noticed a few were discoloured.

I leant closer to get a better look, sniffing at the air as I did so. Then moved away quickly.

Two of them, the ones with unrealistically thin silvery blades, had been tainted by hardened, reddy-brown glutinous lumps that had formed almost perfect spherical droplets on their surfaces.

None of the other tools were discoloured in this way; and none of the other silvery tools looked like anything from any person's toolbox that *he* knew.

Just the view of these tools made me wonder whether Farmer Pengowan's body had been carved up here, in the outhouse, and that thought was promptly followed by the question of who had done it.

You. I heard a distant voice call out in my mind, but dismissed it as a bizarre and ethereal insight that had been induced by the fever I was suffering.

Feeling my bile rise I retreated back to my kitchen; the urge to gather any food today being completely usurped.

I made myself another neat tea and, as I drank it, I looked out of the kitchen window at my small garden and the white fields beyond, without passion and without being. I was completely drained of everything that made me, me.

The light began to dwindle and, automatically, I made my way to bed rubbing my hands together knowingly, a small part of me wishing that, when I awoke, everything that had gone on would disappear as if part of some cruel and vicious nightmare.

Without any energy I collapsed into bed fully clothed and, for a second time a smile crossed my face.

I hadn't the wherewithal to change for bed and I hadn't the wherewithal to be bothered about it.

Chapter 4

My eyes flickered open, in response to the sun hitting them. I think it was the sun but I couldn't move. The ache that *he'd* felt in the passing days had gone only to be replaced by nothingness in *his* limbs.

As my consciousness rose, I felt a tightness on my chest. It was like the shirt *he* wore had become tighter in some way, smaller by a fraction, but I couldn't lift *his* arms to assuage the feeling.

I tried to exclaim; 'What the hell?' but my voice was just a mere whisper of its former self, my throat being terribly dry.

I wondered where I was but, looking to my left, I saw the windows without curtains and knew I was in *his* father's house, lying in *his* bed and all was calm.

Not resisting the paralysis I lay there looking out of the window at this planet's natural day, then, suddenly, my serenity was shattered. The noise sounded like the door to *his* cottage was being smashed in, a rending cracking sound filling the air.

The sirens piercing this new day assailed my ears. I wanted to get up to see what was happening but, every time I tried, nothing moved; my transformation was not yet complete.

Then *his* bedroom door swung back against the room's wall, banging loudly, and people in blue clothing jumped on *us*, turning *us* over, handcuffing *his* hands behind my back.

I tried to ask what was going on but I only exhaled, no sounds coming forth from my mouth.

As they lifted me onto a stretcher and carted *us* down *his* wooden stairs, prone, I heard *him* screaming inaudibly in my head; 'What have I done? WHAT HAVE I DONE?' with no recognition that I was now in control; soon *his* voice would be no more.

And then we were in their vehicle, and travelling; going to who knows where.

As I tried to struggle, only by turning *his* head violently, no other part of *his* body able to move, the image of a blurred man crossed my vision as he leant over me, placing a transparent mask on my mouth, holding it firm.

The man turned to someone behind him, talking, and although the words he said I knew I ought to know, their meaning was lost on me; an alien language to my ears.

I heard a hissing sound and a distantly familiar, almost sweet smell filled my nose, and with each breath I took so light changed into darkness.

About the Author

Simon Woodward

After working consistently in I.T. for over two and a half decades I decided it was time to forego the strictly logical world of computing and take up writing in my spare time.

I don't think I'll ever truly get to grips with this literary world but I'm certainly having great fun finding out about it, though I think my wife, Yve, is not so enamoured by my frequent requests asking 'what do you think of this?'

That said, without my wife, I don't think my three children's books and my adult fiction works would have ever seen the light of day and I wouldn't have enough stuff to be able to have my very own website created.

www.srwoodward.co.uk

Made in the USA
Charleston, SC
09 September 2013